CURSES
and
WARFARE

First Edition
First Printing, 2017

Book design by Christopher Loke
Cover design and illustration by Christopher Loke

Jolly Fish Press, an imprint of North Star Editions, Inc.

Library of Congress Cataloging-in-Publication Data (Pending)
ISBN 978-1-63163-126-9

Jolly Fish Press
North Star Editions, Inc.
2297 Waters Drive
Mendota Heights, MN 55120
www.jollyfishpress.com

Printed in the United States of America

This one is for Reece and Haley Hanzon—for making my dream a reality.

CURSES
and
WARFARE

Jeri Baird

JOLLY
FiSH
PRESS
Mendota Heights, Minnesota

PROLOGUE

Moira

I am called by many names: Destiny, Fate, Fortune; however, I prefer Moira, for it sounds as if I have a heart.

I do not.

I oversee human destinies, and all things happen as I intend. Some try to deceive me, some accept their fate willingly. I am Moira. I will not be cheated.

CHAPTER ONE

Puck's Gulch—November 11, Six Months After His Quest

Zander

War.

Zander rolled the word around in his head and examined it from every angle. No matter how he considered it, the word sickened him.

He grabbed a set of knives and strode to the practice field behind the stable, strapping two to his belt, sliding one into the sheath in his boot, and another up his sleeve. He faced the pell, a six-foot wooden post set in the ground thirty feet away, and flipped the final knife in the air. As it tumbled down end over end, he snatched the handle and threw.

Thud. It found its mark in the heart of the post.

Moira had put the safety of Puck's Gulch in his hands. How could she expect him to turn a group of young men and women not yet twenty into fighters?

Clenching his jaw, he slid the knife from his sleeve and sent it flying. It glanced against the post and toppled into the dirt. Heat flushed through his chest.

He was turning seventeen that day—too young for the responsibility. He snatched the blade in his boot and turned a circle before sending it toward the target. The knife hit low, but a sliced kneecap would still take a man down.

After he'd survived the annual quest Moira designed to test the sixteen-year-olds in his village, she'd offered him a choice—follow his dream of becoming a Protector or train warriors. The Protectors defended the market area from petty thieves and hunted with the elders. Zander's expertise with the bow had made him long to join them. But with Moira's warning of an invasion, Zander had relinquished his dream in order to prepare for war. He'd accepted the burden of his name—Zander, defender of all.

Two-handed, he grabbed the blades in his belt and overhanded them toward the post. One sliced through an imaginary forehead and the other stabbed a cheek.

He gathered the knives, leaned against the wood post, and rubbed his throbbing thigh. During his quest, a boar had gored him and infection had set in, leaving his leg weak. The old wound still ached, and he limped when he was tired. Stars, he hated that it made him look frail! Most days he hid the pain, but the winter cold had seeped into his bone and made the ache barely tolerable.

In the field over, a group of fighters fumbled with steel scimitars, the curved blades lighter than the flat wooden practice blades they were accustomed to. He winced as one of the men swung too quickly and nearly sliced his partner's arm. It had taken six months to forge weapons that matched the blade he'd bought from the Raskan travelers during the last festival. The Puck's Gulch metalsmiths excelled at plow shares, not blades. Zander had paid for the swords himself with coins hard-won at the spring wrestling tournament. A tourney he'd cheated to win. A cheater then, a leader now.

Moira had warned of war, but it was the traveling Raskans who had brought the details to Zander's isolated village. At the last festival, they whispered of fighting among the five tribes Puck had recruited from when he established his utopian society. Founded on peace, his village had never been threatened in their two-hundred-year history. Not until now.

The Raskans' news was that the Kharok tribe had driven the Odwa tribe out of their land. Now homeless, desperate refugees marched toward Puck's Gulch. It seemed certain the Odwans would be the enemy Moira predicted.

He tucked a braid of ebony hair adorned with a single white feather behind his ear and massaged the muscles in the back of his tight neck. After the quest, he'd been pleased when seven of the other questers joined him. With his best friend, Greydon, they'd recruited another three dozen men and a handful of women.

East of the stable, a dozen men and all the women shot at targets in the archery field while the rest of the recruits wrestled in the roundstone outbuilding that doubled as their dining hall. It was from there that Greydon sauntered across the open area behind the outbuilding toward Zander. Calm, with the confidence that came from being the firstborn son to a wealthy elder, Greydon and his friendship had surprised Zander. As the son of a furrier, Zander had held little respect for the elders before he met Greydon. Now, Greydon was second-in-command as they prepared for war.

Zander shared everything with his friend, except the one thing that could make Greydon hate him. Because of Moira's favor, Zander had seen a secret Greydon held close to his heart. Zander had since learned to shield against seeing people's secrets, after spending hours in meditation. He only used his gift when necessary, but he couldn't unsee Greydon's.

"Hoy." Greydon clasped Zander's hand and pulled him in to touch shoulders. Even in the cool winter air, sweat soaked Greydon's blond dreadlocks. He loosened it from a hemp tie and shook his head. "The guys are getting stronger. They're becoming first-rate wrestlers. How's sword practice?"

"They're struggling." The pressure to be ready within the year gnawed at Zander, causing him sleepless nights. "Even with the Protectors' help, I don't see how we can hold off an invasion from men with years of fighting experience."

"We'll do the best we can."

Zander turned to Greydon. "What if it's not enough? Except for your father, the elders ignore us, pretending everything will be the way it's always been."

"They don't like the other part of your plan." Greydon examined his palm, rubbing at a spot of dirt.

Anger bloomed in Zander's gut and tightened his chest. "Puck settled the five tribes to be equals. It's time to honor our founder's vision."

Greydon held up his hands. "It's not me you have to convince."

Before his anger could settle, Zander sensed someone behind him. He turned to the solemn face of Zephyr. The boy was a perfect example of why Zander fought for equality. Following Puck's dream meant there would be no poor and no elders holding the best land.

Though he was almost sixteen, Zephyr was small and malnourished. He bore the red hair and blue eyes of the Odwa tribe, rare in Puck's Gulch. His threadbare jacket identified him as one of the peasants from the shanty houses that ran along the northern rim of the gulch. Zander stared out across the fields at Elder Warrin's large manor. He was one of five elders that controlled the land and employed many of the poor as farm laborers or kitchen workers. But the wages were low and too many went hungry while the elders lived in excess.

Zeph held out a slip of paper. It was a message from Zander's twin sister, Alexa. *Don't forget our birthday celebration tonight. Bring a friend?*

He grinned. She hinted at Dharien, but he wouldn't be the friend

Zander would invite. To Zeph he said, "Tell her I'll be there." He turned to Greydon. "Come to dinner with me?"

Greydon nodded his assent.

Eyes bright, Zeph asked, "Can I see your horse?"

Zander's smile turned wry. He said to Greydon, "Think Helios is up for a visitor?"

"I don't know," Greydon teased. "Maybe it's your backside we should ask."

They burst out laughing at Zeph's worried look.

"Did he buck you off again?"

"Yep, and it took an hour to catch up to him. He'd lathered himself into a mess. Fulk swore at me for another hour." Zander smirked, thinking of the burly stable marshal who'd taken him into his care before the quest, and now helped train the warriors. The warriors reciprocated by mucking stalls and caring for the dozen horses owned by Elder Warrin.

Zeph grinned. "Helios likes me."

Across the field, the warriors carried the swords to a small locked shed. Next up for that group was wrestling. Zander was scheduled to help Greydon, but he could spare a few minutes. He waved Greydon toward the outbuilding. "I'll join you soon."

Zander led Zeph down the row of stalls to Helios's box. Zander had conquered his fear of riding during the quest, but the spirited war horse still threw him every time he mounted.

"All right, Zeph. As long as he's in the stall you can sit on him."

The horse nickered as Zander held a carrot on his opened palm. A white circle scarred the center, a reminder of his near-death in the quest.

Zephyr climbed over the rough slats and slid onto the horse's back. He leaned forward and laid his head of red curls against the horse's black neck. When Zeph whispered to him, Helios's ears flicked back, as if he understood. After a few minutes, Zeph slid off. "I need to get back to Alexa."

Zander's twin treated Zeph like a younger brother, but Zander sensed that Zeph held secrets, and as much time as Zeph spent with Alexa, Zander might need to use his gift. He rolled his shoulders. Stars, he hated seeing others' secrets, but Moira gave him the ability for a reason, and if using it protected Alexa, he'd do it.

Zeph turned to leave, and Zander said, "See you tonight?"

With a short nod, Zeph ran off, and Zander trekked to the outbuilding. He hesitated inside the door. He and Greydon had recruited the young men from the festival tourneys. They sought competitors that fit with their group. It wasn't always the winners they saw merit in. Zander looked for those past their quest who worked hard, had morals, and could take orders.

Pulling off his tunic, Zander joined Greydon's wrestling group. An hour later, soaked with sweat, Zander gratefully quit when Fulk hollered, "Break for noon meal, you pieces of scum, and get your asses over here to set up the tables."

Tired as they were, the men scrambled to obey. The big man's vocabulary could make anybody cringe. In the months before the quest, Zander had frequently been the recipient of Fulk's colorful swearing, but the stable marshal hid a kind heart behind his rough exterior.

After the shared noon meal, Zander had a few moments to relax in his room at the stable. He'd finally gotten around to cleaning the small window, and the patch of warm sunlight stretching across the room was welcome.

"Hey, lazy," he said to the coyote lounging on the blue coverlet covering the narrow bed. Shadow had grown large and sleek, his golden fur tipped in black. His blue eyes matched Zander's.

Zander rubbed under Shadow's neck. "You have another hour to sleep before we train."

Almost a year ago, the coyote had been a gift from Moira. On the first day of the new year, all the sixteen-year-olds in the village began a time of magic in which they earned tokens for good behavior and omens for bad. Moira gave each quester an animal patron to help them in the subsequent quest. He couldn't imagine life without Shadow. They hunted together, and Shadow responded to hand signals. He was even learning to deliver messages to the other warriors. When they went to war, he'd be invaluable.

Smiling down at his companion, Zander slung a dozen bows over his shoulder. He'd spent more of his dwindling winnings for new ones, and he couldn't wait to see the warriors' faces when they saw them. They couldn't win a war if they didn't have suitable weapons. Zander broke out in a sweat. Even with the best bows, he wasn't at all sure they could win.

CHAPTER TWO

The Fortune-Teller's Cottage

Alexa

Embers glowed from the stone fireplace, but the wood she'd added hadn't caught fire yet. Alexa shivered and tightened her scarf. Even in the summer, she wore a woven scarf to hide the jagged scar across her neck from when a black panther had nearly torn her throat out during her quest. If Zander hadn't used the wooden heart token from Melina Odella, Alexa would have died. She hated the ugly reminder and the sympathetic looks from others.

Now, six months later, Alexa apprenticed with Melina Odella. It was in the fortune-teller's cottage that Alexa shivered alone, her teacher having gone to a meeting of the elders. Alexa wrinkled her nose at the politics governing Puck's Gulch. The fortune-teller held equal power with the priest, Father Chanse. Fate and God working together. The council of five elders—three men and two women—collectively held one vote on the rare occasions that Melina Odella and the priest disagreed. Someday, that position would be Alexa's, but Melina Odella was only in her thirties. She'd hold the position for many years yet.

Alexa sat at a table covered with a black velvet cloth and lit a large golden candle. The scent of beeswax combined with smoke and hints of lavender calmed her. Silk cloths in reds, greens, and purples rustled from ceiling to floor against the walls. Alexa wondered what kind of trade Melina Odella had made with the Raskan travelers for such a luxury. Her teacher cultivated mystique as meticulously as the herbs she grew by magic all through the winter. Alexa drummed her fingers against a deck of battered tarot cards on the table in front of her. Reading the cards was one of many secrets her teacher held from her, claiming Alexa wasn't ready for the knowledge.

She carefully shuffled the cards, separated them into three piles, and set her intention. What did Zander's future hold? Drawing one card from each stack, she laid them face down. In the six months she'd apprenticed with Melina Odella, she'd discovered the meanings of the cards came easily, and she understood the truth or untruth as she read them.

Zander never allowed her to read for him, but it was their seventeenth birthday, and the perfect day to see his future. Alexa ran her fingers against the amethyst beads braided into her blond curls to enhance intuition. She closed her eyes and tuned into their vibration. Zander didn't trust her magic, and he had good reasons. During the quest it hadn't always worked the way she intended. She'd nearly killed Kaiya because of a poor decision. But the feeling in her gut that he'd need her help to fight off the invasion had grown stronger. She would divine his future, whether he listened or not.

She turned over the cards and gasped. The Seven of Swords, the Nine of Swords, and the Wheel of Fortune stared up at her. Dread settled like a stone in her stomach. The Seven of Swords foretold a theft. She held the card against her chest, allowing the meaning to come forth. The man carried five swords and had dropped two, which hinted at discovery. If her twin heeded the warning, he could protect himself.

The Nine of Swords vibrated with suffering and despair, but the owl watching from the window allowed for clarity to intervene.

Alexa and the owl were of the night. If Zander accepted her help, he had a chance of lessening the misfortune.

When she regarded the third card, Alexa released a ragged laugh. Of course Moira would appear in the reading. Fate had warned Zander of the coming invasion. The Wheel of Fortune, also known as the destiny card, predicted change. When aspected with the other two cards, it seemed her twin was in for a rough time. It gave no consolation that Moira was pulling the strings. Fate wasn't particularly trustworthy.

A draft flowed through the room. Alexa turned as Zephyr stepped quietly to her side. He fit his name well—soft breeze.

"Zander's coming for dinner. He's bringing a friend." Zeph's large eyes dominated his heart-shaped face. The golden flakes in his somber blue irises reflected the candle flame and appeared to dance. He shifted from one foot to the other. "I saw his horse."

Even with the dire reading foremost in her thoughts, Alexa couldn't help but smile. "How was Z's backside today?"

Zeph grinned at last. "Sore."

"Couldn't you speak your magic into Helios's ear to make him obey Zander?" she teased.

Serious once more, Zeph shook his head. "My words only work while I'm touching him."

Startled, Alexa asked, "Could *you* ride him?" Zeph was a puzzle she hadn't yet solved. His quiet demeanor conflicted with the power she felt hiding under the surface.

He stared past her shoulder, considering the question, before he made a quick nod. "I could."

Melina Odella slid through the black curtain separating her living quarters from the divining room. Her mood, always unpredictable after council meetings, caused Alexa to hold her breath, waiting.

The fortune-teller paused when she noticed Zeph and sighed. "Here again?"

"Zeph brought me a message from Zander." She bit the inside of her cheek to keep from saying more. Zeph was her friend. He could stop by anytime he wanted.

"And how is our young warrior?"

Her teacher's voice fell flat. She'd become distant since Alexa started her apprenticeship, as if she'd lost interest in life. She'd even left off using the dark makeup and charcoal eyeliners she'd often worn, and which Alexa had copied for months. Alexa picked at her thumbnail, knowing she was at least in part responsible for Melina Odella's unhappiness.

She held no hope, but asked, "Come to dinner tonight and see for yourself? Mother's made a feast."

Melina Odella hesitated a moment before shaking her head no. She laid a small package on the table. "Happy birthday, Alexa."

"A present?" The heaviness left her, replaced by excitement. She untied the hemp cord. When Alexa unfolded the rich golden cloth, she gasped. "A calcite?" She clasped the milky white stone in both hands and closed her eyes. The vibration pulled at her consciousness.

"A mineral to help with your studies. Carry it with you to attune to the energy, and I'll teach you to use it soon." Melina Odella pursed her lips. "Do you already feel the vibration?"

The stone sent a strong pulse of energy through her body, but Alexa shook her head. She was no longer a child. She wouldn't receive a snake token for deceit like when she had been preparing for her quest last year. So she lied.

"No. I look forward to your teaching." Alexa turned her back to Melina Odella to find Zeph frowning at the air above her head.

Slipping the stone into her pocket, Alexa understood it would be her true teacher. Since the quest, a power had awakened in her. She'd tried to explain to Zander, her only confidante, but he didn't understand. His thoughts centered on war, not magic. His look of alarm when she told him of the power she felt had surprised her, but she would not hide her gifts from him. She'd lost too many years separated from him to deceive him.

She would lie to Melina Odella about her abilities, but she would not lie to Z. Ever.

CHAPTER THREE
Birthday Celebration

Zander

Zander sucked in his breath before he entered the side door of the bakery where Alexa lived with their parents. He reached down and patted Shadow. The thought of seeing Father made him nervous, but his patron calmed him.

Greydon stepped in behind Zander as Alexa ran to greet them. She gazed up at her twin. "You're taller." She hugged him. "And more muscular."

"It's the training." He rolled his tight shoulders, a reminder of the morning wrestling session. Zeph's visit had distracted him, and Greydon had taken advantage of it and pinned him three times before Zander could get one takedown.

Alexa greeted Greydon with a quick hug and then glanced behind him. Zander draped his arm over her shoulder and whispered, "If I'd brought Dharien, then Paal would have sulked. I need cooperation, not rivalry, among my warriors."

When she blushed, Zander grinned. He'd guessed correctly.

Zeph appeared at Alexa's side and handed Zander a small box made of folded paper. When Zander unfolded it, a tiny carved horse sat nestled in a tuft of wool. Taken aback, Zander remembered the horse token he'd used in the quest. He'd overcome his fear of riding with that token. Out of habit, he rubbed his thigh, remembering that night. He'd barely been able to walk. Without the horse, he and Alexa never would have found Dharien in time to face the black panthers together.

"Did you carve this?" he asked Zeph.

"The Protector named Del is teaching me. It's for luck with Helios."

Greydon laughed and punched Zander's shoulder. "He needs it!"

Alexa's best friend, Merindah, slipped through the door behind them. Her simple dark brown dress, the clothing of the nuns, contrasted with Alexa's red velvet skirt and embroidered black blouse. And while Alexa had dark charcoal lining her eyes, Merindah's face was clear. Her dark skin and curly black hair identified her as descended from the Dakta tribe.

Zander glanced at the others. Four of the five tribes were represented—Dakta, Odwa, Chahda, and Kharok. His thoughts strayed to Kaiya, one of the Yapi female warriors. For more than one reason, he wished he'd thought to invite her.

When Alexa saw Merindah, she rocked up and down on her toes. "I haven't seen you in months!"

"If you'd come to church you'd see me." Merindah's fingers ran over her rose quartz prayer beads. "You've forgotten to give thanks to God."

"Melina Odella doesn't go. Why should I?" Alexa's dark eyes twinkled. "She's teaching me the winter roots to dig. We're alone in the forest on Sundays without the fear of a hunter's stray arrow."

Merindah's lips pressed into a hard line. She hung a dark wooden circle carved with foxglove flowers around Alexa's neck. It jostled with the red heart Zander had used to save Alexa's life in the quest. "Happy birthday. I carved it during solitary time." She handed an identical one to Zander. "To protect you."

He slipped it over his head and felt the wood warm against his chest. "Thanks, Merindah. I'll take all the help I can get."

At his thanks, Alexa grimaced. "Unless the help comes from your sister?" she muttered. "Come, Mother's waiting."

He followed his twin into the main room. Two wrapped gifts sat in the middle of a round oak table set for the meal. Bowls of dried apples and walnuts perched next to them. Zander scooped a handful and tossed them in his mouth.

In the shadow of a blazing fire, Father reclined, a pint of mead in his hand. "Zander," he slurred. "Happy birthday, Son."

Zander flushed at Father's drunken display in front of Greydon and rushed to steady him as he stood. He tried to keep his voice light. "How are you, Father? How's the pelting?"

His father brushed aside the question and the hand that sought to help. "Well, well. How's my warrior son?" He spat the word *warrior* in disdain. "The guilds grumble that you steal their men for your fantasy of war."

Unwilling to repeat the same conversation he always held with his father, Zander held his tongue, but Greydon spoke to defend him. "Moira has assured Zander we will be needed."

"Moira?" Father's throaty laugh filled the room. "You can't trust Fate, now can you lad? She's a fickle mistress indeed." He waved his cup in front of Greydon's face. "What good has Moira ever done for me?"

"Father!" Alexa's face darkened. "She kept Zander and me alive in the quest. Isn't that enough?"

He stumbled and fell back into his chair. "At what cost, Daughter, at what cost? You're off with the fortune-teller when you should be helping your mother in the bakery. And my son? Spending his own coins to play at war." He pointed his finger at Zander. "I hope you don't expect me to support you when your money runs out." Mead splashed from his cup as he gestured to make his point. "And when has our village ever needed warriors?" He paused to drink. "Never."

"The cards confirm it." Alexa glanced at Zander and blushed. "I read Zander's future today."

Heat raced through Zander's chest. "Don't read me without my permission."

"You need to know what the cards say."

"No, I don't. I have Moira whispering in one ear and now you in the other? I don't need it. Even Puck gets in his say."

Their father growled, "Look at my beloved children. They believe they cheated Fate and now they speak for her." He lifted his cup. "Here, here, a toast on their seventeenth birthday."

An awkward silence fell over the room. Zander bit the inside of his cheek. He hated it, but Father might be right. Who was he to take on the task of saving the village?

As Mother entered with a tureen, he scrambled to help, grateful for her arrival. Zander carried the stewed venison to the table as Mother smoothed her blond hair. Alexa had Mother's hair, but Father's dark eyes, while Zander got Father's black hair and Mother's blue eyes. Night and day they'd been called, and it fit.

Zander followed his mother into the kitchen. "Are you sorry Father moved in with you?"

She turned and reached up to cradle his face in her soft hands. He wasn't used to having a mother and, warrior or not, he held back tears that threatened to make him cry like a child.

"Before we separated you and Alexa, your father worked hard and never drank to excess. I thought once we reunited, we could be happy again, but the mead has changed him. I hope for all of us he can find himself." With a sigh, she released him.

He said nothing, but he wasn't at all sure the man Mother had loved was still in Father. Zander carried a plate heaped with warm bread and another with mounds of butter to the table.

Behind him, Mother said, "Shall we feast to celebrate the birth of my twins?"

Zander sat between Alexa and Greydon with Shadow at his feet. Mother and Father sat across from him, Father still glaring. Next to Mother, Zeph's eyes gleamed as he glanced at the heaping bowls of food. Between Alexa and Father, Merindah sat stiffly.

As Father reached for the roasted venison, Merindah bowed her head. "I'll bless the meal." She held up her hands, palms out. "Our God Almighty, who shall be blessed, world without end. We pray for mercy on our table spread, and what your gentle hand has given, let it by you be blessed. All that is good is yours, for you are good. Amen."

Father grunted and stabbed a chunk of meat from the tureen. Mother handed Zeph the bowl of sweet potatoes while Greydon buttered a roll. It was almost like a regular family meal.

Zander glanced sideways to find Alexa watching him. She was a fortune-teller, and he was a warrior. They were anything but normal.

CHAPTER FOUR

Alexa

Alexa lifted her head during the prayer and studied Zander—her brother, her twin. They might be opposites, night and day, but his stubbornness matched her own. She needed to convince him to listen to the cards. And what did he mean that Moira whispered in his ear?

When Merindah finished the prayer, Zander looked up and caught Alexa's eyes. His smile told her he was no longer angry, but that didn't mean he was ready to heed her warnings. She'd find a way to convince him to listen, but not in front of the others.

Instead, she turned to Greydon. "How's your brother?"

Greydon paused, a warm roll halfway to his mouth, and frowned. "Dharien? He's . . ." He seemed puzzled. "I don't talk to him much. He spends a lot of time with Lash." He sat back in his chair. "Why?"

Confused, Alexa hesitated. Greydon trained with Dharien. How could he not know how his own brother was doing? "I—I haven't seen him much since the quest. I wondered how he was, is all." She blushed at Zander's smile.

"I've talked with him," Merindah interjected. "He's working things out." She cocked her head at Alexa. "He's ashamed of his actions before the quest. He comes daily to the church to pray and talk with Father Chanse."

"We all accepted his apology," Alexa blurted. After the quest, Dharien had stood in front of the questers and begged forgiveness. As a group, they'd given it. She wasn't sure if she'd completely forgiven him for stealing Zander's tokens and endangering her twin's life during the quest, but Dharien claimed to love her. If he'd truly changed, she'd like to see if she shared his feelings.

"Sometimes forgiving yourself is harder than forgiving another." Merindah folded her hands on the table. "It's something to consider, Alexa."

Alexa's blush deepened. She glanced around the table. Mother had stopped eating, intent on the conversation. Zeph ate, head down, ignoring it. Her twin seemed amused, but Father growled, "Not the kind of talk for the table."

They finished the meal in silence, which left Alexa too much time to think. She ate slowly, hardly tasting the food. Merindah made it clear she didn't approve of Alexa apprenticing as a fortune-teller. Well, Alexa didn't approve of Merindah's choice either. Once, they'd been best friends, but it seemed they'd let this come between them. Moira and God might work together for the benefit of their village, but they weren't working together for Merindah and her.

Zander nudged her from her thoughts as he leaned in to whisper, "I'm ready for dessert. How about you?"

Father scraped his chair away from the table and grunted, "Good meal, Lark." He grabbed his mug and stumbled to his chair by the fire.

With Father gone, the mood lightened. Zeph looked up from his plate for the first time, and Merindah actually smiled when Mother brought out a layered carrot cake, which she cut into thick wedges and passed around the table.

Greydon clutched his belly and moaned. "Lark, you bake the best cakes in the village. Mother's cook sneaks off to buy from you when we have celebrations."

Laughing, Mother added another slice to his plate, and although he protested, Greydon had no trouble finishing both.

After the cake was gone and the table cleared, Mother handed a small package to Zander and one to Alexa. Zander encouraged Alexa to go first. She unwrapped the purple cloth to find hanks of silk embroidery ribbons dyed in rich shades of purple, red, and green and two skeins of fine gold and silver thread.

"Mother! Silk? They're beautiful!" She held the ribbons to her chest. They hadn't come from the Puck's Gulch market. "Where did you find them?"

"This morning, a Raskan woman asked to trade for seed cakes. She said the silks came from across the ocean. She asked about you both. Her name was Tshilaba."

Beside her, Zander startled at the name, but she felt a joy rise in her heart at the memory of the fortune-teller. She rushed to hug her mother. "I've never had a more beautiful gift. I know just the scene I want to stitch."

Zander scowled.

Alexa held his gaze. "I made mistakes in the quest last year. I learned from them." The magic in her embroidery had proven difficult to predict. She wouldn't admit to him that she still struggled with the outcomes.

Mother turned to Zander. "Open yours, Son."

He unfolded the black cloth and jerked his head up to stare at their mother. "Where did you find it?"

She beamed. "Last week while I searched the gulch for rose hips, I tripped and fell. As I rubbed my knee, I saw it next to me." Her voice dropped. "Is it the one?"

Zander held up the black and white stone. "It is." He explained to Greydon and Zeph. "It's the stone that saved my life." His face darkened. "It came from Moira, and Alexa insisted on using it even though we didn't know the outcome."

"You would have died without it." Alexa held up her hand to show the white circle burned in the center of her palm from using the stone.

Zander lifted his right hand with the matching mark. "I didn't mean to leave it, and I've gone back to search for it many times. Thank you, Mother."

In Alexa's pocket, the calcite vibrated. A certainty flowed through her that she didn't understand. It was no accident Mother found the stone.

Winter dark came early, and Merindah agreed to stay the night. Zander and Greydon would walk Zeph to his home in the shacks. Those who hadn't quested had a curfew of dark, and no one was allowed in the market square after closing, but the Protectors patrolling the area allowed the warriors to pass through.

Before he left, Zander pulled Alexa aside and pressed a sharp object into her palm.

It was a brooch with a single garnet surrounded by cut quartz stones. Gold leaves held the stones in place. Alexa was stunned. She'd wanted it so badly at the last festival, but didn't have the money.

"I saw you lusting over it." He laughed. "Good thing we don't get omens anymore."

She pinned it to her tunic and hugged him. "You shouldn't have spent your money, but I love it." Already she sensed the vibrations of the gold mix with the stones pulsing with energy. "Thank you, Zander." She pulled a plaited necklace of lavender stems beaded with amethyst from the bag she carried at her waist. "To calm you. Maybe Helios will soon let you ride." She kissed his cheek. "Don't wait so long to come back?"

"I don't know, Alexa." He rubbed the back of his neck. "How do you stand it here with Father, drunk the way he is?"

"You lived with him all those years." She searched his eyes. "I guess it's my turn. Mother hopes he'll come to his senses, but I think the mead has too strong of a hold on him." She hesitated. "Does Moira really speak to you?"

He rolled his eyes. "She comes in my dreams, like after the quest. She doesn't always bring a message, but she watches me. And at the end she whispers, *Zander, defender of all.*"

Her twin seemed to forget that "defender of all" included her. Father had told them that the names Alexa and Zander combined carried that meaning. She touched his arm. "But sometimes she gives you a message? What does she say?"

"That time is short." His bleak eyes sought hers. "It seems the displaced Odwans will invade us. They're used to war. How can we defeat them?"

"We'll do it together, just as we did in the quest. Our path is still the same."

He shook his head. "War is no place for you."

"I may not fight with bow or sword, but I will fight in the way I know."

"Through magic? Is Melina Odella teaching you how to defend against an enemy?"

"There is magic in me that Melina Odella knows nothing of. Ask Fate in your nighttime trysts. It comes from her, does it not? She speaks to you in dreams, but speaks to me through cards, stones, and embroidery. The sooner you see the wisdom in that, the sooner you'll be prepared for war."

"First the quest and now war." He searched her eyes. "It seems we have no choice over the direction our lives have taken."

"We have a choice, Zander, but at what cost? The quest was for naught if we didn't learn that lesson."

"And yet you still try to control through your embroidery?"

"Yes." She averted her eyes. As in the quest, she would do everything in her power to protect him.

"I hope I know what I'm doing." He hugged her. "I often doubt that I'm enough."

She couldn't help but tease him. "With Fate whispering in one ear and me in the other, how can you fail?"

CHAPTER FIVE

Zander

Zander sauntered with Greydon and Zeph through the market, waved at the trio of Protectors, and headed north toward the gulch. Despite the chill, it was a fine night to be out. Gentle flakes of snow reflected the moonlight as they drifted to the ground. Zeph lived in the opposite corner of the village from Elder Warrin's estate and the training grounds. He tried to convince Zander to let him walk alone after they passed the market, but Zander would have none of it. Getting caught out after curfew meant a night in jail. Zander wouldn't let Zeph take that chance.

They turned east at one of the two taverns that served the village. With the Raskans in town, the stone building bustled with activity. The travelers spent seven weeks in Puck's Gulch, coming before the winter snows to get settled for the Twelve Day Celebration that began on the first day of the new year.

Zeph stared at the ground as they passed the noisy tavern. His mother worked there as a barmaid. It was the tavern that Zander's father spent his time in and, like Zander, Zeph must have learned to take care of himself at a young age.

The music and laughter spilling out the door called to Zander. He was seventeen. He should be having fun, not be weighted with the safety of the village. He was permitted after completing the quest to enter the tavern, but his fear of turning into a drunk like Father kept him away. That and the responsibility of training warriors. But there were times he'd like to enjoy the music with his friends and maybe dance with a girl. Kaiya came to mind, but he pushed the thought away. Any fun he envisioned had to wait until the war was fought and won.

They passed the tavern without comment. When the mud hut Zander had grown up in loomed in front of him, the smell of lye hung in the damp air and stung his nose. His eyes blurred at memories, good and bad. Farther on, they reached the row of shack houses that housed the poorest workers. Most worked for Elder Terrec, the harshest employer in the village. The shacks held single mothers, and sometimes fathers, struggling to feed children who had little hope of a better life. Zander glanced at Greydon, who frowned, lost in his own thoughts. Greydon hadn't known a hungry night in his life.

Zander nudged his friend. "This is what we fight to protect. These people barely survive now, and their lives will be worse yet if we're conquered."

Greydon looked up and his face twisted. "I wish I didn't know of this." He nodded toward Zeph and whispered, "How does he survive this place?"

"The better question is why the rest of us allow it." Zander clenched his jaw. It might be easier to win the war than to change the village hierarchy.

After leaving Zeph at his shack house, Zander and Greydon walked south. By the time they arrived at the training grounds, they would have walked the entire perimeter of the village.

Zander pondered Alexa's words. Why was she so sure when he was so full of doubts? *Training* for war was one thing. He loved pushing himself and the others to do their best. There was an art to the swordplay that calmed him, and the hand-to-hand combat cleared his head of the worries that kept him awake at night. But the thought of real war invaded his dreams and haunted his thoughts.

Musing aloud, he said, "Alexa believes her magic can help with the war."

"Is her magic strong enough? She's only had six months of training."

Zander shrugged. "She thinks so."

"She should leave it to Melina Odella." Greydon slapped Zander's shoulder. "Dharien likes her."

"I'm not sure he has a choice." Zander grinned. "Did you know she gave him a love potion last year?"

Greydon snorted. "He told me, but he swears it no longer holds him. She's turned into a beauty. Paal and Lash watch her as well."

"Not Lash!" Zander kicked at a rock and sent it spinning down the path. Last spring Zander had seen Lash's secret—his father, Elder Terrec, beat him, but that didn't excuse Lash for acting like an arse.

"She could do worse." Greydon shrugged. "As the eldest son he'll inherit more than Dharien."

Zander pushed Greydon against the wall of the church and held him under his stern gaze. "Never say that. Melina Odella makes her own living as a fortune-teller. Alexa will never need to marry except for love."

"And what about you? Maybe *you* should marry for money the way you spend on bows and swords." Greydon chuckled and then turned serious. "You should ask for a tithe from the guilds."

"They'd never give it—not until they're convinced of our purpose."

"Yet, you don't mind asking my father to spend my future inheritance?"

"Stars!" Zander released him and stepped back. "Is that what this is about? You fear losing your fancy manor when the village could lose everything? If you don't believe in our cause, you should leave."

"I believe in you, Zander." Greydon held up his hand when Zander started to interrupt. "I defend you when others claim your madness will ruin us. I just think others should share the cost."

Zander slumped against the bricks. "And how do I convince them if they think I'm mad?"

"We need someone to liaise between the warriors and the guilds." Greydon spread his hands. "You don't have time, and you know I get tongue-tied when I speak in public."

Zander snorted. "Asking for money is hardly public speaking." He rubbed at his temples. "Let me guess. Lash?"

"He can be charming when he wants something." Greydon smirked. "He's our man."

"Just keep him away from my sister."

"As long as your sister agrees, it's a deal."

"She'll agree," Zander grumbled. "She knows an arse when she sees one."

They walked in silence. Something had been bothering Zander since Elder Warrin had given him the war horse. "Greydon? Do you mind that your father gave me Helios? He was meant for you."

"Hells, no. That horse is wild. I'm relieved Father will never expect me to ride him. You'll be lucky if he doesn't kill you."

Zander snorted. It was going to take a lot more than luck to ride that horse, and Zander had to break Helios, and soon. Elder Warrin bragged to the villagers how his horse would lead the fight. Zander had to ride Helios to earn the respect of not only the warriors, but the whole damn village.

"I feel unprepared to fight." Zander leaned his head back and cracked his neck. "I hate conflict and my stomach turns at the thought of killing a man. Why would Moira pick me?"

Greydon reached out to take Zander's arm. Shadows from the quarter moon fell across Greydon's face. "Would you rather Terrec led the men?" He laughed, but there was no mirth in it. "Or my father? Or the Protectors?" When Zander shook his head, Greydon continued. "My friend, you have the kindest heart of anyone I know. It seems to me that only a man of peace can be trusted to go to war."

CHAPTER SIX

Zephyr

Zeph woke in a sweat, panicked from his dream. Several minutes ticked by before he calmed enough to slow the pounding in his chest. Men in tattered jackets, with red hair and beards, marched down the north side of the gulch with bows and swords.

He turned on his straw tick and lay face down on the coarse fabric. The smell of mold made him sneeze, but he remained still, remembering as many details from the dream as he could. He must warn Zander. The dreams Zeph experienced right before waking always came true. Always.

Chilled from cold and fear, he shivered under the thread-worn coverlet. In forty-eight days, on the eve of the New Year, Zeph would turn sixteen. He shuddered at what his time of magic would bring. Already he possessed abilities he didn't want. The dreams, the . . . he shook his head, not wanting to think about the pain his second ability caused.

After dressing in the cold shack, Zeph kissed his mother's sleeping cheek. She served mead at the tavern and stayed after closing to drink. He wouldn't miss breakfast for there would be none. He didn't mind. He felt stronger because of it. He was glad he didn't have a father. The fathers in the shack houses were quick to beat their kids. His mother had never hit him. Not once. She loved him at least that much.

He had no reason to think Zander would believe him, but before he could change his mind, Zeph hiked across the village, cut through the market, and jogged to Elder Warrin's estate. Rushing into the warm hallway at the stables, he bumped into Greydon carrying a tray of steaming sausages and biscuits.

"Whoa, Zeph. Take it easy. What's the hurry?" Greydon placed the morning meal on the smooth oak table where Zander and Fulk huddled around cups of hot cider.

Zander's eyes shifted toward him, and he waved Zeph to the table. "Zephyr? What brings you so early?"

Zeph stared at the biscuit dripping with butter Zander offered and remembered the first time Alexa had given him a roll after he'd shown her the fortune-teller's door. She'd thought him shy, but he'd been mesmerized by the silver shimmer surrounding her. A shimmer of gold encompassed Zander now, and Zeph didn't know what to make of it. He shook his head at the biscuit, but the grumble from his stomach betrayed him.

"Sit. Eat. No messages until after breakfast." Zander nodded at the chair next to him.

Between mouthfuls of sausage, Fulk eyed him. "Boy, you look like you've seen a ghost." He pushed a mug at him. "Skin and bones, you are too, not much more than a spirit yourself."

The cider warmed his belly, lulling him into thinking he could ignore the dream that had driven him to the stable. As he listened to the discussion on the day's training schedule, he choked down a final bite of sausage, his nerves catching up to him.

After the last crumb disappeared, Zander turned to Zeph. His sharp gaze unsettled him. "Well, Zeph? What message does my sister send so early? A warning from her cards?"

"It's private." Zeph blushed when the three warriors stared in surprise.

Greydon's eyebrows rose, but he stood. As he and Fulk left through the stable doors, Zeph heard the marshal mutter, "He's a strange one, that boy."

If Fulk knew the truth, he'd think Zeph more than strange, which was why he kept his one ability a secret. After he was sure Greydon and Fulk were out of the stable, Zeph met Zander's eyes. "I had a dream."

Zander leaned his chin into his hands. "You, too?"

The urge to run rose from deep in his belly. He gripped the edge of the table to remain seated and blurted, "A group of red-haired men came down into the gulch." Zeph smoothed his own red hair, aware his ancestors were Odwans. "They carried bows and swords and long sticks with shields. The trees were green. They'll be here soon." He slumped against the chair, his energy deflated, now that he'd delivered his message.

"So it's true. The Odwans will invade." Zander rubbed at his temples.

Zeph's heart nearly thumped out of his chest. "You believe me?"

"You confirm the rumors. Moira pushes me to train harder. I know it's coming." Zander released a long sigh. "We need more men."

"I can help," Zeph blurted.

Zander glanced at Zeph, startled. "Zeph, you'll soon enter your time of magic. That will be enough of a challenge. You won't have time to train."

An unusual courage bloomed in Zeph's chest, and he persisted. "Quester class is only two mornings a week. I know the gulch. I could scout for you."

Sitting back in his chair, Zander's eyes narrowed while he drummed his fingers on the table. "If we're to win this fight, we'll need all the help we can find. I accept your offer, Scout Zephyr. Come back at the noon bells."

For a few seconds, Zeph couldn't breathe, but he hid his excitement. He nodded to Zander, stood, and forced himself not to run when he left. He'd prove to Zander he could help.

As the noon bells rang, Zeph rushed into the dining hall. A bonus of joining the warriors: he'd eat every day. While the other warriors filled their bowls with thick rabbit stew, Zeph's mouth watered. He couldn't help himself—he was always hungry. But first, he went to find Zander.

As the last stragglers hunkered down to eat, Zander stood at the front with Zephyr and rapped on the table. Unused to having so many eyes on him, Zeph shrunk back, but Zander laid his hand on Zeph's shoulder and kept him at his side.

Kaiya and the women sitting at a table near the front smiled, and Zeph took comfort from their support. It hadn't been easy for them to be accepted as warriors. They'd understand how he was feeling.

When Zander had everyone's attention, he announced, "I've learned the Odwans will most likely attack from the north, through the gulch. It will be spring or early summer at the latest."

The warriors murmured until Zander held up his hand. "We need new recruits, and Zephyr has volunteered his help." At their laughter, he tightened his hold on Zeph's trembling shoulder. "He hasn't quested yet, but Zeph is strong of will, and he knows the gulch as well as I. He'll train with us, but I want you to account for his size. Zeph is our scout."

At a table in the back, Lash snorted.

Zander cocked his head and asked, "You have a problem?"

"No problem," Lash said. "We'll treat him like a warrior." He smirked at Dharien and a man named Koe, who sat with him.

Koe blanked his face and said, "I think it's a great idea to have a scout. Zeph's one of us now."

A black shimmer hovered around the man's head. That was the ability Zeph kept hidden. He'd learned at an early age that the shimmer meant a lie. And people lied all the time. The surprise was that Lash had told the truth.

Zander's jaw tightened. "Zeph, get your stew and sit with Greydon. I'll join you soon." He strode to the back table.

From the way Zander stood, Zeph guessed he wasn't happy. Zeph hadn't been there an hour and he'd caused a problem. He clenched his fists and dug his fingernails into his palms. He'd do everything he could to make Zander proud of him.

When Zander joined Zeph at the table, he said, "You let me know if Lash or Koe give you any trouble. Hear me?"

He nodded, but it would have to be bad before Zeph would bother Zander. His leader had more important things to worry about than Zeph being bullied.

After the meal, Zander split the men and women into four groups. The women he sent with Fulk for archery. Ten grabbed knives for hand-to-hand fighting with Geno, a large man with a scar across his neck, who scared Zeph just looking at him. Ten others, who'd been nice to Zeph at lunch, went with Greydon to the pells with wooden practice swords.

The rest, including Zeph, followed Zander to the stables. They scooped manure from the stalls and hauled bales of straw for the floor. Together they oiled every piece of leather tack. Zeph's shoulders ached, and his fingers cramped, but he'd never been happier. With the chores finished, they saddled the horses.

"Do you want me to help with Helios?" Zeph asked Zander.

Zander rolled his eyes. "I'll work with him later, when there aren't any witnesses." He showed Zeph how to saddle Lady. "She's a good horse for your first ride. Greydon's bay is steady."

Nervous at first, Zeph soon found he rode as well as most of the men. He urged Lady into a trot and then a full gallop down the sides of the fields. Relishing the feel of Lady's strength under him, Zeph whooped when she jumped a short brick wall and continued past Zander's surprised face. Back at the stable, he dismounted, sorry the training was over. He brushed Lady and treated her with a carrot he'd stuck in his pocket during the meal. As she crunched, Zeph leaned his head against her side and scratched her neck. Lady's soft nicker filled Zeph with a contentment he'd rarely felt.

With the horse already drowsing, Zeph followed the other men to the wrestling building. Relieved that Zander taught him privately, Zeph surprised himself at how quickly he learned the moves. Zander outweighed him, but Zeph was quick and got more than one takedown by ducking out of Zander's grasp and grabbing his legs. He couldn't hold Zander for more than a second, but Zeph was content not to embarrass himself.

Even Fulk complimented him. "For a scrawny lad, ye did good," which was high praise from the marshal.

Only one thing marred his day. Zander may have called him a warrior, but Zeph could tell the others weren't yet convinced yet. Their looks were skeptical, not approving.

Before Zander sent Zeph home, he rummaged around in his dresser and pulled out a pair of sturdy pants and a tunic. "Here, these should fit. See you at breakfast."

Although he walked tall, Zeph's shoulders ached and muscles he didn't know he had throbbed. As he left, he heard Zander mutter, "Not so different from me a year ago."

Fulk roared, "And now look at ye, a warrior."

With his back to Zander and Fulk, Zeph allowed a grin to light his face. And now he was a warrior, too. He'd prove it to the others, no matter how hard he had to work.

CHAPTER SEVEN

Alexa

Two days after her birthday celebration, Alexa trekked to Melina Odella's cottage. She stopped at Zeph's shack house and knocked timidly, knowing his mother slept during the day. When he didn't come to the door, Alexa set a basket of sugar biscuits on the stoop and trudged on, dreading her lesson.

She wasn't the only one who found the fortune-teller moody and sharp-tongued. Not all in the village trusted Melina Odella, and she seemed to enjoy intimidating them with her haughtiness. As a fortune-teller, Alexa would cultivate an air of mystery, but she would not be aloof. She wanted to guide even those who couldn't pay much. Melina Odella wouldn't approve. It was another secret Alexa would keep from her teacher.

The closer Alexa came to the cottage, the more her stomach churned. Being an apprentice wasn't supposed to be like that. She should be excited to learn from her mentor, not worried about what mood she'd find her in. As soon as Alexa stepped into the cottage, she sensed a dark aura. Depressed energy swirled around Alexa and slowed her steps.

In the middle of the room, Melina Odella sat facing the door, head down, shoulders hunched, flipping card after card onto the table. Her scowl deepened with each toss. Unaware of Alexa, the fortune-teller muttered, "Fortune, Tower, Moon, Death." Then she glanced up and her scowl turned to anger. "You spy on me?"

Stepping back, Alexa shook her head. "I only now entered."

Melina Odella stood and swept the cards into one pile. With barely controlled anger, she spat, "Get your journal. We'll work on spells."

Not spells. The only use for the spells Melina Odella taught Alexa were to make hair fuller or grow faster, or ridiculous things like keeping a knife sharp or a pot shiny. Alexa wanted to learn how to grow herbs in the winter, or at least how to make an arrow fly true. She held in her sigh, knowing it would make Melina Odella angrier, slumped into a chair, and opened her journal. She flipped through the pages of potions. Who needed a potion for pretty feet? She skimmed recipes for smooth skin, plump cheeks, and removing warts. She wanted a spell to *give* warts. That would be amusing.

With a thump, Melina Odella sat across from Alexa and opened her own book. For several moments, she stared at Alexa. "I know you want to learn more important spells."

Alexa jerked her head up. "I–I think I'm ready."

With a snort, Melina Odella said, "You're not. You have to build a foundation. Master the small spells first. Walk before you run."

Alexa recoiled as if her teacher had slapped her. She pursed her lips and, with uncharacteristic control, kept her thoughts to herself. Mother had told Alexa once that Alexa ran as soon as she stood. Walking had never been her way. She didn't think Melina Odella would appreciate the analogy.

For two hours, Melina Odella droned on about spells for making bread rise in cold weather, keeping spiders out of a house, and getting a hen to lay an egg a day. There were five separate spells for keeping a goat from chewing on laundry hung outside to dry. Alexa wrote each down, growing more despondent. She didn't care about a goat eating towels. Keep the damn thing in a pen!

The only distraction came when Elder Nhara came to the door and whispered for a potion. When Melina Odella disappeared behind the red curtains that led to her stockroom, Alexa leaned forward and turned a few pages of the fortune-teller's book. She saw a spell that might actually come in handy. Luckily, she could read upside down. She wrote it quickly in the back of her own book and flipped back as Melina Odella strode into the room. If Alexa could get her hands on that book for a day or two, she'd learn something worth knowing.

As Elder Nhara left, the potion clutched in her hand, the noon bells rang. Melina Odella dismissed Alexa with the flip of a hand. "Enough for today. Don't come tomorrow, I have duties."

Relieved to be released, Alexa rushed to the market. She wove through the crowd to the west side to find the temporary homes of the travelers who'd arrived for the upcoming Twelve Day Festival. She'd forgotten Tshilaba until Mother mentioned trading for the ribbons. Even though she could read the cards for herself, she liked getting another's perspective, and Tshilaba had plenty of experience.

She hesitated when she came to the black tent with red symbols painted on the sides. She recalled the reading she and Zander had received in May before the quest. As she stood outside, the flap pulled back, and Tshilaba smiled from inside.

"Alexa!" she called. "I hoped to see you." Her dark skin contrasted with her pale blue eyes. Embroidered snakes swirled around her black velvet skirt.

Alexa eyed the stitching. When she earned the right to tell fortunes on her own, she'd sew one like it. With her favor, the snakes would actually move. She smirked. Melina Odella would hate that.

She stepped into the square tent, blinked a few times to get used to the dark, and studied the space with a fortune-teller's eyes. A table covered with a rich purple cloth sat in the middle of the room. White candles provided the only light. Baskets overflowing with bottles of potions and jars of salve filled one corner, while drying herbs hung from another, infusing the room with exotic scents Alexa couldn't place. Although stark compared to Melina Odella's room, Alexa felt a rapport she didn't feel with her teacher.

Two figures perched on low wooden stools in a third corner next to a potbelly stove that vented out the side. They stood when Tshilaba motioned to them. One was the red-haired girl who worked the Wheel of Fortune booth during the festivals. Unusual hair color for the Raskans. The other, a boy who looked a couple of years older than Alexa, wore a scowl and a braid running from his left temple to behind his ear. The rest of his dark blond hair was twisted up into a bun. They both had brown skin, common in the Raskans.

"This is my daughter, Sophia," Tshilaba said. "And my nephew, Jess."

Alexa stared at the silver rings Jess wore on every finger. Zander would never wear jewelry like that. When she looked up, his gray eyes startled her. She'd never seen eyes that color.

"What's your problem, Chadha girl?" He glared at her, and Sophia giggled.

"Be kind, Jess." Tshilaba nodded to the back of the tent. "Leave us."

Chadha girl? Jess said it like a swear. As Sophia and Jess slipped out a hidden flap, Alexa collected her thoughts. Other than Tshilaba, she'd only seen the Raskans at the festival booths or trading with the merchants. They kept to themselves when not working. Maybe they didn't like the other tribes.

"My Sophia is our Chosen One." Tshilaba's eyes lit up. "Her destiny is foretold to hold great magic. She'll bring honor to our people."

A year ago, at the May Festival, Sophia had given Alexa a star for her quest. She'd said then that Moira spoke to her. Alexa hadn't believed her, but maybe she'd spoken true.

"It is rare for our tribe to have a red-haired fortune-teller—the Chosen One comes only once every few generations." Tshilaba's many bracelets jangled as she brought her cards from her pocket. "You came for your future, yes? Let's see what the cards say."

A shadow at the back of the tent caught Alexa's attention. Remembering her first reading with Tshilaba, she frowned. "Where's the black panther?"

Tshilaba raised her eyebrows. "Panther?"

"The black panther that sat next to your table when Zander and I had our reading."

"I've never had a panther." Tshilaba cocked her head. "Perhaps it was a phantom warning only for your eyes."

Alexa snorted. "We didn't listen very well."

"Come, sit." Tshilaba shuffled the cards and splayed them across the silken cloth. "Choose your cards."

People who agonized over every card, afraid of picking the wrong one, annoyed Alexa. With no hesitation, she intuitively turned over five cards.

Tshilaba studied the cards, as did Alexa. The deck differed from the ones she used, but the meanings remained the same. The Tower, the Five of Swords, the Devil, the Five of Cups, and the Magician spread across the table.

"You still try to control," said Tshilaba.

Alexa nodded.

"Youth is the time to rebel." Tshilaba patted Alexa's hand. "To believe you know better than Fate."

Leaning forward, Alexa asked, "And what of you? Do you always trust Moira?"

"Trust? That is entirely different from acceptance. I trust that Moira will do as she desires, and I accept that I may not like it."

Alexa laughed. "Well put."

The Raskan's gaze turned serious. "You must learn to use your gift quickly. The village will need you far sooner than one of your age would be ready."

"What of Melina Odella?"

"It is you who will fight in this war."

"I don't trust her." Alexa hesitated. Did she trust this fortune-teller enough to confide in her? Her gut feeling was that she could, so she said softly, "She betrayed Zander before the quest."

Tshilaba closed her eyes and after a few moments spoke in a voice that drifted from deep within. "The Devil lies between the Fives. She will betray you once more."

Sudden dread clutched Alexa's heart and she started to tremble. "How will I know?"

"Pay attention. Question everything she teaches. Don't defy her, but keep your secrets. Her betrayal will be less dear if you're prepared."

She had felt it. She would be careful with Melina Odella. Her teacher wouldn't catch her unaware.

Tshilaba interrupted her thoughts. "The silk ribbons? Did you like them?"

Thrown by the sudden change in conversation, Alexa's stuttered, "Th-they're beautiful."

"They are for your magic. Not for others. Understand?"

"Yes."

"I wish you could apprentice with me, but your place is here for now." Tshilaba hesitated. "When I return, will you travel with me? Let me teach you for six months. Sophia could use the challenge of another student."

Shock rolled through her body. Leave her twin, their parents? Leave Dharien? "Six months?"

"It's a big world out there, Alexa."

"Can I think about it?" If Jess's reaction to her reflected the other Raskans, she might not be welcome.

"It will be as it will be." Tshilaba swept up the cards and motioned Alexa to the bench behind her. "I have a gift for you."

When Alexa sat with her, Tshilaba pressed her palm against Alexa's forehead. "Close your eyes."

A tingle started in the center of her forehead and turned into a throb. Alexa watched images behind her eyes turn into a story. The pictures flashed through her life, starting with the day she and Zander had been separated—a day she didn't even remember. She watched as she cried herself to sleep, afraid of the dark without her brother. She watched her mother weep, as heartbroken as Alexa.

The scene flipped through each birthday as she watched herself become more and more unhappy with her mother's expectation that she become a baker. When she reached her sixteenth, she saw the ungrateful child she'd become. Her cheeks flushed. The scenes flipped quickly through the six months before the quest, showing her schemes and plans. Tears rolled down her cheeks when she and Zander discovered they were twins.

Scenes from the quest showed her still trying to control her own destiny as well as the others, and she grimaced at the way she'd tried to get Merindah to bend to her will. She threw her body in front of Zander to protect him from the panther. She cringed as she saw his horror at the viciousness of the attack that tore her throat. She saw another figure she'd not been aware of—Moira stood at her feet and gazed intently at the happenings. Fate whispered to Zander, "The red stone," and then "use the heart." And when Zander sat back on his heels, Moira flicked her wrist and the snake appeared next to him. She whispered, "Shadow" and after the snake struck, she held out her palm as if to prevent a second bite while Shadow grabbed it.

Remembering how sure she was that Zander was dying, Alexa's eyes filled with tears. Moira whispered, "The final stone, Alexa." In her vision, as Alexa held up the black and white stone, Moira appeared ghostlike in front of Zander. When Alexa pressed the stone between her palm and her twin's, Moira spread her arms across them. Then Alexa saw her stand back and smile.

Tshilaba released Alexa's forehead, and Alexa fell forward. "Tshilaba, did you see . . ."

"No. It was for you alone."

"Can you teach me to do that?"

Tshilaba's eyes held the promise of secrets.

Alexa yearned to know them with a desperation that surprised her. She whispered, "Yes, I'll go with you next year."

CHAPTER EIGHT

Zephyr

Zeph could scarcely believe Zander had asked him to train with the warriors. Excitement had kept him awake until after Mother came home from the tavern, and then he overslept. He ran all the way to Elder Warrin's estate and rushed into the outbuilding, blushing at the laughter he felt directed at him. He grabbed a cold biscuit and a slice of ham as Zander assigned him to archery practice. He had it eaten before he reached the practice field.

Zander handed Zeph a bow. He tripped over the end and nearly fell as he lined up with the women down one side of him.

Zeph's cheeks burned when Lash took the space next to him and called out, "Hoy, little warrior. Sure you're ready to play with the men?" Lash turned to Koe and laughed. "What was Zander thinking, recruiting a baby?" He swiveled back to Zeph. "What are you, twelve?"

"Almost sixteen," Zeph mumbled.

Zander strode to stand behind Zeph. His voice rang out down the line of archers. "Get ready to shoot." He adjusted the bow in Zeph's hands and frowned. "This will never work. It's too long for you." He took the bow and headed to the shed where they kept the supplies.

At Lash's muffled laughter, Zeph felt the sting of his earlier words. He might be almost sixteen, but he did look closer to twelve.

The only thing that kept him from bolting was remembering Zander's words. "*He'll be invaluable to us during a battle.*"

When Zander returned, he handed Zeph a smaller hunting bow. Zander said loud enough for everyone to hear, "A scout needs a smaller bow so he can hide more easily from his enemy."

As Zander called out, "Nock, draw, release," Zeph fumbled with the arrows, shooting one into the ground instead of at the target. At least with Zander standing behind Zeph, Lash didn't dare laugh. He soon got the hang of nocking the arrow, as well as pulling and releasing almost smoothly, but his arrow often hit the ground before getting as far as the target. Zander was patient, like Zeph imagined an older brother might be, had he been lucky enough to have one.

Zeph was thankful when the noon bells rang and Zander called a halt to session. His shoulders ached as he stood last in line to put away the bows. He stepped into the windowless shed and hooked the bow on a nail. Before he could turn, the door slammed. The bolt clicked shut and familiar laughter filled his ears.

He stumbled in the dark to the door, knowing it was hopeless. The others had already rushed to the outbuilding for the midday meal. He sat on the rough wooden floor and waited. Minutes went by and then half an hour. Zeph lowered his head and sat stoically. He'd be found when the next group came for their bows, but he dreaded the laughter that was sure to come, or worse, pity.

Soft steps outside the door made Zeph jump to his feet. The bolt shot to the side. When the door opened, one of the women warriors stared open-mouthed at him. A large crow sat on her shoulder.

Kaiya's look of surprise quickly turned to one of anger. "Who did this?"

He shrugged and stepped out of the shed, blinking in the sudden light.

She grabbed his arm. "We're going to Zander."

He rolled away from her. "It was a prank. I'm fine."

She narrowed her eyes. "I have an idea who it was. Promise me—if he pulls something like this again, you'll tell Zander?"

He'd never whine to Zander about something so small. He mumbled, "I'll take care of it," and hoped Kaiya would accept it.

She seemed to when she nodded. "Lucky for you, I left my jacket in the shed." She grabbed the brown wool garment off a hook and pulled it on over her hemp tunic. "No one else needs to know."

Relief flooded Zeph at her understanding. Kaiya lived in the row houses, one step up from the shacks. She'd understand how much he wanted to fit in.

"You missed the noon meal." She glanced at the warriors pouring out of the outbuilding. "We're with Greydon next." She wrinkled her nose "Swords. Come on. I'll walk with you."

When they reached the practice field, the women split off to the side to drill with each other. They didn't have the muscles of the men, and Zeph wasn't sure it was a disadvantage they could overcome. Greydon sent Zephyr to their group, and to his surprise, Zeph found them better swordsmen than he'd ever be. What they lacked in strength, they made up for in speed and finesse. His shoulders already burned from pulling the bow earlier that day, and as he swung, the wooden practice sword grew heavier with each passing minute. By the end of an hour, his head dropped in shame.

"Don't worry, Zeph," Greydon consoled him. "I wasn't any bigger than you when I was fifteen. You'll grow, and it'll get easier."

A black mist surrounded Greydon's head. Disgusted, Zeph turned away. People lied all the time about things that weren't important. Greydon had always been tall for his age.

As he trudged to put the sword away, Zeph's feet were swept out from under him. He fell hard to the ground. The wooden sword bounced up and smacked his lip. He leaned out so the blood dripped on the ground and not on his tunic.

In a flurry, Kaiya was in Lash's face, poking her finger in his chest. "You do that again and you'll answer to me."

Lash stepped back and spread out his hands. "I don't know what you're talking about. I didn't do anything to the little warrior." He backed away, laughing. "Not my fault he's clumsy."

Zeph slumped against the ground, confused. Lash was lying, but no black shimmer showed around his head.

CHAPTER NINE

Zander

While leaning against the stable door, Zander watched the men and women head for home after another long day of training. The throbbing in his thigh angered him. Damn boar.

Greydon strode toward Zander, looking as weary as Zander felt. He slumped against the wall next to Zander. "Rough day."

Zander shoved away from the door to face Greydon. "Another day closer to a war. Every night I ask myself if we'll be ready."

"We push them as much as we dare." Greydon gestured at the path leading to the stable. "Here comes your newest recruit."

Zeph broke from the group and trotted to the stable. "Thanks for letting me train."

Zander clapped Zeph's shoulder. "Hope today wasn't too tough for you. Will I see you tomorrow?"

After a moment's hesitation, Zeph nodded.

Zander held on to his shoulder. "Zeph? We have an extra room in the stable. It's small, but do you want to move in here with me? You could bring your things tomorrow."

Uncharacteristically for Zeph, he grasped Zander's hand and touched his forehead to it. Zander almost couldn't hear his words.

"Yes." Zeph turned and walked stiffly down the path leading to the village.

"I'm not sure why I did that." Zander rubbed the back of his neck.

Greydon's smile lit his face. "Fate knows the boy can use some attention."

Zander groaned. With his invitation to Zeph, Zander's private time at the stable would be non-existent.

"He's not the only one that worships you. Most of the men think you're the next best thing to God. Defender of all."

Zander's head snapped up at Greydon's words. "I hope I don't disappoint them. Do you think we'll be ready?"

"If we're invaded, we'll have to be."

"If?"

Greydon studied his hands. "We don't know. You're basing your gulch strategy on a boy's dream."

Zander ran his hands through his dark hair. The owl feather he'd tied on the side caught in his fingers. "It makes sense. The marsh beyond the gulch will be impassable until early summer. Have you looked in Zeph's eyes? He carries secrets."

"Like you?"

Greydon was too close to the truth. Zander ignored the question. "I believe in him."

"Just don't tell everyone what your source is."

Zander grinned. "I'm not stupid."

Greydon grew serious. "We still need to talk about Lash."

Zander swore. "It's time, I guess. Help me pitch some manure. It seems fitting."

They grabbed pitchforks and tossed manure into a cart to be taken later and spread on the alfalfa field. Between stalls, Zander asked, "Do you believe he'll do right for us? I don't trust him."

After a long toss that missed the cart, Greydon said, "I don't either, but I've thought on it, and I still think he's our best choice.

You don't want to do it, and I can't. The only other sons of elders are Paal and Dharien. Neither have the money sense of Lash."

Another forkful of manure missed the cart. "What's Dharien doing hanging out with Lash?" Zander thought he and Dharien had settled their differences after the quest. Dharien had seemed eager to make a fresh start and joined the warriors when he could have taken the easier path of becoming a Protector. Zander glanced at Greydon's scowl. "What?"

"I don't know if even Dharien knows what he's doing. He won't talk to me." Greydon tossed the pitchfork at the wall. "We used to be close. The quest changed him, but he won't confide in me." He twisted his mouth. "I don't suppose you'd tell me?"

Dharien would have died if Zander and Alexa hadn't found him on the final day of the quest. The three had fought their most dangerous omens, the black panthers, together. Zander shook his head. "It's better left unsaid."

"Somehow I doubt that. Maybe I can get you to the tavern. A few mugs of mead might loosen your tongue."

Zander snorted. "Not likely. I won't be a drunk like my father."

"Drinking a pint now and then doesn't make you a drunk."

"Not going to happen."

They finished the last stall in silence, and Greydon leaned against the rail. "What about Lash?"

Ignoring the warning twist in his gut, Zander said, "We'll talk to him tomorrow." He stepped back and landed one boot in a pile of manure that had missed the cart. The smell wafted up and burned his nose.

"And Zander?"

He looked up from scraping his boot against the cart to see Greydon's furrowed brow. "What?"

"It's your call, but what will you do about Alexa?"

"What do you mean?"

"At least three men can't keep their eyes off her when she visits." Greydon hesitated.

"And?"

"Maybe you could encourage her to promise to a man outside our ranks?"

Incredulous, Zander stared at Greydon. "You want me to tell my sister who to love?"

"What does love have to do with it? Find her a good match and convince her of the wisdom. Then she can forget about meddling in your affairs."

"You really don't know my sister, do you?" Zander went over the conversation he was not having with his twin. Telling Alexa what not to do was a sure way of getting her to do it.

"I know she's distracting our men. And my brother is one of them."

"So talk to Dharien. I won't tell Alexa what to do."

CHAPTER TEN

Alexa

While sitting across from her mentor, Alexa copied yet another useless spell as Melina Odella recited it. Seriously, who needed bread to rise more quickly? She forced a smile. Melina Odella didn't respond well to anger.

"I've been practicing reading the cards."

Annoyance flitted across Melina Odella's face. "Understanding the cards takes years of study." She flipped a page in her journal and recited the words to a spell for keeping a floor clean.

Useless, useless, useless. It was all Alexa could do to write the spell. She was wasting her time with Melina Odella's teachings. A war loomed. She needed spells that made arrows fly true. Spells that protected the village, not a floor from dirt. Spells that saved lives. Without thinking, she sighed.

Melina Odella snapped her book shut. "If I'm wasting your time, you can leave."

Alexa met her teacher's angry eyes. "The village is in danger. Zander will need my help."

Stone-faced, Melina Odella leaned toward Alexa and wagged her finger in her face. "You aren't ready now and you won't be ready for a very long time. *If* the village is invaded, Zander will fail. He's seventeen. He can't lead a war."

A wave of dizziness washed over Alexa. She grabbed the edge of the table to steady herself. "Moira picked him. She believes in him."

Melina Odella's mocking, high-pitched laughter filled the room. "Moira. Still you trust her?"

Did she? Uncertainty rose like flood waters, fast and furious. Just as quickly, it receded. She trusted Moira more than Melina Odella. Alexa sucked in a deep breath. "If we're invaded, we have no choice but to trust her. Zander's our only hope." She steeled herself for Melina Odella's reaction, but the fortune-teller only pursed her lips. "Why is that, Melina Odella? Why has Fate given Zander the task of protecting our village when you, the priest, and the elders should be the ones to save us? Tell me why?"

Melina Odella leaned back in her chair. "You're the one who gave Chanse a love potion and ruined my life. You're the one who disgraced Chanse in front of the church. You're the one who cheated in the quest and brought everyone home safely when half of you should have died."

What did those things have to do with protecting the village? And how did Melina Odella know about the quest? Jumbled thoughts rolled around inside Alexa's head. She needed to be careful with what she said next.

Before Alexa could speak, Melina Odella slapped her hands on the table. "You do not speak for Moira. I do." She twisted her hands together and glared at Alexa. "I've devoted my life to Moira's wishes. You will not usurp me."

Her teacher had gone mad. Melina Odella paced the room and Alexa's throat tightened. Suddenly, Melina Odella seemed to calm, but the fire in her eyes denied any peace.

"You think you're ready?" Melina Odella threw the cards onto the table. "Let's see." She jerked the chair away from the table and sat hard.

Suddenly nervous, Alexa took the deck in trembling hands. She fought the urge to heave while she shuffled the cards and spread them across the table.

Melina Odella snapped up the cards one at a time until five faced up. She glared at Alexa. "What say you?"

Alexa laid them in a line. The Sun, The Lovers, Two of Swords, Nine of Pentacles, and the Queen of Wands.

With a pounding heart, Alexa studied the cards. It seemed her teacher had intentionally chosen wrong. They made no sense. And if she misread them, Melina Odella would declare her unfit. She closed her eyes and fingered the red heart at her neck. A vision of the future flashed behind her eyes. Melina Odella fleeing the village. Melina Odella hiding in a rocky canyon. Melina Odella spelling a curse that surrounded the village.

Alexa's eyes flew open. She dropped her gaze to the cards to avoid looking at her teacher and picked up the first card.

Later that night, alone in her room, she had no memory of what she'd said to Melina Odella. Only that her teacher declared with a great deal of satisfaction that she needed more practice.

But the images that had flitted through her head couldn't be forgotten. Alexa felt the evil of the spell even as she remembered it. Would that be the betrayal Tshilaba had warned against?

She shuffled her cards and asked a question—What need I fear from Melina Odella? She chose one and turned it over. The Five of Swords. Betrayal and Deceit.

CHAPTER ELEVEN

Zephyr

Zeph trudged to the archery field. As hard as he'd tried, he wasn't getting any better with the bow. He lined up next to Zander. Maybe this would be the day he'd do it right.

Behind Zeph, Greydon's voice rang out. "Ready to shoot." Twelve archers came into position.

Zeph eyed Zander's stance and tried to copy it. Feet shoulder length apart, right leg slightly behind the left.

"Nock."

He pointed the bow down. The arrow bounced to the ground before he could settle the notched end into the hemp cord. His cheeks flushed. He was the last to be ready.

"Mark."

He raised the bow and focused on the target thirty yards in front of him. He turned his head from side to side trying to get a fix on it.

"Draw."

His right arm pulled back the string, muscles trembling. Maybe this time he'd hit a bulls-eye.

"Loose."

As he released the arrow, Zeph's arm jerked up. His heart sank as his arrow flew over the target.

Greydon continued with "Nock. Mark. Draw," until all twelve

arrows had flown. A few of Zeph's hit the target, but none close to the center.

After the warriors collected their arrows, Zander stood next to Zeph and frowned. "You write your letters with your right hand?"

He didn't understand what writing had to do with shooting, but Zeph nodded.

"I want you to try something." Zander took the bow from Zeph's left hand and placed it in his right. "Pull back the string without an arrow a few times."

"It feels awkward." He hated that the others stared.

After Zeph drew a few more times, Zander said, "Try it with an arrow."

Zeph fumbled with the arrow. It flipped out of his hand. Guffaws rang out behind him. It seemed he was the morning's entertainment.

Zander stooped to pick it up and handed it back to him. "Take your time."

When Zeph had the arrow nocked, Zander called out, "Mark. Draw. Loose."

Zeph watched his arrow fly true to the target. Almost a bullseye! His mouth dropped, and he whirled around at Zander's whoop.

"Again. Nock. Mark. Draw. Loose."

Arrow after arrow hit the target.

Zander grinned. "You might use your right hand, but you sight with your left. I should have thought of it sooner."

Zeph couldn't stop smiling.

He'd trained for six weeks with the warriors. Zeph slumped on his bed in the stable. His wrestling had improved, but he couldn't get a takedown. At archery practice, he hit the target every time, but not often the center. The only place he felt comfortable was with the horses or alone with Zander. And neither happened as often as he'd like.

Every man in training demanded Zander's time, and after the day ended, Greydon stayed to talk strategy. Lash and Dharien joined them more often now, and, for many reasons, Zeph didn't like Lash. He was sure Lash lied to Zander, but no telltale black mist appeared over his head. Zander obviously didn't trust Lash either. Zeph watched him force his body to relax when Lash joined them.

It was almost the New Year. Zeph's birthday came the day before, forcing him into his time of magic as the youngest quester. He hated that he'd miss training for the quester class, but his battered body was ready for the break they'd take for the Twelve Day Feast.

He headed to the pells and picked up the wooden practice sword Zander had special made for him. It was smaller than the others. He hated that, hated being smaller, hated the special treatment because of it. He sucked in a deep breath. He couldn't help his size, but he could control how hard he worked.

He approached the pells single-mindedly. Twelve round posts stuck in the ground and most were being attacked by other warriors. Zeph found a free one in the middle. He stared at the six-foot post and imagined it as Lash. He thrust his blade where a man's heart would be and then jabbed at what would be the thigh. He twisted and cut behind the "knee," imagining his foe dropping. Sweat poured down his temples and back, and still he swung the blade.

He felt a hand on his shoulder. "Whoa, Zeph. Take it easy."

Zeph blinked through glazed eyes. "Zander?"

"Who else? You looking to kill the pell?"

The adrenaline rush gone, Zeph's muscles trembled. The fury that had fueled his fight drained. He leaned against the wooden blade he'd planted on the ground and wiped sweat from his face.

Zander's eyes swept Zeph's body and returned to study his face. "Everything all right?"

Zeph nodded. He wasn't a tattler.

"You'd tell me if something was bothering you?"

Or someone. Zeph stared at the ground and nodded again.

"Hoy, Zander!" Greydon strode to the pells. "You're needed at the archery range."

Grateful for the interruption, Zeph dragged the wooden blade across the grounds and returned it to the outside rack. The practice blades weighed twice as much as the steel scimitars. His muscles complained, but Zeph managed a grin. At least he had muscles now.

His smile faded when he heard two voices inside the shed. One was Lash. Zeph pressed against the rough wood.

"Greydon's a fool if he thinks I'm giving him everything I collect from the villagers."

Laughter, and then another voice murmured. Zeph crept closer to listen.

Lash continued. "A few coins from each guild's bag won't be missed."

Zeph heard the men's boots at the door. He slunk to the other side of the shed. Lash strode toward the manor. Greydon's brother, Dharien, laughed next to him.

Zeph could go to Zander now, or he could wait. Lash would deny it, and Zeph had no proof. He would wait.

CHAPTER TWELVE
Two Days Before the New Year

Alexa

It had been a week since Alexa had a lesson. She'd trekked out to Melina Odella's cottage early that day only to be banished again with the excuse her teacher had a council session. So instead of learning magic, Alexa spent the day baking. Mother was exhausted trying to meet the demands for her special breads and cakes for the Twelve Day Celebration. With the last round of sugar biscuits cooling on the counter, Alexa filled a basket with warm cinnamon rolls. She pulled the hood of her green cloak over her head and made the trek to Elder Warrin's estate. She missed Zander. She wouldn't mind if she ran into Dharien, too.

Dusk rolled in as she made her way to the stable. Zeph stood outside the door. Since he'd joined the warriors, she rarely saw him. He'd grown a couple of inches, and his too-thin frame had filled out a little. His genuine happiness to see her warmed her heart. She smiled at the feather tied in his hair. Just like Zander's.

"Alexa! What are you doing here?" He took the basket from her and leaned in to sniff. "Cinnamon?"

She laughed for the first time in a very long time. "Cinnamon rolls. They taste fine, but they rose lopsided." She rolled her eyes. "Mother would be ashamed to put them out for sale. Although if

I'd told her I was taking them to Zander, she would have insisted I bring the good looking ones."

Zeph cocked his head at her. "Don't they taste the same?"

Indeed. But the elders who could afford the rolls wanted only the best. She reached into the basket and pulled one out. "See for yourself."

The look of rapture that crossed Zeph's face as he took a bite made her laugh again. "Isn't my brother feeding you?"

He mumbled around the roll. "Not like this."

She turned to find Dharien and Paal coming up the path behind her. Both men were sweaty, their bodies lean and muscular under their training clothes, but it was Dharien who drew her gaze. He'd always had that effect on her.

She gave them each a quick hug. "It's been months. How are you?"

"Ready for a break." Paal groaned. "Zander pushes us to our limit." He patted his belly. "Lost the last of my baby fat."

Dharien grinned. "With the way you eat, I don't see how." When he looked back to Alexa, his grin faded and sadness filled his eyes. He touched the scarf around her neck. "Why do you wear this?"

"Because I hate that scar. It reminds me every day of the panther attack. It's ugly." She flushed, aware that Dharien must hate his own scar that ran across his cheek where he couldn't hide it. She whispered, "Dharien, I'm sorry!"

He pulled back and stared at the ground. She wanted to reach out and take his hand, but it had been so long since they'd talked, she felt shy. An awkward silence fell between them.

"Alexa?"

She'd forgotten Zeph standing behind her. She spun to face him. He held out the basket. "Want me to take these to Zander?"

"Uh, yeah. I'll go with you." She turned back to Dharien and Paal. "Maybe I'll see you at the Welcoming Ceremony?"

Paal brightened. "Let's meet for the noon meal?"

Dharien hesitated and then nodded. "Sure, let's meet up."

"I'll look for you." She'd find a way to make up for her careless words. He had to understand it was different for boys. He looked strong with the scar on his cheek. She walked with Zeph to the stable. Although her heart ached at the pain she sensed in Dharien, she resisted the urge to look back.

Inside, Zander sat with Greydon and Fulk. Maps covered the table, held at the corners with stones. The three leaned in, studying the gulch and northern border of the village. Shadow slept at Zander's feet.

Zeph set the basket in the middle of the map. "Alexa brought cinnamon rolls."

Zander looked up then. Alexa gasped at the dark circles under his eyes. "Have you not been sleeping?"

He rubbed his temples. "I'll catch up during the break. Greydon insists we stop training during the celebration."

"He's not the only one exhausted." Greydon regarded Zander. "Weary men make poor warriors."

She interjected, "And women. You have women warriors as well."

Fulk grabbed a roll and scraped his chair back, as if pulling away from a fight. Zeph disappeared into his room.

Greydon looked up at her defiantly. "War is no place for girls."

She crossed her arms. She didn't come to argue with Greydon, but she couldn't let that slide. War was no place for anyone—male or female.

Before she had a chance to speak, Zander half-rose and leaned forward to glare at Greydon. "I'm tired of this argument. Moira chose them. They stay."

"And when they die in battle? It's not Moira who'll tell their families." Greydon didn't wait for a reply. He jumped from his chair and strode toward the door. "See you after the celebration. Maybe you'll have come to your senses by then."

Stunned, Alexa slumped into a chair. She'd never known Zander and Greydon to have words. She laid her hand on Zander's arm. "I didn't mean to start an argument."

He dropped his head into his hands. "You didn't. It's a daily discussion." He reached into the basket.

She waited until he finished the roll and was licking icing off his fingers. "I need to talk to you about Melina Odella."

Fulk grabbed another roll. "I'm off to the tavern." He patted Alexa's shoulder and nodded toward Zander. "A pint would do him good. Maybe you, too." He whistled as he left.

Zander turned weary eyes to Alexa. "What about Melina Odella?"

He looked so miserable Alexa couldn't bring herself to cause him more worry. She'd deal with Melina Odella without his help. "It's not important. Get some sleep." The relief on his face convinced her she'd made the right decision. "We're celebrating Zeph's birthday on the eve of the New Year. I'll see you then?"

"I'll be there." He stood. "Come on, Shadow. Time for bed."

He disappeared into his room, and Alexa sat for a moment alone. Before she told Zander he couldn't count on the fortune-teller's help, she'd come up with new plan. Zander needed her on his side.

CHAPTER THIRTEEN

Two Days Before the New Year

Zander

Zander leaned against the open door of the stable sipping a cup of hot cider. It was nearing mid-morning, and the grounds were empty except for Shadow chasing a hare. It had been a month since they'd hunted. Now, with two weeks off, maybe they'd have time. He massaged the back of his neck. Every day the warriors didn't train left them that many days short of being ready for an invasion. And after twelve days of feasting the men *and* women would come back out of shape and out of practice.

Greydon's words still rankled Zander. Moira wouldn't have picked the women if they weren't going to be needed. He flinched thinking of spirited Kaiya hurt or worse. She trained as hard as any of the men and had emerged as a leader among the women. Kaiya. What he'd give for a few minutes alone with her. He sighed and tossed the dregs of the cider into the yard. Until the village was safe, he had no business thinking about her in that way.

Another problem with having all those days off: too much time to obsess about all the things that could go wrong. If the invaders attacked, everyone he loved was in danger. It was his responsibility to protect them.

He grabbed a pitchfork and headed for a stall. He'd taken on

Fulk's duties so the marshal could have a real holiday with his family. Zander sure wasn't spending it with his. Father would be drunk, Mother overworked, and Alexa badgering him about his destiny as foretold by the cards.

Stumbling out of his room, Zeph yawned. "Did I miss breakfast?"

Zander snorted. "It's near noon." He nodded toward the small kitchen. "One cinnamon roll left. Help yourself." He smiled at the look on Zeph's face. The boy liked sweets as much as Zander did. He was quiet, too, which Zander appreciated. He'd enjoy spending more time with him. As much as Zander liked Greydon, his friend talked as much as Alexa. Sometimes they both wore him down.

As Zander finished the last stall, Zeph wandered out of the kitchen with icing smeared on his cheek and headed straight to Helios's stall. He fed the horse wrinkled apples and chuckled when Helios licked the sugar off his face.

Zander thought back to a year ago when he was Zeph's age and ready for his time of magic. He would have volunteered without a second thought if the village was in danger. Maybe Zeph was old enough to make the choice.

Watching Zeph with Helios, Zander sighed. Over the holiday he'd work at breaking the war horse. Helios still didn't tolerate more than a few minutes with Zander in the saddle. At least Zeph would be the only witness when he hit the ground.

He joined Zeph at the gate to Helios's stall. "How's our favorite horse?"

Zeph lay his ear against Helios's neck. "He's ready for a ride."

Huh. Was he joking? When Zeph's solemn face turned, Zander saw the truth of his words. "Let's get him saddled."

Zander pulled the reins off the wall, and Zeph slipped the bit between Helios's teeth while Zander saddled the horse. He checked the girdle twice—not so tight as to be uncomfortable, not so loose it would slip.

When Helios pawed at the ground, Zeph kept hold of the lead. Hesitant, he searched Zander's eyes. "He's nervous because you're nervous. Until you're calm, he's going to throw you."

His racing heart told him Zeph spoke true. Zander rubbed his forehead. "It's hard to stay calm when he throws me every time I ride."

"He won't throw me."

"I can't take the chance," Zander said. Alexa would never forgive him if Zeph were injured.

Zeph pleaded, "Let me try."

The boy stood there with a calmness that Zander couldn't begin to summon when he thought of riding the war horse. If Zeph could ride Helios, Zander would know it was his nerves that were the problem. He sucked in a deep breath. "Just around the circle."

Zeph swung up into the saddle, and Zander led Helios into the outside ring. He flipped the reins to Zeph. "Walk him."

Dumbfounded when Helios didn't buck with Zeph, Zander said, "Let him trot."

The horse moved into a cantor, elegant and magnificent. Zeph seemed to blend with the horse. Zander realized what he must do if he was ever going to ride the stallion. The tension he carried weighed him down. He needed time in the forest to release the knot in his gut.

He'd take Zeph with him. Zeph hid the same pain Zander felt at that age. Meditating in the forest, away from the clamor of the village, would be the answer for both of them.

CHAPTER FOURTEEN

Zephyr

Zeph trotted Helios around the ring. On Helios's back, Zeph joined with the horse's power and grace. He soaked it in as a plowed field welcomes spring rains, and the feeling settled into his bones and strengthened him.

When Zander motioned him to the stable door, Zeph reluctantly slowed Helios to a walk. He leaned forward and laid his head against the horse's neck. He whispered so Zander wouldn't think him foolish. "I love you, Helios." Helios turned his head and nickered softly.

As Zeph slid off the horse, Zander said, "After we groom Helios, let's take the palfreys to the gulch."

Zeph brushed the horse, paying particular attention to Helios's long black mane, untangling the knots with a gentle hand. He hoped Zander couldn't hear his pounding heart. Zander went to the gulch when he was stressed, and he always went alone. What did it mean that Zander asked him to come with him? He gave Helios a bucket of oats and then saddled Lady.

Outside the stables, light snow fell as the two trotted across Elder Warrin's land and crossed the hand-wrought fence into Elder Terrec's. As Shadow loped beside them, they skirted along the edge of the village until they reached the trail heading down.

Zeph's bay followed Star down the steep path. Pebbles tumbled down in front of them. Lady slid, but quickly recovered. Unlike Helios, she was steady, but Zeph would have gladly traded her calm for Helios's spirit.

"Almost there," Zander called back.

At the bottom of the gulch, Zeph followed Zander along the frozen creek bed east until they reached an old gnarled oak. A few stubborn brown leaves clung to the branches. Sheltered from the winds, the stagnant air was thick with the musty scent of rotting leaves. Zeph sneezed, disturbing the quiet of the sleeping winter forest.

"This is the tree Alexa had the questers meet at during our quest." Zander dismounted and tied Star loosely to an evergreen. She hoofed at the dusting of snow, searching for green shoots.

Surprised that Zander mentioned his quest, Zeph tied Lady next to Star and waited. None of the questers from last year talked about their challenges from Fate. He knew only they had all returned, and Zander had announced to the villagers that Moira had called him to train warriors to save the village.

"Zeph . . ." Zander's voice trailed off.

His energy rushed out and Zeph slumped against Lady. Was Zander unhappy with him? He didn't want to return to the shacks.

"You're doing great in training. I couldn't ask for a harder worker." Zander rubbed the back of his neck. "Come, let's sit."

Zander laid two coarse blankets on the ground and sat cross-legged with his back near the trunk of the oak. Shadow curled up next to him.

After sliding down, Zeph imitated Zander's posture. Straight spine, hands relaxed on his knees.

"Do you meditate?"

Zeph wasn't sure what Zander meant, so he just shook his head.

"Follow what I do." Zander stilled. "Breathe in your nose for five counts, and hold it for six counts before breathing out through your mouth for seven counts."

Zeph's exhalation created a cloud of vapor in the cold air. He shivered. Couldn't they have meditated in the warm stable?

After three counted rounds, Zander said, "Now, breathe normally, but as you do, imagine the energy from the earth filling you. Let it flow into your chest and out into your arms and legs."

He couldn't figure out what earth energy felt like. If Zander had said the energy Zeph felt from Helios, he could have done it. He scratched at a sudden itch on his arm. Lady whinnied, and he opened his eyes. He couldn't do this.

As if reading his mind, Zander said, "This is your first time. You'll get distracted. Each time you find yourself thinking of something else, bring your attention back to your breathing."

The longer they sat, the easier Zeph found it to let go of the thoughts running through his head. When his shoulders softened, the earth filled him with a warm energy that thrummed through his body, leaving him both calm and alert. His senses sharpened. He peeked at Zander. He sat straight, with his body relaxed. The worried look he often wore had disappeared. Maybe there was something to this.

When Puck's ghost whispered through the trees, Zeph didn't flinch like he usually did, but his calm was broken.

"Zander," the voice floated from the east. "Unite the tribes and save the village."

"I'm trying, Puck. I'm trying."

"The boy can help."

Zeph's heart quickened. Puck was talking about him?

"Make the boy an assassin." Puck's voice faded away with, "Heed my words."

An assassin! Adrenaline raced through Zeph's body, chasing the calm until it was only a memory. He trembled with the suddenness of it.

Zander stared at Zeph. He looked as shocked as Zeph felt.

A sudden clarity filled him. "I want it. Make me an assassin."

As if he hadn't heard Zeph, Zander stood. "So much for meditating. Let's head back."

They spoke not a word on the ride up the gulch wall. Back at the stables, they groomed Lady and Star in silence. In the quiet, Puck's words repeated through Zeph's head. *Make the boy an assassin.*

Zander left for the manor and returned with roasted pheasant, glazed potatoes, and hot buttered rolls. They ate at a small table next to Helios's stall. Three times Zander started to speak and stopped. He looked everywhere but at Zeph.

He could take the silence no longer. Zeph cleared his throat. "What do I need to learn to be an assassin?"

Startled, Zander looked up and turned red. "I'm not sure." He stared at Zeph. "I can ask Geno."

The man with the scar. Zeph didn't like the idea of spending more time with Geno, but he couldn't expect Zander to know how to train an assassin. He set his fork down. "Why do you think Puck said that?"

"I don't know." Zander rubbed the back of his neck. "Zephyr, you don't have to do this. Puck's been dead for ten generations. Maybe he doesn't know what he's talking about."

"I can do it." And even though fear coursed through his body, pride made him stand a little straighter. As an assassin, he'd be important in the war. He cocked his head. Could he kill another? What if that person threatened the village or Zander?

When Zander left to hunt with Shadow, Zeph had never felt so alone, and yet at the same time so much a part of a grand plan. His place in the village was suddenly bigger than he could have imagined.

CHAPTER FIFTEEN

Day Before the Twelve Day Feast

Alexa

Alexa dropped two loaves of apple cinnamon bread from the wood-fired oven onto the cooling counter. Expecting a lesson with Melina Odella, Alexa had woven malachite and azurite beads, meant to enhance visions, into the long braid hanging down her back. She was a fortune teller, not a baker, but here she was, sweating in a hot kitchen.

When she'd gone to Melina Odella's cottage that morning, her teacher had dismissed her, saying, "I have other responsibilities during the feast days. I don't have time for you to tag along."

The words had stung and ignited in Alexa a fury she still carried. She muttered, "I have power. I'll show her I'm not a trifle." She slid a tray of rolls into the oven and slammed the door.

"Alexa! Be careful." Mother grabbed the second tray of breads Alexa had picked up. "What's wrong with you today?"

Mother's canary chattered in the ornate cage hanging in the corner near the door. She reminded Alexa that she no longer had her own patron, and her anger heightened. "This isn't my calling. I should be with the fortune-teller, not stuck in this infernal kitchen baking for arrogant rich people."

"Watch your words. If the elders don't feel welcome, there are other bakers on whom they can spend their coin. It's not the peasants we earn our living from."

"Zander's going to change that. Soon, the elders won't have all the power in the village."

"Hush." Mother glanced around the kitchen as if someone would hear. "That's nonsense talk. The elders have always held the land. That's not going to change."

Alexa bit the inside of her cheek. Zander *would* change things. A thought crept into her mind. She could stitch an embroidery that would help. She needed to talk to him.

"Mother? Are you caught up?"

Pursing her lips, Mother nodded. "Eva's coming to help. You can leave."

"Thanks. I need to see Zander."

"Zander?" She brightened. "Take him this carrot cake. And make sure he's coming tonight?"

"I will." Alexa rushed from the kitchen before guilt made her stay. But stars! She was a fortune-teller, not a baker. She shouldn't have to justify it.

She ran up the stairs to her room, slung her bag of cloth and thread over her shoulder, and slipped out the back door to avoid seeing Father drunk in his chair. She carried the cake in a woven basket covered with a yellow cloth to hide the treat. Today was supposed to be a day of fasting.

The day before the Twelve Day Feast was meant for reflection. The market was empty, and only a few stragglers walked the streets. She clutched her cloak against the frigid breeze, hurried south on the market road, and then skipped over to the path that ran behind the Yapi alley toward the stable.

She slowed when Melina Odella, with her patron wolf, Sheba, and an old woman Alexa had never seen, crossed the path ahead of her. They disappeared into a deserted, ramshackle hut. Drawn to follow, Alexa couldn't help eavesdropping from a broken window in the back.

"Your student has potential for great power," said the old woman.

"She's impatient and unwilling to learn the basics," scoffed Melina Odella.

"Be careful or she'll surpass your abilities and take your council position."

"I'll never allow it."

"Take care that you don't. She's already . . ."

Sheba growled at the window, and Alexa fled, missing the rest of the conversation. She ducked between two huts and pulled her hood up around her face. Who was that woman and how did she know about her power?

Shaking, she wound through the alley heading toward Elder Warrin's estate. When she reached the road leading to the stables, Alexa pushed the overheard conversation from her mind. She'd come to convince Zander her magic could help unite the tribes. She rubbed the brooch he'd given her. The garnet warmed at her touch. He couldn't have known when he gave it to her that the stone would increase the creativity of her embroidery.

The stable door opened as she reached for it, and Zeph stepped out. Before he saw her, Alexa noticed the worry etched across his face. He was starting to look like Zander, but with a shock of red hair instead of black.

"Alexa! What are you doing here?" His smile chased away the worry lines.

"Happy birthday!" She hugged him. "How's my second favorite warrior?"

"Better than your favorite. Helios threw him again this morning."

Alexa groaned. Zander would be in a bad mood.

Her twin appeared in the doorway and leaned against the door with a smirk. "He threw me, but thanks to Zeph, I set a new record before my butt hit the ground."

His mood was infectious, and Alexa and Zeph laughed with him.

"Join us for our noon meal." Zander stepped to the side and motioned her in.

"We're to fast today." She said it out of habit, aware of the cake in her basket. "And to reflect upon the past year." It had certainly been one to remember. Alexa had learned she had a twin, survived the quest, and become apprenticed to the fortune-teller.

Zander rolled his eyes while Zeph tried to hide his smile. "Who's to know? And we'll be celebrating Zeph's birthday tonight. I'm sure Mother's been cooking all day for it." He took the basket and sniffed. "Is that carrot cake?"

They sat at a small oak table in a kitchen between Zander's and Zeph's bedrooms. Zander brought out cold rabbit, pickled beets, and slaw. After they finished, he sliced off three large pieces of cake.

As they finished the treat, Alexa glanced from Zander to Zeph. She sensed they shared a secret. Only six weeks ago, she'd been Zeph's best friend. Now Zander had taken her place. She pushed down the pang of jealousy that prickled her chest. Zeph lived with Zander. It was right that they'd grown close.

Both sweets-lovers, Zander and Zeph scraped the crumbs from their plates. Alexa hated to break the good mood, but she didn't know when she'd next be alone with Zander. She brought her bag from the corner where she'd dropped it.

"We need to talk." When Zeph stood to leave, she said, "Stay? Maybe you'll help my argument."

Zander groaned. "What argument will we be having today?"

She couldn't help but grin. "I can help unite the tribes." She pulled out the silk ribbons Mother gave her for her birthday. "Tshilaba said these have special power."

"No, not your magic stitching." Zander rubbed his thigh. "That didn't work so well in the quest."

"I've learned to cast spells as I stitch." She laid a cloth with doves circling the church on the table. "In the quest, I was trying to thwart Moira. There's no reason it shouldn't work now."

Zeph leaned forward and peered at the moving picture. "You stitch magic scenes?"

She nodded. "Puck says we have to unite the tribes to save the village. If I stitch it, it will happen."

"Or you could make it worse." Zander crossed his arms over his chest and tipped his chair back. "You don't know what will happen."

"I can control it, I know I can."

"Control? Since when does Moira give control of anything to anybody?"

Shock ran through Alexa like bolts of lightning. "You don't believe Moira gives us choices? You had a choice after the quest. You chose to be a warrior."

A ragged laugh escaped him. "Moira is tricky like that. Making you think you're choosing when she's manipulated you into what she wants. How could I not have chosen warrior?"

In his quiet manner, Zeph said, "She always gets her way."

Zander's chair legs hit the floor. "Does she speak to you, too?"

Zeph turned red. "In my dreams."

"Great stars! You and Zander both?" Tradition held that Moira spoke through the fortune-teller holding the council seat. Each villager heard from her once at the end of the quest when she gave them their apprenticeship. Now, she spoke to Zander and to Zeph. And to Alexa. "She speaks to me through magic." She pleaded with Zander, "I have my favor for a reason. We have to use everything we can to win this war."

"I think she's right," Zeph said. "I have my role and you have yours. Let Alexa use her magic."

When pain twisted Zander's face, a shiver ran down Alexa's spine. What was Zeph's role that made Zander look like he had sucked on a lemon?

Zander slumped back in his chair. "Can you make my men better fighters?"

Yes! She'd win him over one embroidery at a time. "I think I can. I'll work on it over the feast days."

Later that afternoon, Alexa laid aside her embroidery and brewed a cup of chamomile tea with honey. She sat cross-legged in her favorite stuffed chair under the shuttered window in her bedroom. The muscles in her shoulders relaxed as she sipped her tea. Scattered across the floor, were the results of her stitching. She regarded a scene of ten archers with bows drawn. It wasn't pretty, but then, it didn't need to be. It just had to hold her spell.

She set down her cup and stitched each arrow with the silk from Tshilaba. She spoke in a clear voice, "Arrows fly true, hit the target, don't skew." The spell wound through each ribbon and settled invisibly onto the scene. With a fine gold thread, she stitched a line from the tip of the arrow to the center of the target. As she made the final stitch, she whispered, "As it will be done."

On the next cloth she quickly stitched men with swords without regard to how it looked. It only needed to carry the spell. As she needled the swords, she cast, "Sharp sword, struck deep, blood poured." She frowned. That didn't sound right for practice. She didn't want the men killing each other. She'd save that spell for the war.

Last, she cut a cloth and stitched ten men fighting hand-to-hand with knives. She sat for several minutes searching for the right words. When the spell didn't come, she set the cloth aside.

Then, she thought of another and grinned. She stitched a regal black horse and upon his back, Zander. She spelled, *Ride the horse, cannot fall, stay the course, all for all.* Her words weren't that great, but it was the intention that made them work. Zander would see the value of her magic when she was the reason Helios allowed him to ride.

As she stitched the final thread, a knock at her door startled her. She shoved the cloths under her coverlet and opened the door. "Father?" The heavy smell of mead nearly gagged her.

"Zander will be here soon with the tag-a-long. Your mother needs your help."

Zeph. "Don't call him that." She'd hated it when Melina Odella said it to her.

"That's what he is, that's what I'll call him."

She followed Father down the steps as he stumbled and grabbed at the walls to stay upright. For all the times she'd wished for a father, Alexa had never imagined he'd be a drunk.

CHAPTER SIXTEEN

New Year's Eve

Zander

Zander walked with Shadow to the bakery. If it wasn't for Zeph's birthday celebration, he would have stayed at the stable. Zeph hadn't said another word about Puck's message, but Zander could tell the boy was thinking on it. Alexa's noon visit had been a nice diversion, even if she was determined to get her way in using her magic.

He smelled the bakery before he saw it. The competing aromas of yeast bread and honey-sweetened fruit pies wound their way down the street, found his nose, and made his stomach grumble. The church decreed this to be a day of fasting, but Mother had to bake days ahead to keep up with the demand for the Twelve Day Feast. No one would notice if she happened to stuff a little rabbit meat into a pie.

He reached the bakery and took a deep breath before he opened the side door. It would be all he could do to keep his calm with Father's drunken tirades. Just before he stepped in, Zeph ran up behind him.

"I smelled bread all the way from the tavern." Zeph's eyes sparkled, and he opened his hand. Three bronze coins nestled in his palm. "Mother gave them to me. I've never had more than one coin at a time." He stuffed them in a leather bag tied at his waist. "I'll keep them with the tokens I earn."

Zander laughed at Zeph's enthusiasm. "Good thing you don't earn omens until tomorrow. I have a feeling you're going to overeat tonight."

"I hope so." Zeph nodded so hard his curls bounced against his shoulders.

They entered the kitchen together and stopped short. Zander had never seen so many baked goods. Trays of cinnamon rolls and sweet biscuits lined the counters. Pies cooled on the rack. Too many kinds of bread to count filled the ceiling-high shelves. The highlight of Mother's baking—the cakes—sat like masterpieces on every other available surface.

Shadow's nose quivered upward at the smells. Zander herded him from the kitchen. The coyote was generally well-behaved, but the temptation might prove hard to resist.

He entered the dining area and found himself face-to-face with Father. An odor of a different sort assaulted Zander. The alcohol he expected, but did the man never bathe? Zander turned his head and took a step back.

Father grumbled, "Your mother baked all day. I hope you appreciate it."

When he could breathe again, Zander gaped at the table. Meat pies, roasted potatoes and carrots, dried apples with walnuts, and steaming pumpkin soup surrounded a three-layer cake on the round table. At the side table, a modest pile of gifts waited for Zeph.

Beside Zander, Zeph stood transfixed. "This is for me?" he blurted.

Zander's chest grew tight. Zeph was a boy who'd had nothing. He was finding a family with him and Alexa, and now, because of Puck's damnable interference, the boy had taken on one of the most dangerous roles in war. It was one more point, driven like a thorn into Zander's heart, that life was not fair.

During dinner, Zander kept his head down and ate. He felt sorry for Alexa having to live with Father's drunkenness. Zander could spend a few hours tolerating it and leave.

When Father compared the warriors to the worthless Protectors, Alexa glanced at Zander as if expecting a reaction. He shrugged. What was the point? He'd wasted too many hours trying to convince Father the warriors would be needed. Mother winced each time Father banged his fist on the table. Only Zeph seemed unperturbed, eating two wedges of meat pie along with everything else, and thanking Mother each time she passed a bowl.

Stars! How could the boy stay so calm? Puck had asked him to become an assassin, and he hadn't even taken time to think it over. He just agreed in that quiet way of his and went on with life as if nothing had changed.

At last, Father retired to his chair next to the fire, and soon snores rumbled from the room. Zander's shoulders relaxed for the first time since the meal began. The table was cleared and the gifts transferred to sit in front of Zeph, who couldn't stop grinning.

The first he opened came from Alexa. An embroidery of Helios prancing around an apple tree while sparrows flitted around the branches left Zeph mesmerized. He shook his head. "It's beautiful." He leaned over and gave Alexa a hug.

Mother gave him a small basket filled with dried fruit and nuts saying, "Growing boys can never have enough food." Another package from her held a carved wooden slingshot. At his quizzical stare, she blushed. "I know you're learning real weapons now, but every boy needs a slingshot for fun."

Zeph tucked it in a side pocket and reached for a folded paper. He read it slowly and looked up at Zander, eyes gleaming.

Always impatient, his sister asked, "What is it?"

"An hour a day alone with Helios!"

Alexa turned to Zander, and he knew the question before she asked it.

"Is that wise? Shouldn't you break him first?" She leaned in and whispered, "I stitched a scene to help you."

To help him? Not the men? "I don't know, Alexa."

"You want to ride Helios, don't you?"

He leaned his head back and cracked his neck. Tempting. "Tomorrow? The stables will be deserted."

Her smile almost chased away his doubt.

He looked back at Zeph. "Maybe after Zeph spends time with Helios, that horse will be calm enough to try."

At Zeph's shy smile, Zander said, "Open your last gift."

Mother sat forward, intent, as Zeph picked up the gift. Soft and bulky, a piece of yellow cloth wrapped it. When he untied the hemp twine, Zeph gasped. He tried to speak and couldn't.

A new set of quester's clothes sat folded in front of Zeph—soft hemp pants dyed green from the roots of sorrel, a yellow undershirt, and a brown tunic with a braided belt. Zander had seen the set Zeph had in his bedroom. They'd been used countless times and were threadbare and faded. He glanced at Mother's shining face. Gratitude filled Zander for her kindness. Zeph could go to the Welcoming Ceremony and not feel like a kid from the shacks.

Zander watched Mother punch down the yeast bread she'd bake later that night for tomorrow's Welcoming Ceremony. Shadow stood alert at the open kitchen door, sniffing at the nighttime smells.

Zeph stood next to the cage holding Mother's patron, peering at the yellow canary. Zander laughed as Zeph tried to whistle. It came out as a whoosh.

"I never did learn to whistle." Zeph stuck his hand in the cage and the bird hopped onto his finger. "I wonder what patron Moira will give me?"

"Probably something big and bad," Zander teased. "You'll know soon enough. I got Shadow on New Year's Eve day. That'd be a great birthday gift for you."

"She'd better hurry." Zeph's eyes shone. "I hope it's a coyote like Shadow." Gently, Zeph put the canary back in her cage. She tucked her head under her wing and went back to the sleep he'd interrupted.

A movement caught Zander's attention. Alexa stood inside the door. A shadow crossed her face as she stared at the cage. She'd given up her patron after the quest to save Shadow, and Zander could never repay her for that sacrifice. She crossed the room and tucked a cloth in his hand. When he unfolded it, he saw a stitching of himself on Helios's back. This was going to help him ride?

"Carry this when you ride. He won't buck you off."

He folded the cloth and placed it in his jacket pocket. "Thanks. Time for me to get back to the stables."

Mother covered the last bowl of dough. "Won't you stay the night?"

Zander glanced at Zeph's cocked head and hope-filled eyes. Stars knew Zeph could use some mothering.

"I promised Fulk I'd stay at the stables with the horses." He hid his smile at Zeph's crestfallen face. "But there's no reason Zeph can't stay."

When Zeph looked uncertain, Mother put her hand on his shoulder. "Yes, stay, Zeph. We'll have sausages and sugar biscuits for breakfast."

"Sugar biscuits?" Zeph turned to Alexa. "Like the ones you brought to the shacks last spring?"

"Even better. They'll be hot from the oven." Alexa's eyes sparkled.

"Then we'll go to the stables and watch Zander ride Helios before the Welcoming Ceremony."

His sister was as single-minded as she was stubborn. "Only if you bring me some of those biscuits." He snapped his fingers at Shadow. "Come, boy."

After leaving, Zander sauntered through the deserted market and behind the quiet row houses. The crisp winter air and nearly full moon cleared Zander's head. He didn't remember the last time he'd been out alone at night. He wound past the bare fields until he picked up the north path.

Within sight of the stables, Shadow's ears pricked forward. The hair on his back bristled.

"What is it, boy?" Zander peered through the dark. As they drew closer, Shadow growled low in his throat. Zander stopped and held out his hand, palm down, the signal for quiet.

Together, they crept forward. Suddenly, the stable doors flew open and Helios charged out. "Hoy!" Zander yelled.

Alerted to a noise behind him, Zander turned in time to see a wooden practice blade swing toward him. It caught him on the side of the head, and he hit the ground.

CHAPTER SEVENTEEN

Zander

Zander woke, face down on the ground, confused, with a mouthful of dirt. His thigh ached and his head throbbed.

By the way the moon lay in the west, he'd been out for an hour or two. He squinted, unable to see out his right eye, and shivered. The ground had sucked all the heat out of his body, and a light dusting of snow covered him. Pushing into a sitting position, he tried to whistle for Shadow. No sound escaped his dry lips.

Puzzled, he stared at the open doors to the stable. An image forced its way through his foggy brain. Helios had raced out right before Zander had been clubbed. He tried to stand, but dizziness forced him back down. Who did this? He probed his swollen cheekbone. He'd have a helluva black eye.

A whimper drew his attention. A dark lump lay twenty feet in front of him. Zander half scrambled, half crawled to his patron.

Shadow struggled to raise his head, his breath slow and labored. He pulled himself across the cold ground to meet Zander and then collapsed, whining.

"Stay quiet, boy. Let me check you out." Zander ran his hands over the coyote's legs. Nothing broken. He brushed down his sides, and Shadow yipped in pain.

When he lifted Shadow's head, thick, sticky blood caked his left ear. Zander knelt next to him. He slipped both arms under the heavy body and lurched to his feet. He cradled Shadow to his chest and stumbled to the stables. He'd worry about Helios later.

Shadow moaned.

"Easy, boy. You'll be all right." Zander fought back tears. He'd lost Shadow in the quest, and Moira's magic had brought him back at Alexa's cost. He couldn't lose him again.

Zander limped into the stable and laid Shadow on the bed. He heated water on the wood stove and added dried lavender, rosemary, and yarrow. His right eye had swollen shut and everything looked blurry out his left. Collapsing into a chair, wave after wave of nausea rolled over him.

As the water heated, the smell of herbs filled the room. Zander leaned over the pot and inhaled the healing fragrances. The rosemary cleared the fog from his brain.

Just before the water boiled, Zander dipped a clean cloth into the pot and wrung it out. He walked back to Shadow and gently wiped the blood from his fur. It took several trips before he had Shadow clean and could see the wound. It needed stitches. Zander's stomach flipped. He wasn't at all sure he could stitch Shadow on a day when his own head wasn't splitting from pain. Fulk was the one who stitched the horses on the rare occasion of an injury, but the marshal would be gone for days.

Dizziness rolled over him. He hated needles. The blood had clotted. It could wait a few hours. Zander dipped two clean cloths in the hot water. One went on Shadow's wound. Zander crawled into bed next to him and draped the other cloth over his swollen eye.

He slept.

"Zander? Zander!"

Someone shook his shoulder. He threw his arm out and almost

knocked Alexa in the head. The horrified look on her face reminded him of the last night.

"What happened?"

"Where's Helios?" Zeph paced behind Alexa. "His stall's open and he's gone."

Zander winced. "Right before I was attacked, I saw Helios charge out and gallop north."

Alexa sat next to him and appraised his face. "Do you have salve?"

Salve. Why didn't he think of that last night? Because he couldn't think last night. His brain was fuzzy still.

"I'll get it," Zeph said.

Alexa smeared the thick oily paste over his face and swollen eye.

Shadow whined, and Zander twisted his fingers into the thick fur at his neck. "Shadow's hurt, too. I need to stitch him."

"I'll do it. You forget. I'm handy with a needle."

Zeph handed Fulk's kit to Alexa. She rubbed numbweed on the gash. As she stitched, Zander lay back and held Shadow's head in his lap. He closed his good eye. It made him dizzy to watch.

As she knotted the last thread, Alexa twisted to look at Zeph. "Stop pacing."

"I found tracks. We have to go after Helios."

"Zander's not going anywhere." She raised her chin. "Helios has hours on you. You won't find him."

With his head clearing a bit, Zander said, "I didn't see a rider, but someone wanted him gone. All the doors were open."

Zeph snorted. "No one can ride him but me."

Alexa bristled. "Zander can ride him now that I spelled the embroidery."

Someone tried to kill him, Helios was missing, and still Alexa argued for her magic. Zander glanced at Zeph. He felt sure his face showed the same doubt he saw on Zeph's.

CHAPTER EIGHTEEN

Zephyr

Zeph had paced the length of Zander's room as Alexa stitched Shadow's wounds. He breathed in and out like Zander had taught him. He tried thinking calm thoughts, but one kept intruding—he had to go after Helios before it was too late. The horse had been gone for hours.

"Zander?" Zeph winced when Zander turned to look at him. His face had to hurt. "Can I take Lady to look for Helios?" He tapped his fingers against his thigh. If Zander didn't say yes, he might explode.

Before Zander could answer, Alexa said, "No. It could be dangerous."

Through his one good eye, Zander stared at Zeph and nodded. "It might be dangerous. Take Fulk's horse. Tipper's faster. And take a bow and a knife."

Relief flooded Zeph. Zander trusted him, and Zeph wouldn't let him down. He'd find Helios and bring him home.

Alexa twirled to glare at Zander, but as she started to speak, Zander interrupted her. "He's training to be a warrior. He'll face worse when war comes. If Zeph wants to search for Helios, he can go. Hard to know when I'll be able to look. I can't stand without getting dizzy."

In five minutes, Zeph had Tipper saddled and headed for the

door. A sheathed knife hung at his belt. He grabbed his bow and quiver from the peg along the side wall.

As Zeph mounted the horse, Zander hollered, "Remember, Zeph. If you run into trouble, get back here, and we'll send for Fulk."

Steam rose from the fields as the mid-morning sun burnt away the snow. Zeph followed the tracks north until he lost them in the hard ground. He slid off Tipper and knelt. A faint hoof print led north. Tipper followed as Zeph searched for signs. He reached the line separating Elder Warrin's property from Elder Terrec's and hesitated. Elder Terrec didn't tolerate trespassers. He thought of Zander. He never let Elder Terrec intimidate him. Zeph wouldn't either.

He mounted Tipper and followed the prints into the north woods. Zeph could tell by the spacing of the hoof prints that Helios had slowed to a walk. Once he rode into the thick undergrowth, Zeph lost the tracks.

Zeph stared into the sky. "Moira? I could use a hound dog." He didn't expect an answer, and he didn't get one.

As he rode deeper into Terrec's land, he hunched over Tipper's neck. Maybe he should have waited for Fulk. At a distant sound, he cocked his head. Voices floated through the trees. He pulled back on the reins and strained to hear. He recognized Lash's harsh laugh. Nothing good would come of running into Lash on his father's land.

Then he recognized a whinny that could only be Helios. And he was skittering. Zeph pulled the bow into position and took a calming breath. He urged Tipper toward the sound.

Zeph broke into a small clearing. Lash and Elder Terrec stood with their backs to Zeph. Hobbled and tied to a branch, Helios jerked his head and squealed.

When Tipper snapped a stick on the ground, Elder Terrec spun to face Zeph. Recognition lit his eyes, and he smirked.

The lord's hair had faded with age, but without his usual cap, the red was unmistakable. Understanding sank into Zeph's belly like lead. Elder Terrec was the only man in the village besides Father Chanse with red hair.

Lash practically snarled. "Get out of here, tag-a-long. Tell Zander we found his horse."

"Found it or took it?" Zeph nocked an arrow, hoping his shaking hands didn't betray his nerves.

"Why, you little weasel." Lash lunged toward Zeph.

Elder Terrec grabbed Lash's arm. "Go back to the manor."

Disbelief colored Lash's face. "But Father . . ."

The elder shoved him, and Lash stumbled to his knees. "Go. I want to talk to the boy alone."

After a moment's hesitation, Lash stomped from the clearing. He threw Zeph a look of hatred over his shoulder before disappearing into the trees.

Elder Terrec turned to Zeph and sneered. "Lash may not have my red hair, but he has my temper. How about you, Zeph? Is there some fire under that red hair of yours?"

Hardly able to breathe, Zeph lifted the bow.

"Put that down," Elder Terrec commanded. "You've nothing to fear from me but the truth."

Zeph lowered the bow to his side, but kept the arrow nocked. He stared at Elder Terrec. He didn't want to hear his truth.

"Don't talk much, huh? That's fine. You need to listen. I've been keeping an eye on you. Wasn't happy to see you take up with Zander and his foolish ways." He stroked his chin. "But that might prove useful."

Heat flushed Zeph's face. Still, he kept quiet.

Anger flashed across Elder Terrec's face as he strode to stand in front of Tipper. "Stars, boy. Did your mother never tell you about me?"

Blackness washed over Zeph. He grabbed the pommel of his saddle to keep from falling and managed to croak, "Tell me what?"

Elder Terrec laughed then, and Zeph hated him. He pulled the reins to turn Tipper, but Elder Terrec grabbed the bit.

"I'm your father."

No black mist hovered over Terrec's head. He told the truth.

"I have no father." Zeph yanked the reins and Tipper pulled his head up and away from Elder Terrec. They bolted across the clearing.

Elder Terrec yelled after him, "Blood wins over friendship, Son. You'll see the wisdom in that soon enough."

Tipper raced through the woods until Zeph slowed him at Elder Warrin's gate. His heart beat as if he'd run beside the horse. Mother would tell him Elder Terrec lied. Zeph laid his head against Tipper's neck and let his tears soak into the mane. It didn't matter what Mother said. He knew in his gut—Elder Terrec was his father.

Panic swept through him, and he started to shake. When Mother lied to him, he never saw the black around her. His gift didn't work with blood relatives, and Lash was his brother. Lash could lie and Zeph wouldn't know.

Zeph rode down the wall of the gulch and followed the almost dry creek bed. Tipper labored to climb back up to the shack houses. He stopped at his house, but knew Mother wouldn't be there. When he wound back through the woods to Elder Warrin's stables, Alexa paced out front.

She waved him in and ran to meet him. "Where have you been?"

The noon bells rang. Stars! He was late for the Welcoming Ceremony. The villagers would see him rush in late. He hated being watched like that. He pulled Tipper to a stop next to Alexa.

"Quick! Run in and change into your quester clothes," Alexa said. "If you ride, you might make it to the Quinary before the ceremony's over. I'll bring Tipper back."

After he changed, Zeph raced back and vaulted onto Tipper's back. He grabbed Alexa's outstretched hand and drew her up to sit behind him. He kicked his heels against Tipper's flanks. "Go!"

Zeph urged Tipper to the edge of the market. The mingling villagers made it impossible to go any farther. He slid off and handed the reins up to Alexa. Then he ran to the Quinary.

Six questers stood in line across the pavilion. Father Chanse and Melina Odella stood in front, ready to share the duties of the yearly ritual. Wearing the traditional black robe and white cap, the priest began. "I represent God, the Church, and tradition."

Zephyr's face burned at the laughter from the crowd when he tripped as he joined the line of questers. He found a place behind Father Chanse. Only two men in the village had red hair: Terrec and the priest. Self-conscious, he pushed his own hair behind his ears. Did everyone but him know that Terrec was his father? He glanced down the row at the other questers. Another embarrassment—everyone had a patron but him. Oddly, they were all assorted species of birds.

Melina Odella stood next to Father Chanse. Sheba sat by her side, black eyes intent on the questers. A long, purple embossed tunic flowed over the fortune-teller's black skirt, tied by a gold cord at her hips. A scarf of gold velvet covered her hair. As she gazed across the crowd, the villagers grew silent.

The fortune-teller began the speech she repeated every year. "I embody Moira, our Fate, and things hidden. On this day, the priest and I remind you of the balance between the faith and mystery upon which our village was founded." She paced erratically in front of the questers.

The priest frowned, but kept to his part. "Ten generations past, our God protected Hedron Puck as he led the Five Tribes in his dream to create a utopian society by the Merope Sea. His destination changed after they camped in our gulch during a lightning storm."

Melina Odella continued the history. "While they were climbing the steep sides of the gulch, every wagon broke a wheel. Only Moira works in this way. Our ancestors built the village on the upper rim of the gulch. The first building Puck constructed was this Quinary with five living oak trees to support it. The five equal sides represent the five tribes. He dedicated it to both the God who led them to safety and to Moira who kept them here. Unfortunately, Hedron Puck died in a hunting accident in the gully before he could establish his dream of equality for all."

Puck. Zeph wished the old codger had stayed dead. The ghost wouldn't rest until he got his way.

"With the village without a leader, five elders stepped in and created our order based on tradition." Melina Odella's mouth twisted. "Puck's vision of each tribe having an equal voice died with him."

Clearing his throat, the priest said, "At the first New Year celebration, Moira came in a vision to the priest and the fortune-teller to explain the purpose of the quest she designed for our youths. Moira would reward and punish the sixteen-year-olds with tokens and omens for their actions. She gave the priest and fortune-teller the duty of teaching the questers how to use them in the five-day quest. Only the teens worthy of joining our society as adults would survive. Each year since, it has been our tradition."

"Today we celebrate our past and look to our future," Melina Odella said. "These young men and women standing before you with their animal patrons represent our hopes for a productive society."

Zeph's heart thumped. Where was his patron?

"Let us pray." Father Chance raised his arms, fingers pointing to the sky. His green eyes drifted across the crowd as his voice boomed. "We bless these questers and ask our God to keep them safe. May their good actions and pure thoughts bring the tokens needed to survive their quest. Purify their sinful nature, that they shall take their productive place among us. And if they refuse to bend to thy will, we release them to the fate of the quest."

The priest strolled across the stage, sprinkling holy water on each bent, submissive head, blessing them. When he came to Zeph, Zeph felt a nudge in his back, and a warm head pushed under his arm. A small gray donkey, with a white face and big ears that stood straight up, nuzzled Zeph's face. Great stars! Moira gave him a donkey as a patron?

The priest stopped as if surprised and then smiled. He sprinkled the water over Zeph. "Blessings, my child, in your time of magic."

A young acolyte followed, swinging a metal censer. Zeph swallowed a cough as the smoke of the burning sage flowed over him.

Moira gave him a donkey.

The fortune-teller seemed to float down the line. One by one she gazed into the questers' eyes. She gave each a single word to symbolize his or her journey through the quest. "Dove, rose, lavender, rock, copper, sun." Melina Odella hesitated in front of Zeph, as if listening. "Diamond," she whispered.

Diamond? What did that mean?

As if she read his mind, and maybe she did, Melina Odella said, "Light-bearer."

Skirt swishing, she turned to the villagers. "I present to you your questers. May their bravery save them."

The villagers turned to each other in confusion. Those weren't the traditional words Melina Odella used to end the ceremony.

All Zeph could think of was—Moira gave him a donkey.

He didn't stay for the meal. He needed to talk with Zander. As he walked to the stable, the donkey ambled beside him, stopping to grab a few bites of grass or sniff at a tree. As he walked, the donkey's name popped into Zeph's head. Dorothy. He looked underneath. She was a jenny. It was bad enough he got a donkey, but even worse, she was a female. Questers always got patrons the same sex as themselves. Always. Even Zander would make fun of him for having a female patron.

And if the day couldn't get any worse, there was Lash, his half-brother, coming from the other direction, leading Helios to the stable.

CHAPTER NINETEEN

Alexa

Alexa sat cross-legged on the end of Zander's bed and watched him sleep. He hadn't finished the meal she scavenged for him before he curled up next to Shadow and started snoring. It hurt her to look at them. The swelling in Zander's face had gone down from the salve, but the bruises were darkening. If only he'd listened to the warning from the cards. The Seven of Swords had foretold a theft, and Helios was gone.

On the wild ride to the Quinary, Zephyr'd said Lash had Helios. Too many questions rolled through her mind. As hard as he slept, Zander wouldn't miss her, so she slipped off the bed and headed outside, hoping the crisp air would clear her mind.

When she stepped out, she saw two figures coming toward her. One was Lash, leading Helios. From the other direction came Zeph, dawdling as if trying to avoid Lash. With his hood thrown back, Zeph's red hair reflected the sun. A pang of regret hit her that she hadn't been at the Welcoming Ceremony to support him, but Zander needed her. She squinted. Was that a donkey following him?

As they drew near, Lash stopped and waited for Zephyr. His laugh sliced through the quiet. "Don't tell me that's your patron?"

Zeph nodded and turned red.

"An ass?" Lash slapped the donkey's flank. "Fitting, very fitting."

Anger at seeing Zeph made fun of boiled up in Alexa. When

Lash sauntered up, pulling Helios's rope halter, she took a deep breath.

"Hoy, Alexa." Lash smirked. "Is Zander missing his horse?"

"And how did he happen to end up in your hands?"

"Don't accuse me. I didn't do it. He was wandering on Father's land. Lucky for Zander, he didn't get sick the way he was lathered."

"Lucky?" Alexa glared at him. "Zander was beaten half to death with a practice sword."

The smirk left Lash's face. "What?"

"He spent the night unconscious on the cold ground. He's *lucky* to be alive." She shoved her finger in his chest. "You know anything about that?"

Lash shook his head, but he wouldn't meet her eyes.

Suspicious.

"I'll take Helios." Zeph reached for the rope.

Lash jerked back. "I'll take him in."

Zeph straightened. "He's not your horse." Zeph grabbed the reins away from Lash.

Good for Zeph, Alexa thought smugly.

Lash grabbed Zeph's arm and jerked him close. "I heard Father this morning. You're the bastard son of a barmaid and nothing more. You'll never be as good as me!"

What was Lash talking about? Alexa stepped between them and pushed Lash back. "Go home to your feast. You don't belong here today."

Rage crossed Lash's face. "You don't belong on an Elder's land. Not you, not him, and not your brother. If somebody gave him a beating, he deserved it." He turned and walked stiffly away.

Alexa watched until he was a small speck. She turned to Zeph. "Moira gave you a donkey?"

He grimaced. "A jenny. Dorothy."

"Oh, my stars. Let's tell Zander. He could use a laugh."

"First, we take care of Helios."

Zeph's expression sobered Alexa. He was right, of course. The war horse, worth a small fortune, came first. She followed Zeph, Helios, and the donkey into the stable. A donkey for a patron? Moira had a wild sense of humor.

The little jenny scooted forward to walk next to Helios down the aisle of the stalls. He reached over and nipped at her ear. Unperturbed, she butted his shoulder and moved in front to lead. Alexa stifled a laugh. Maybe Moira knew what she was doing, after all. If Zeph's patron had the courage to take on a war horse, what could she do for Zeph?

Side by side, Alexa and Zeph groomed Helios. She brushed the mane as Zeph checked each leg and hoof for cuts. He gently combed the cockleburs out of his tail.

A comfortable silence fell between them. Zeph had become like a younger brother. Soon, he'd earn tokens and omens and then go on his quest. Could she stitch an embroidery to protect him, or would that be cheating? She couldn't risk Zeph earning a black panther omen for her mistake.

Satisfied at last that Helios would be all right, Zeph shut the gate to the stall and turned to the donkey. "There aren't any open stalls. Where do I put Dorothy?"

"Usually the patrons stay with their quester so they can bond."

Zeph's eyebrows rose. "In my room?"

Just then, Dorothy lifted her tail and dropped a warm pile at Zeph's feet.

"Not in my room."

Alexa burst into laughter. "Maybe not."

They cleaned out a tack room that had once been a stall. Soon Dorothy was happily munching on oats while Alexa and Zeph checked on Zander.

When they walked in his room, Zander sat cross-legged on

the bed with his back against the wall. One side of his face had turned purple and both eyes shone black. Alexa hesitated. He was meditating. She didn't want to interrupt.

Zander opened his good eye. "We need to talk. You, me, and Zeph."

CHAPTER TWENTY

Zander

Zander waited while Zeph brought a chair in from the hall. Alexa sat at the edge of his bed, and he ignored her stare. She'd know soon enough what was on his mind. She and Zeph were two of only a handful of people he trusted.

His head pounded and his body felt like Helios had thrown and then stomped him. How could he have been so stupid to let down his guard? If he'd been at war, he'd be dead.

When Zeph sat, Zander looked from his somber face to Alexa's. "We have a traitor among the warriors. Whoever did this knew where to find the practice blades. I'd moved them into the dining hall for the break. Thank the stars I had the key to the shed with the steel blades." He rubbed his cheek and winced. "I'd be dead if he'd used one of those."

"Do you think it was one person?" Zeph squirmed in his chair.

"Maybe two. I saw the stable door fly open right before I was hit." He stared at Zeph. "Have you heard anything during practice that might give me a clue as to who would do this? I suspect Lash."

Alexa leaned forward. "Lash looked surprised when I told him you were clubbed."

"What do you think, Zeph?"

The boy sat still. Zander didn't need his favor to tell that Zeph was sorting through his thoughts. Zander blocked seeing other's secrets most of the time and only used it when needed. That was why he'd been meditating. With his concentration scattered, it took more effort to close it down.

Zeph stirred. "I don't think he lied. Helios wasn't hidden, and Elder Terrec would never be able to claim him. Everyone in the village knows he's your horse."

"Not Lash, then. Stars, I wish it had been. I'd love an excuse to throw him out."

"But you can't trust him." A deep frown crossed Zeph's face.

"No, I can't, but I need proof he's doing something wrong."

"Isn't it enough that his father threatened you after the quest?" Alexa crossed her arms. "I hate Terrec."

Was it his imagination or did Zeph blanch? He looked back at Alexa. "Elder Warrin counseled me to keep Lash close."

"I did hear something. I . . ." Zeph fell silent.

"Go on. It's safe here. Nothing you say will leave this room."

"Not even to Greydon?"

Zander hesitated. There were few things he kept from his friend, but if Zeph was uncomfortable, Zander would keep his secret. "Not even Greydon. You have my word."

"I heard Lash bragging about keeping some of the money he collects from the elders and merchants."

Zander stiffened. Why hadn't Zeph told him before now?

"I wanted proof before I told you. It would have been his word against mine."

His anger dissipated. "I'll always believe you over Lash."

"I know that now. I wasn't sure then."

Alexa sat back, eyes narrowed. "Who was Lash bragging to?"

Zeph's tension filled the room. "Dharien."

The words settled deep in Zander's stomach, and he could tell by Alexa's face she was dumbstruck. He thought Dharien had changed since the three of them had formed an alliance in their quest. He took a moment to breathe and gain his composure before he glanced at Alexa. "Maybe it's not as it seems."

Blinking back tears, Alexa stood. "I should have known not to believe he'd changed. He's still the arrogant elder's son he was before the quest." Her shoulders slumped. "Will you be all right? I should check in on Mother."

When Zander nodded, Zeph joined Alexa at the door. "I'll walk with you to the village." He turned back to Zander. "Moira gave me a donkey." He stared at the floor. "Don't laugh. Her name's Dorothy."

Poor Zeph, but Zander couldn't hold back a snort. "I'm sure Moira knows what she's doing."

After they left, Zander dropped his head in his hands. Not only did he not know who had clubbed him, now he had to deal with traitors. He should have known Dharien hadn't changed, the way he chummed around with Lash.

A soft knock at his open door startled him. "Kaiya?" He jumped off his bed and winced at the shooting pain in his head.

She crossed the room to touch his arm. "I was on my way out to practice shooting. Alexa told me what happened. Who would do this?"

Damn, he hated her seeing him like this. "It's nothing. I'm fine."

She looked at his face, appraising what was undoubtedly a nasty looking mess of black and blue. "Yeah, it looks like nothing."

"I don't want to talk about it." He cringed at the hurt that crossed her face and took her arm. "Let's go outside. I need some air."

They sat on the stone wall outside the stable while Kaiya's patron crow, Korble, glided on the thermals above them. Shadow limped to a spot in the sun, turned a circle, and plopped to the ground. Kaiya's tentative glances at his face threw him off balance. He took her hand. "Look, don't worry. I'm going to be fine."

She pulled her hand away. "I also came to talk to you about the warriors."

He sucked in a deep breath. He was pretty sure he didn't want to hear what she had to say.

"The women aren't happy. You're babying us." She held up her hand when he started to speak. "Moira called us to be warriors just like you. We can't help if you don't let us learn the same things as the men."

She was right, but Zander couldn't stand the thought of Kaiya going into battle. And he wasn't the only one. Elder Warrin had warned him of the villagers' displeasure at women being put in danger. "Stars, Kaiya. What can I say?"

"Just be honest. Why aren't we training like the men?"

Anger wound up from his gut to his chest. "You want the truth? War is ugly." He pointed to his face. "You think this is bad? What do you think will happen if we have to fight a band of war-hardened Odwans? Our people will be hurt far worse than black eyes and bruises. Damn it, Kaiya, people will be killed or maimed." He stood and faced her, matching her glare. "Do you think I could live with myself if you were hurt? Or worse?"

Her cheeks flushed. "And yet, you want me to sit back in safety while you take that risk?" She pulled away. "I was called, Zander. I was called." She jabbed his chest with her finger. "Just like you, just like all the men." She stepped back and narrowed her eyes. "You're going to need me. And all of the women."

He took a deep breath. And then another. Moira wouldn't have called the women if they weren't going to be helpful, but it didn't have to be in battle. He needed time to sort it out. "I'll talk to Fulk and Greydon. You'll be treated as equals in training."

Kaiya slumped in relief. "You won't be sorry. You'll see how hard we can work."

Zander promised to let her train, but he hadn't promised she'd see battle. He felt like a traitor.

CHAPTER TWENTY-ONE

Last Day of the Twelve Day Festival

Alexa

Alexa dumped a scoop of oats in Helios's trough and pushed her sweaty hair behind her ears. She'd come every day since Zander's attack to help with his chores. It kept her mind off Melina Odella's continued rejection during the festival.

After tossing the last pile of dung from Helios's stall, Zander hung the pitchfork on the side of the wall. He joined Alexa as she washed at the small basin, and bumped her shoulder. "The warriors return tomorrow. I won't need your help."

"What? I'm not good help?" she asked as she dried her hands. At the table, she slathered fresh butter on slices of apple walnut bread and handed one to Zander. "You look better," she said, peering at his face. The purple had faded into an ugly yellow, but his eye was open now. "Are you ready to try my magic?"

Zander choked on a mouthful of bread. "I'm not ready to add to my bruises."

"Trust me. You can't fall off." She flinched at his withering stare and softened her voice. "You have to ride Helios sometime. No one's here to see except me."

Wincing as he stretched his arms over his head, Zander said,

"I'm still sore." He sighed. "But Fulk would love it if I had Helios broken when he returns."

She eyed Zander, hopeful. She needed a distraction from thinking about Dharien. Zeph had shocked her when he said Dharien knew Lash kept money from the donations. She'd skipped the festival, hiding out at the stable, mainly to avoid Dharien.

She pushed Dharien from her thoughts. She could never be with a cheater. A flush started in her neck and spread to her face. She and Zander had cheated once, but they earned the worst omen to fight in the quest and learned their lesson.

Zander snapped his fingers in her face. "Let's do it." He brought out tack from a side room and had Helios saddled in minutes. After he checked the straps three times, he held out his hand. One eyebrow rose. "Embroidery?"

She ran to get the small square of cloth from his room. The scene with Zander on Helios's back held a spell that guaranteed Zander would stay in the saddle. She tied it over his wrist with a red silk thread and pulled his sleeve down to hide it. "See? No one will know."

Zander led Helios out of the stable and into the training yard. As Zander placed his foot in the stirrup, Alexa murmured the spell she'd woven into the cloth. *Ride the horse, cannot fall, stay the course, all for all.*

Zander pulled up into the saddle.

Helios's tail swished from side to side, and he lowered his head.

Adrenaline raced through her body. Alexa yelled, "Wait. Don't go!"

The warning came too late. Helios sprinted off on a run. Zander stared at Alexa and her horror reflected in his face. He grabbed at the pommel as the reins slipped from his hands.

The horse raced for the fence, turning at the last moment. Helios planted his front feet and kicked his back legs straight out, breaking a board. Zander slipped sideways. Helios reached back to nip at Zander's knee.

Without the spell, Zander could have slid off. Instead, he pitched to the side. Helios bolted across the pen, bucking and jumping, tossing Zander up and down. He smacked his nose into the pommel. Blood flooded down onto his tunic.

Helpless to do anything but watch, Alexa flattened her body against the wall. How could she have been so stupid? The spell kept Zander in the saddle, it didn't help him ride. Zander would never trust her again.

In a frenzy, Helios raced again for the fence. He twisted, trying to scrape Zander off. Alexa cringed when Zander's leg was crushed between the fence and the horse's flank.

She had to do something to correct her mistake. When Helios stilled for a moment, sides heaving, she dashed in and grabbed the fallen reins. He reared and jerked them from her hand.

"Get out! Zander yelled. "He's going to kill us both!"

Helios butted Alexa, and she fell. When he rose up to trample her, she rolled into a ball and recalled the wild boar in her quest that almost killed her. There was no one to save her this time.

"Settle, Helios."

Alexa looked out from behind her hands. Zeph held the bridle. Foam lathered Helios's nostrils as he trembled.

Zander ripped the embroidery from his wrist and slid to the ground. Blood smeared across his face. He held his hand out to Alexa and pulled her up. "Never use your magic on me again. Never." He limped to the door and disappeared inside.

Shaking, Alexa turned to Zeph. "What have I done?" she whispered.

CHAPTER TWENTY-TWO

Zephyr

Zeph laid a wet cloth across Helios's face and walked him in circles until he cooled. He ran his hands down Helios's legs, checking for injuries before he brushed him. It would take a long time before the horse would trust a rider. Zeph led Helios to his stall and lured him in with an apple.

Alexa had left in tears after Zander refused to talk to her. Zeph had never seen Zander so angry, but he didn't blame him. If he hadn't come back when he did, Alexa and Zander both would have been injured. He leaned against Helios and sent calm energy to the antsy horse.

After he felt certain Helios was unharmed, he turned to Dorothy and scratched behind her ears. He'd had her eleven days and still didn't understand why Moira gave him a donkey. Zander had Shadow, who was useful for hunting. What could Dorothy do? He led her outside and together they wandered the perimeter of Elder Warrin's land, stopping when Dorothy found a spot of green grass. She didn't need a harness—she seemed happy to follow Zeph.

Looking across the frozen fields, Zeph imagined it split into smaller parcels. Zeph had heard enough of Zander talking with Greydon to know Zander wanted to do away with the elders holding all the land. If each family in the shack houses had their own plot, they wouldn't worry about being hungry. Guilt jolted through him.

Since he'd joined the warriors, he'd forgotten what it was like to go to bed with an empty stomach.

He stayed out until dusk. When Zeph returned to the stable, Zander's door remained closed. Zeph ate the cold rabbit he found in the small kitchen, put Dorothy in her stall, and went to bed.

When Zeph woke the next morning, Zander was gone. Zeph ate a slice of oat bread as he fed Dorothy and gave her a quick brushing. He rushed out the stable and down the path to the village. He passed the open door of the dining hall. Zander welcomed the warriors back for their first training in twelve days. Zeph hated missing training, but he'd be back after quester class for the noon meal.

He followed two boys to the white stone church. Round windows curtained in purple silk flanked each side of the thick oak door. An X embedded with dark and light pebbles graced the top of the door, representing God and Fate working together. Zeph wound through the dark halls to the classroom, where seven oak chairs formed a circle. He clutched the purple journal that had appeared at his bedroom door on his first day of magic.

Once all seven questers were seated, Father Chanse rapped his knuckles against the wall. "We're here to help you understand the tokens and omens you will receive in the coming months."

Pacing behind the circle of chairs, Melina Odella said, "Some of you may have already earned tokens for good deeds. It's important you keep them safe, for if lost or misplaced, they cannot help you during the quest. However, the omens you earn for bad behavior will appear during the quest whether you carry them or not. As you accumulate these trinkets, we'll play games of strategy using your tokens to defeat your omens. This is theory. The quest will play out as it will, and is always full of surprises. Moira will test you."

Zeph's bag was empty. He'd earned no tokens, no omens.

"The most common way to receive omens is by committing the five deadly sins." Father Chanse's boots clicked on the stone floor until he stopped behind Zeph's chair. "I'll begin with the sin of pride. When you think only of yourself as better than another, or that your gifts come from yourself and are not given by God, you are prideful. The omen for pride is a peacock."

Zeph felt his face heat when the other students stared at him. Was Father Chanse making an example of Zeph by standing behind him?

"Humility cures pride. Allow other's needs to come before your own." Melina Odella held out a sparrow token. "You'll receive one of these for being humble. It may seem foolish, but when you're tired and alone in the forest, a muster of peacocks can overwhelm you with their pecking. Tossing out one sparrow token will vanquish one peacock."

The priest continued his pacing. "The second sin is envy, the longing to possess something belonging to another. The omen is a scorpion."

"And the cure is kindness," the fortune-teller added. "The token being a dove. If a scorpion appears during the quest and you throw out a dove token, the bird will eat the scorpion."

"The third sin is anger, represented by the hornet," the priest said. "Too many stings in the quest can be fatal."

Melina Odella quirked her mouth. "Patience cures wrath. The token is a turtle. The lowly turtle loves to snap up hornets. You may receive other tokens and omens. Moira likes to get creative."

One of the girls raised her hand. "What about our patrons? Does the kind we get mean anything?"

"Your animals are given by Moira as extra encouragement to do good deeds." The priest rubbed his hands together. "One of your tasks is to discover how your patron might help in the quest. They are a token you can use if your life is in danger."

"However," Melina Odella added, "if you use them in the quest, they disappear. You will bond with your animal. You need to earn enough tokens to avoid the heartache of losing yours." She walked around the room and handed each teen a wooden token representing their patron. "Guard these well."

Zeph shook his head at the small carved donkey. Dorothy. What help could she be?

"Still having your patron after the quest strengthens your favor." Melina Odella nodded at the silver wolf sleeping in the corner. "Sheba has been my constant companion. And because of Moira's magic, your patron will live as long as you do, so it's your lifetime friend."

One of the boys spoke up, "If we...." He swallowed. "If we don't survive the quest, what happens to our patron?"

Sympathy softened Melina Odella's face. "If that happens, the patron is dissolved."

"They die?"

She nodded and the questers looked at each other with grim faces.

What if he died in the war before the quest? Would Dorothy survive? Zeph's chest tightened. He didn't want to know the answer.

"Since we're talking about our patrons, Chanse and I had a surprise visit from Moira. She wants us to train you with your patrons."

Train? Zeph sucked in his breath. Dorothy?

"She's assured us the patrons will be important in this quest. Next week we'll meet at the Quinary. Bring your patrons."

The other questers perked up. Zeph recounted their patrons. A sparrow, a crow, two owls, a snipe, and a hawk. And Dorothy.

Father Chanse dismissed class. "We'll finish with the deadly sins next class."

When Zeph stood, Father held up his hand. "Zephyr?"

"Yes, Father."

"Your donkey will be a special challenge. He ..."

"Not a he."

Father Chanse wrinkled his forehead. "What?"

"My donkey's a jenny."

"Are you sure?"

Zeph's cheeks burned. "I can tell."

"Well, uh, then . . . she's not a patron we've seen before, but Moira doesn't make mistakes. We'll trust she'll show us how to use a donkey in the quest."

Melina Odella smiled. "I'm sure she'll be fine, Zeph."

As Zeph rushed out the door, he heard Father Chanse mutter, "A female donkey?"

Melina Odella's reply didn't surprise Zeph. "The cards have confirmed that this quest will not be normal."

That afternoon, Zeph practiced archery. After dinner, he fed Dorothy and brushed her soft coat. She nuzzled against his shoulder, leaving slobbers on his tunic. He couldn't help it. He already loved her. If he died in the war, what would happen to her?

CHAPTER TWENTY-THREE

Alexa

Alexa couldn't shake her humiliation at failing Zander. He'd never been so angry with her. She had to earn back his trust or he'd never let her help with the war. And she knew, just knew, he was going to need her help.

She trudged the path to Melina Odella's cottage. A year earlier, she'd pledged to help the children who lived in the shacks she passed. Smoke rose from chimneys barely held together with mud and crumbling bricks. Cloth doors swung in the cold breeze. A child peeked out a cracked window. Alexa smiled and waved, but the face disappeared. How could the elders allow such squalor?

It was then her heart spoke. Once she'd brought sweet biscuits. She could bake them again. She'd ask Zeph what else she could do. Could she help with her enchanted embroidery? She shuddered. Maybe not yet. She needed more experience before she tried changing lives.

Past the shack row, Alexa wound through the brambles while she chewed on her thumbnail. She hadn't seen Melina Odella in two weeks. What mood would her mentor be in?

After turning left at the wooden post carved with a moon and stars, Alexa followed the path until she stood at a mustard-colored door marked with runes. Rosemary, thyme, and ginger grew behind a short brick wall. Melina Odella had yet to share the spell she used to grow herbs in the winter while other plants lay dormant. The stone-walled cottage might have been inviting if Alexa didn't dread what waited for her inside.

She took a deep breath to settle her nerves before she opened the door and slipped in. A single candle flickered on the center table. Melina Odella sat hunched, absorbed in the cards spread across the purple velvet. The fortune-teller picked up card after card before dropping them in a haphazard pile. She dropped her head to her hands.

Although she felt like an intruder, Alexa couldn't help glancing at the cards. She gasped when she saw the Lovers card on top.

Melina Odella spun to face Alexa. She swept up the cards and slapped them face down. "How long have you been standing there?"

"Not long." Time enough to understand why Melina Odella was agitated. The Lovers?

"Hmpf." Melina Odella stood and shoved the cards into the bag that hung at her waist. She strode to the back room and snarled over her shoulder, "Potions today."

It wasn't potions Alexa needed to work on. She'd memorized all the formulas the first month of her apprenticeship. She steeled herself for Melina Odella's response and asked, "When are you going to teach me something useful?"

The fortune-teller whirled to face her. She hissed, "You can't expect to learn everything in your first year. You're too impatient, and I might add, arrogant, to think you're ready for anything more than simple potions."

The words stung Alexa like a slap to her face. "My brother is training warriors, and I'm stuck here learning how to make a love potion."

Melina Odella sneered. "It wasn't so long ago you desired a love potion."

"And that turned out well."

"I warned you."

"There's a war coming, Melina Odella. Do you care that the village will be invaded? Zander needs help."

"You think I don't know this? You're only an apprentice." Melina Odella flicked her hand. "You can't be ready by then."

"But you do believe the invasion is coming? Has Moira spoken to you?"

Rage crossed her face, and Melina Odella raised herself up. "It's no business of yours if Fate speaks to me." She crossed the room to confront Alexa. "You think you know Moira? I've had twenty years of her controlling my life. You'll regret your choice, as I do."

Alexa stepped back, stunned. She knew Melina Odella was unhappy, but this hatred for Moira?

"I have villagers who depend upon the potions I concoct. The cobbler wouldn't get out of bed without the drink that helps him forget losing his twin in the quest. The blacksmith would be blind without my help. Even your mother uses a potion to concoct the recipes that the elders' wives clamor for. If you're too good to help, then leave. Come back when you're ready to be the student and not the master."

Alexa turned and bolted out the door. Did Melina Odella truly believe she wasn't ready, or was she worried Alexa's powers would surpass her own?

CHAPTER TWENTY-FOUR

Zander

Zander paced in front of one of the long dining tables. The knot in his stomach took root and held fast like a gnarled oak tree. He went to bed with it and woke with it. The oats he'd eaten at breakfast threatened to come back up.

Hunched over the table, Greydon, Fulk, and Geno frowned at a roughly drawn map of the village. Lash and Dharien stood behind, staring over their shoulders. Since the New Year, this was the core group that met each morning before the warriors arrived for breakfast. Two of them, Zander didn't trust.

Zander stopped to point at the forest north of the gulch. "With the cliffs to the west and east, this is the only area from where we can be invaded."

Fulk rubbed his chin. "We could set traps. Won't stop 'em, but it might slow 'em down."

"Greydon? Could you rig a rabbit trap big enough for a man?" Zander shuddered at the image of a man hanging by his heels.

Greydon's eyes lit. "I think so. I'll talk to the rope maker about dyeing the hemp green. Then I'll need to find the right trees." He twisted to stare at Dharien. "It'll be like when we were boys and hunted for play."

It was a stark reminder of the difference between Zander and

Elder Warrin's sons. Zander hunted as a boy so he and his father didn't go hungry.

"The gulch will be our strength and their weakness." Geno stabbed at the map. "I can make a machine capable of lobbing metal scraps at them."

Zander nodded. "Do it. Fulk? What are you thinking?"

Fulk met Zander's gaze. "We won't be ready. Some of the warriors aren't taking the training seriously, and their attitude affects the others. You need to kick out the sluggards."

"Dismiss them?" Zander rubbed the back of his neck. "Any other ideas?"

"I agree with Fulk." Greydon grimaced. "Father says the field workers are more motivated by fear than kindness."

Another difference.

Lash rocked back on his heels. "The women are a distraction."

The other men glanced up at Zander, waiting for his reaction. It wasn't the first time Lash had accused the women of disturbing the men, and every time Zander had shut him down.

"The women aren't the problem." Zander glared at Lash. "The men need more discipline."

Lash held up his hands and smirked. "I know the women want to help, but the men spend more time trying to impress them than learning new skills."

Fulk stood. "Those women work damn hard every day. It's not their fault the men turn into idiots around them."

Surprisingly, Dharien nodded his agreement with Fulk.

"And who will do most of the fighting? Five women or three dozen men? The men need to focus on learning to fight, and if that means moving the women somewhere else, then I think that's what we should do," Lash said.

Pressure built in Zander's head until he thought he'd explode.

He'd expected the warriors to work as hard as he did and to understand the stakes. He sucked in a deep breath. "I'm sick of this! If the men won't see the urgency, I'll give them the boot." Never had he felt the burden of his name more than at that moment.

"There's another reason for moving the women somewhere else. If you allow them to fight and they're disabled or killed, can you live with that?" Greydon sat, arms crossed over his chest, sullen. "Can't you find something safer for them than fighting?"

"I'll think about it." He was tired of arguing.

When the warriors broke for the noon meal, Zander still didn't know what he'd do about the women. Looking at it objectively, he hated to admit that Lash might be right. The men were distracted, but did he need to punish the women? They were focused and trained hard every session. And he'd promised Kaiya. She'd never forgive him if he sent them away.

He strode to the front of the dining hall and waited for the talk to die. The warriors glanced at each other as Zander stood silent in front of them. He hated this part of leading, but Fulk was right. The warriors would be stronger if he was tougher on them. "The village is in danger."

From the back table, Koe hollered, "You've been yammering about that for six months." He crossed his arms over his chest. "Yet we see no signs, no proof."

The anger Zander had pushed down into his gut ignited and rose to his throat. Koe made this easy. "And you treat training as a joke." He pointed to the man and jerked his head to the door. "Get out."

Koe stood and shoved the table. "I gave up working in Terrec's stables for the promise of steady meals." He charged down the aisle toward Zander.

Alarmed, Greydon and Fulk rushed to Zander's side.

Zander sucked in a deep breath and rested a hand on the pommel of his knife. "Don't be a fool, Koe."

The man hesitated and then made a show of turning and stomping out the door. The remaining warriors turned shocked faces to Zander.

"Anyone else? If you're only here for the food and don't believe in our cause, it's better I know now." He held his breath as two others slunk out. Only three, and good riddance. He met each of the remaining men's eyes before he looked at the five women.

They stared back nervously, except for Kaiya, who met his gaze without wavering. Lash was wrong. It wasn't the fault of the women if the men found them distracting. They didn't deserve to be sent away. But Greydon had a point. If they died in the war, he'd be at fault for allowing them to fight. How could he live with himself if Kaiya were injured or worse? Stars, she was going to hate him.

He took a deep breath and, even though his gut warned him he was making a mistake, he said, "I have a new plan for the girls."

Kaiya's eyes narrowed.

"I'm moving you to the healers."

"No!" Kaiya stood and planted her feet. "Moira called me to be a warrior. Not a healer. You have no right to change that."

Zander held up his hand. "You'll still be in the war." He glanced at the floor and took a breath before he looked at her again. This didn't feel right. He resisted the urge to rub his aching thigh. "You just won't be fighting. I want the girls behind the lines."

"No. We're warriors."

He felt the heat rise in his chest. "It's not your decision."

Kaiya hurled a bowl of stew at Zander's head.

He jumped to the side in time to avoid the collision. It splattered on the floor behind him.

Kaiya stormed out, leading the other women. He'd betrayed his promise to treat them as equals. Why had he listened to Greydon? Many of the men nodded at his decree. He couldn't change his mind, or he'd look weak.

Kaiya turned before she reached the door. "And stop calling us girls. We survived the quest. We're women."

CHAPTER TWENTY-FIVE

Alexa

Alexa glanced out the front window as she loaded a tray of buns onto the bakery shelves. To her surprise, she saw Kaiya leading a group of women straight for the bakery. By the way Kaiya strode, she wasn't happy. Alexa tossed her apron on the table and went outside to greet them.

"Your brother threw us out of the warriors." Kaiya's eyes flashed. "He can't do that."

Bindi and Yarra from Alexa's quest year, plus Gia and Rosa from the year before, crowded in a circle around Alexa and Kaiya.

Bindi slapped a knife against her thigh. "Moira chose us. He has to let us train with him."

"Melina Odella isn't training me either." Alexa chewed the inside of her cheek. "I have an idea." She brushed the flour off her hands and stuck her head inside the kitchen. "Mother? I'm leaving." When Mother nodded, Alexa motioned the others to follow and led them through the side door to the stairwell.

They thumped up the steps to her room, filling the bed, chairs, and floor. Alexa stood in front of her dresser and pulled an embroidery out of the top drawer. She held it out for the women to see the scene as it moved across the cloth.

"I'm sure the elders' wives will love it," Rosa scoffed. "What does it have to do with us?"

Kaiya took it and peered, intent, at the scene. "This is Paal, Lash, and Dharien training with bows." She looked up, puzzled. "What are you doing?"

"I know I can help the war if I stitch the right scenes. This one helps them shoot straight."

Bindi sat up straight. "I never hit the bulls-eye. Can you help me?"

"I think so, but I haven't quite got my spells right. I'm not using the right words."

"Merindah could help." Kaiya handed the cloth back to Alexa. "Have you heard her prayers during Sunday mass? She has a gift with words."

"I haven't been going." Alexa shook her head. "I'm not sure she'll help if it involves magic."

Yarra stood. "Stay here. I'll get her. She owes me a favor."

While they waited for Yarra, Alexa passed around the embroideries she'd stitched of the warriors training. The women laughed at the scene of them using practice blades on the pells.

"You're good at this." Gia rubbed her finger across the cloth. She glanced up at Alexa. "I never could get my stitches straight, and I kept poking my finger with the needle."

"When I get in a hurry, I prick myself, too," Alexa said, holding out her left hand. A dozen blood spots scattered across the pad of her index finger. She lifted her velvet skirt to show the scar in her knee. "I also don't carry a needle in my hem anymore."

"That was awful in the quest when Zander had to pull out the needle. I thought I'd faint." The others laughed with Kaiya, but Alexa sobered. Zander. What was he thinking? He'd alienated the best group of women she knew. He was going to need all of them in the war. And Melina Odella, too. Alexa hated the thought, but she needed to stay close to the fortune-teller. She dropped her skirt as Yarra walked in with Merindah.

She puzzled over Merindah's changed appearance. She wore the usual plain brown dress, but she'd added a black scarf that covered her head. There were dark circles under her eyes as though she had not slept in days, and she compulsively fingered the amethyst beads tied in a loop around her waist. Merindah glanced at Alexa and dropped her eyes.

When she moved to give her friend a hug, Alexa gasped as she put her arms around her thin body. "What happened to your hair?"

Merindah stiffened and pulled away. "Hair is a vanity." She yanked off the scarf to reveal her shaved head. "It would benefit all of us to spend less time on appearances and more time in prayer and meditation."

The room grew silent. Alexa ignored the jab. "We need your help."

"If it doesn't interfere with my vows, I'll try. Yarra said you have a plan to help Zander stop the invasion."

"You believe the village is in danger?"

Merindah nodded. "I know it is. God speaks to me in my meditations."

Stunned, Alexa stuttered, "God speaks to you? Moira speaks to Zander." Alexa wasn't ready to share her own visions from Moira. She'd never felt the presence of God. She hesitated, unsure if she wanted to hear Merindah's answer, before she asked, "What does he say?"

Merindah lifted her eyes heavenward. "We must unite the tribes as Puck envisioned. Only together, as one soul, can we defeat the invaders and preserve our village."

A shiver ran through Alexa. "Puck also speaks to Zander, but I think my brother has forgotten his directive."

Merindah turned sorrow-filled eyes to Alexa. "Then we will fall."

"No." Kaiya paced at the door. "We won't. We'll find a way to remind Zander, and we'll train on our own." She grabbed Alexa and Merindah's hands. "Together. If *we* can't get along, what hope do we have to unite the others?"

Unite the tribes. What did that even mean? Members of five tribes lived in Puck's Gulch. Tshilaba belonged to the sixth tribe, the Raskans, who called no land home. In Puck's Gulch, they'd found peace, but not unity. Although the tribes had intermingled, they still identified with the tribes by their appearance. Yarra was Chadha like her. Kaiya was Yapi, Bindi was Kharok. Merindah and Rosa were Dakta. Gia, with her bright red hair, was one of the few Odwa in their village.

Hope blossomed in her chest and spread until she felt the warmth flush her cheeks. Alexa caught each of the women's eyes. "We have all the tribes right here. Let the men train for war. We'll train for peace."

Alexa brought out the journal she'd used in the quest. Lavender scent drifted from the pages of the black book. "This isn't so different from the quest. We'll list our strengths and our weaknesses." She cocked her head and looked around. "Moira is preparing us for war. I have my embroidery. What favors did she give each of you?"

"Zander says I shoot straighter than most of the men." Kaiya's grin lit up her face. "I hunt better, too, because I step quieter than most."

"I see in the dark." Bindi looked around as if expecting the others to question her.

"That's an awesome favor." Alexa wrote it next to Bindi's name. Rosa's favor was exceptional hearing.

"Gia?"

"I'm good with a sling." When Alexa's eyebrows rose, Gia tipped her chin up. "I was good before the quest. Now I'm amazing."

Alexa wrote it down. "Moira gave it to you, I'm sure it will be useful."

They turned to Merindah. She ran her fingers along the strand of beads at her waist. "I pray."

Alexa almost snorted. "Everyone prays, Merindah."

She stiffened and stood as if to leave. "My prayers work."

Silence settled over the room. "What do you mean?" Kaiya asked, moving to stand with Merindah. "Can you change things?"

After a short nod, Merindah stared at Alexa. "You control with your embroidery without regard for consequences. I influence events after hours in meditation, when I'm certain of God's will. My way is better."

Indignant, Alexa jumped up to face Merindah. Merindah referred to the time Alexa used her stitching to help Zander win the tournament with disastrous results.

Kaiya held her hands between them. "Together. We need to work together." She glanced from Alexa's to Merindah's faces. "We can't do this if we blame each other or claim only one way as right."

When Merindah dropped her eyes, Alexa felt the fight leave her. She slumped to the bed and whispered, "Merindah, we were friends once. Can we work together for the good of the village?"

Tears welled in Merindah's eyes. She took Alexa's outstretched hand. "I want that. But your way isn't the way of God."

"It's the way of Moira. Puck's Gulch was founded on both equally. Have you forgotten? Moira and God working together with the tribes united." Alexa jolted upright. "If we can work as equals ..." she gestured at the others "... and include all the tribes, we can do this." She jumped to her feet and hugged her friend. "We'll prove to Zander he's wrong to leave us out."

Merindah looked at her strangely, but nodded.

The group turned to Yarra, who shrugged. "I don't know if I can explain what my favor is. When Zander talks strategy, I see it in my head. It's like I understand how doing one thing affects another."

Kaiya's eyes lit. "That's brilliant. I never know what he's talking about, but Yarra—if you understand Zander's strategy, we can make a solid plan to help." She pumped her fist in the air. "We *will* win!"

After Alexa wrote Yarra's favor on the page, she said, "The seven of us will do it together."

Merindah gasped. "Seven? That's the number of spiritual connection. God and Moira, prayer and magic. This is why we've been called to work together."

They made plans to meet the next morning at dawn. The other women left, and Alexa spread her cards across the bed. She pulled one to guide their path. The image was a woman sitting on a platform supported by two beasts—one white and one black—representing two opposing forces. The Chariot card foretold of triumph, but only with great effort and self-discipline.

It was the card associated with the number seven.

CHAPTER TWENTY-SIX

Zander

The look on Kaiya's face as she left haunted Zander, but he didn't have time for regrets. He split the men into four teams and sent them out. He and Greydon walked behind their group on the way to the archery range.

"Did you see the men's faces? It never occurred to them they could lose a spot with the warriors. They're determined to work harder than ever." Greydon playfully punched Zander's shoulder. "And nothing will distract them."

Zander stopped. "Who distracts you, Greydon?"

The words were out before Zander thought about what he was saying.

Greydon turned to face him, blushing brilliantly, but he held Zander's eyes. "What are you talking about?"

"It's not the women, is it?" He only brought it up now because of the twist in his own gut. He never should have listened to Greydon. "Is it Odo? I see the way you watch him."

He didn't have time to duck before Greydon's fist connected with his chin and knocked him to his butt. Greydon looked as shocked as Zander felt. They'd argued, but never come to blows. Zander rubbed his jaw. "Nice hook."

"What the hell, Zander!" Greydon extended his hand and pulled Zander to his feet.

"Am I wrong?"

When Greydon stared back at him stone-faced, Zander leaned in. "Look, I don't care. I just think you're being a little holier-than-thou about the girls—I mean the women." He pulled his hair back and tied it with a leather strap. "I don't care, Greydon. You're my best friend. I don't want to fight about this."

"Is it obvious?" Greydon slumped. "Do the others know?"

"I don't think so. And it only matters if it bothers *you*."

"It matters to my father. You don't know what it's like being a firstborn son."

Zander's eyebrow rose. "And what am I?"

"You know what I mean." Greydon had the grace to look away. "There are certain expectations for an elder's heir. I need to marry and produce the next heir."

"Well, then, all the more reason to bring down the current system, hoy? I bet Puck's picked this time to resurrect his dream just to get you out of the heir business."

That brought a grin. As they walked, Greydon grew quiet. He mumbled, "You really don't care?"

"I care a lot more about avoiding your fist." Zander stepped to the side to bump Greydon's shoulder. "I've known for a long time. I don't care, Greydon."

Greydon grabbed Zander's arm and pulled him to a stop. "How long?"

This was a conversation Zander never should have started. He shrugged Greydon's hand off his arm. "Long enough."

"How?" Suspicion clouded Greydon's face. "I've never told anyone, and Odo's the first man I've been truly interested in. How did you know?"

Damn. How could he get out of this without revealing his own secret? "Look. Sometimes I just know things. I–I . . . saw it in your eyes when we met at the archery tournament."

"That long?" Anger flashed in Greydon's eyes. "Who have you told?"

"No one. I swear."

"Why would you keep that secret when we weren't even friends then?"

Zander felt his own anger rising into his chest. "Damn it, Greydon. Everyone has secrets. You think that's the worst one I know? It's not." He should stop talking, but the words flew out. "Moira gave me a favor I never wanted. It's a curse, not a gift."

"I don't believe you." Greydon stepped back and rocked on his heels.

What the hell? If Zander wasn't careful, he was going to lose his best friend. He sucked in a deep breath and tamped down his anger. It wound down into a familiar place in his gut, tight and pulsing. He had to confess to Greydon and hope he'd understand. He pulled energy from the earth and embraced the calm that flowed through his chest.

"During my time of magic, Moira gave me the favor of seeing a person's deepest secret when I looked in their eyes." He held up his hand when Greydon started to interrupt. "I hated it. I didn't want to see your secret. But sometimes it helped me. I found Alexa because of what I saw in Father's eyes. After the quest, I begged Moira to take it, but she insisted I'd need it yet." He rubbed the back of his neck. "I've spent hours learning to control it. I only see secrets when I let down my shield." He searched Greydon's eyes. "I never let it down with you. Never."

Disbelief washed across Greydon's face. "How would I know?"

"You have to trust me. I give you my word."

Greydon stared at the ground. "It's a lot to ask."

And there it was. The one thing Zander feared. If Greydon wouldn't trust him, no one else would. "Will you at least keep my secret?"

Greydon nodded without looking at Zander. He glanced across at the men waiting at the targets for instruction. "Let's get to work." It unsettled Zander that Greydon obviously felt betrayed. If he exposed Zander's secret, it would undermine any trust Zander had built with the warriors. But then, Greydon wanted his own secret kept. Once he calmed down, Greydon would realize it.

Zander spent the next two hours improving the men's stances and giving encouragement. It was two hours that Zander could forget the suspicion on Greydon's face and the anger on Kaiya's.

At the end of the afternoon, when the men had all gone to their own homes for the night, Zander limped to the stable. He rubbed the welt on his thigh. Scars were like secrets. Everyone had them. Some were on the outside, exposed, and some hid deep inside. It was a relief to have Greydon know. He'd find a way to make it work between them. Now, if he could figure out how to make things right with Kaiya. Somehow, he didn't think a punch to his jaw would do it.

In the privacy of his room, Zander pulled a stone from the pouch on his nightstand. Tshilaba had given it to him before the quest. It was two-colored: the red reflected love and the black represented his anger. He'd used it during a meditation to release the anger he'd held onto for years and the stone had transformed to all red. Now, he turned it over and over in his palm. The black took up nearly half of the stone. If he didn't deal with his anger, he'd lose control. And he couldn't afford that.

CHAPTER TWENTY-SEVEN

Zephyr

"Come on, Dorothy."

His patron had stopped to smell the winter bloom of the witch hazel that wove through the fence separating the village from Elder Warrin's land. When she pulled off a blossom and chewed it with a determination only a donkey could have, Zeph chuckled. "Eva will switch you for that. The healers need it for remedies."

A knot formed in the pit of his stomach. With war looming, the healers would need more than a tonic for bruises. And while Zander trained the warriors, Zeph was stuck going to quester lessons with the most stubborn donkey he'd ever known. He patted Dorothy's head. "With all your faults, I still love you."

Dorothy's response was to lift her tail and leave a steaming pile in the snow.

Thank the stars no one was watching. As he drew closer to the Quinary, Zeph's steps slowed. Moira had changed the traditional classroom lectures to include patrons. The classes had not changed in two hundred years. Why now?

Even with his new quester clothes, Zeph felt uncomfortable with his fellow questers. They were supposed to be equals during the time of magic, but he couldn't relate to the others. His classmates knew him as the dumb kid from the shacks. He preferred it over what they would think if they knew the truth. No one would tolerate his presence if they knew he saw their lies, had always seen them. If it was a gift from Moira, it was one he'd always had. No, it was better to be thought stupid than to be feared.

Dorothy nudged his shoulder as if sensing his mood. He leaned his head into her neck and scratched her ears.

Why did he think he'd make any difference in the war? He was nothing but the bastard child of a cruel elder. Even Moira must think so. He'd not received a single token or omen since beginning his time of magic.

Zeph had barely returned from class when Geno charged into the stables carrying a small cage.

"Zephyr," he growled. "Get your bow and come with me."

What had he done? Still in his quester's clothing, Zeph grabbed his bow and stumbled down the aisle past the horse stalls. He paused at Dorothy's pen where she munched from a pail of oats. It looked like Zeph was going to miss his noon meal.

"Leave your donkey. You don't need your patron for this." Geno marched out the back door.

Zeph grabbed his jacket from a peg on the wall. Geno was taking him to the training ring.

At the center, Geno turned to face him. "Zander said to train you as an assassin." He glared at Zeph, appraising him from head to toe. "Let's see if you have it in you. Get your bow ready."

The bow flipped out of Zeph's hand, clattering against the hard ground. When he bent to pick it up, his arrows slid out of the quiver, landing in a pile at Geno's feet.

Geno snorted. "Some assassin." He opened the cage and a wild pup skittered out and raced for the fence, searching for a hole.

"Shoot it," Geno ordered.

Zeph lifted his bow and then lowered it. He couldn't kill an innocent pup.

"You think it'll be easier to kill a man? Shoot." Geno stood with his arms crossed over his chest. "Or shall I tell Zander to find a new assassin?"

Shaking, Zeph positioned his bow and drew back. He sighted and closed his eyes as he released the string. A sickening thud and squeals of pain filled his ears.

He opened his eyes. The pup lay, whimpering, with an arrow in his side. Why couldn't he have missed?

Geno held out a knife. "Kill him."

He shrank back. "I can't."

Unwavering, Geno stood with the knife, handle out. "If you'd shot with your eyes open, you might have made a clean kill. He's in pain. Finish it."

Zeph took the knife and knelt at the pup's side. Soft brown eyes stared up at him. If he didn't do it quickly, he wouldn't be able to.

He slit the pup's throat.

Smirking, Geno nodded. "You might make an assassin after all. That was lesson one." He strode back to the stable.

Lifting the dead pup, Zeph choked back sobs. He couldn't bury it in the frozen ground, but he could take the body to the woods. He carried it out the corral door and into the trees where he kicked aside the blanket of leaves. He wrapped the pup in his blood-stained jacket and laid him to rest.

He could never kill a man. Never.

CHAPTER TWENTY-EIGHT

Alexa

Alexa woke as a rosy dawn graced her window. She snuggled under the warm coverlet, holding onto her dream. She'd sewn half the night, and would rather go back to sleep, but Kaiya and the other women were counting on her help. She had the stitchings. If Merindah helped with the words, Alexa could spell them into the cloth.

The dream danced in her mind, fuzzy and out of reach. Sometimes it was her and Zander, sometimes her and Merindah, but always they walked ahead of her, and she couldn't quite catch up. Frustration at not understanding the meaning drove her to throw back the covers.

In the chilly winter air, she dressed, grabbed the bag of embroidery, and ran downstairs. Mother had baked as late as Alexa had stitched. The still-warm oven heated the kitchen, and fragrances of yeast and sugar filled the air. Sturdy loaves of bread lined the shelves, ready for market, and Mother's special cakes and feather-light rolls filled the front tables. Moira had favored Mother with the knowledge of how to blend herbs and flowers into her baking so that the scent delighted the nose and the taste dazzled the tongue. Alexa knew the recipes, but lacked the imagination to create. Thank the stars Moira had called her to be a fortune-teller and not a baker.

She sliced two thick pieces off the not-perfect oat loaf on the center table. All her life, Alexa had eaten the bread that didn't rise quite right or the rolls that over-browned from sitting too close to the oven wall. They tasted fine and filled the belly, but Alexa chafed from always feeling second-best, as though she wasn't worthy of the good stuff. She hesitated only a moment before she grabbed a sweet roll from the shelf reserved for the elders' wives and scurried out the door.

As she walked through the market, the Protectors changed shifts. The ones leaving exchanged information with the replacements, who rubbed sleep from their eyes. Cobie's father, the coppersmith, clanged his pots as he set up shop. Cobie should have followed in his father's tradition. Instead, Moira had called him to train as a healer. After their quest, the village had gone from one healer to four. All in preparation for war.

A shudder rolled through her that wasn't from the cold. What if Zander failed to protect the village? He was foolish to dismiss the women from training. They needed Fulk and Geno's knowledge. And she had to prove to him that her magic would help. Stubborn brother.

She skirted past a horse pulling a cart of root vegetables and headed catty-corner across the market toward Paal's father's estate. He'd agreed to lend them use of his archery range for the mornings.

The sun burst above the trees and blinded her just as she glimpsed Merindah's dark clothes ahead. "Hoy, Merindah."

Alexa ran to catch up. The dream flashed back to her. When Merindah turned to greet her, Alexa stumbled. Circles under her friend's eyes appeared purple against her dark skin. Was she not sleeping at all?

They continued to the range. Alexa asked, "Did you have any trouble getting out of morning prayers?"

"The priest understands. I do what I need to do."

Alexa blinked. That didn't sound like Father Chanse, but he'd changed since Alexa had disgraced him in front of the church. He'd gone into seclusion for two months, and when he returned, he was subdued and contrite. At that same time, Melina Odella had withdrawn from Alexa.

As Alexa struggled to find a response, Merindah placed her hand on Alexa's wrist and squeezed lightly. "I'm the anchoress, Alexa. Father Chanse and the nuns understand I follow God's will, not theirs."

A vision of the Queen of Swords card superimposed itself over Merindah's face—the people's champion, but not a person to cross. Alexa clutched Merindah's hand. "You're not going through with that, are you?"

Merindah tipped her head and examined Alexa. "Of course I am. It's my destiny."

The Death card hovered between them. The end of one phase of life for another.

They walked in silence. Alexa's thoughts swirled round and round. Merindah choosing to enter a cell, Zander choosing to fight, and the village in danger. Was her role more than stitching magic scenes?

They found the five warriors already in practice. Kaiya stood at the first post, stance strong but relaxed, her auburn hair gathered into a top knot at the crown of her head. She held her bow in position and called out for the others—"nock, draw, release." Five arrows whistled to the targets. Only Kaiya's flew true and hit the center.

Alexa dug in her bag and pulled out five small squares of embroidery. The women gathered around her, chattering and laughing at their depictions on the cloth. Each scene showed a woman with bow aimed at a round target.

"I need to add the spells." Alexa glanced at Merindah. "Will you help? I have trouble getting the words right."

Merindah hesitated.

Kaiya held out her square. "Think of it as a prayer. Ask God's blessing upon us."

It would take more than a prayer, but Alexa kept the thought to herself. If Merindah composed the words, Alexa could add her magic.

Merindah closed her eyes. She held her palms out and in a clear voice chanted, "Arrows from God, fly true. Target hit, not askew."

Quickly Alexa threaded a needle with a single strand of the gold silk thread from Tshilaba. As she stitched a line connecting the arrow to the center of the target on Bindi's cloth, she joined her voice with Merindah's. In her mind, Alexa watched as the words blended into the thread. She tied the knot and handed it to Bindi. "Try it." As the worst shot, Bindi would be the best test of the magic.

After tucking the small square up her sleeve, Bindi moved to the post. She fumbled with her arrow and dropped it. "I'm nervous with all of you watching."

Kaiya moved next to her and drew her bow. "We'll do it together." She planted her feet. "Nock, draw, release."

Two arrows sailed to the target. Two arrows flew true. Two satisfying thuds as they hit the bulls-eye.

"Take that Zander!" Bindi whooped as the women surrounded her. "We'll show him we can be better than the men."

This wasn't about the women against the men. Alexa stepped back away from the group. They needed to work together. But the women's excitement was contagious, and she couldn't help but join in. She finished the rest of the embroideries while chanting with Merindah.

Shot after shot, every arrow hit the center circles. With each success, Alexa's smile grew larger. Even Merindah looked pleased.

Kaiya spun in the opposite direction and aimed at a tree twice as far away as the target. "Let's see what happens."

As Kaiya released the arrow, Alexa realized her mistake. Halfway to the tree, the arrow jerked up and flew backward. Kaiya ducked as the arrow whizzed past her and on to the target to hit the bulls-eye.

Wide-eyed, Kaiya twirled to face Alexa. "This isn't going to work."

Alexa held up a hand as the babbling women surrounded her. "I made a mistake. It can be fixed."

"A mistake?" Yarra snorted. "You nearly killed Kaiya."

To Alexa's surprise, Kaiya grinned. "I've survived Alexa's mistakes before."

She referred to the quest, when Alexa's plan to fight their omens together almost caused Kaiya to be attacked by a snake. Alexa appreciated Kaiya's confidence, then and now. "I need to take out the target and stitch something that will work on anything you aim at."

"You could stitch a man," Gia suggested. "That's who we'll be aiming at if we're attacked."

"What if the arrows fly toward our men?" Rosa asked.

Bindi sniffed. "It would serve them right for throwing us out."

No. That wasn't what Alexa wanted. "We need to work with the men, not against them."

Merindah tapped her hands at her sides. "It needs to be something the shooter can think of as their target in any situation. Let me see one of the cloths."

"What if you took out the target and stitched an X?" Rosa handed hers back to Alexa.

Alexa cut out the stitches for the target and replaced them with a large black X. Then she stitched a tiny third eye on the figure of Rosa. "You need to concentrate on the target you want." She wasn't sure it would be that easy, but it was a start.

"Watch out." Rosa faced the tree.

The others scooted away from the targets. Rosa squinted as she drew her bow. She breathed in deeply and held it before she released the string. The arrow stayed true and hit the trunk with a resounding thunk.

As the others cheered, Alexa let out the breath she didn't realize she held. Using magic to control the arrows had been trickier than she'd expected. She'd need to be very careful with what she planned next.

CHAPTER TWENTY-NINE

February Festival of Victoria

Zander

Zander reached the top of the gulch and bent over to catch his breath. He and Shadow had been scouting places to lay traps. It had been weeks since he'd sent Kaiya to work with the healer Eva. He'd heard nothing from either of them.

"Hoy, Zander!" Greydon called out to him from the trees on Elder Terrec's land line.

He squinted. Damn. Alexa was with him. They wanted him to join them at the Festival of Victoria. Before the quest, the festivals were his favorite time of the year. Now, he avoided them. Too many people made it difficult to keep his shields up, and he hated seeing all those secrets. Even worse were the looks from the merchants who resented his taking three dozen men who should have been working in guilds. And he really didn't want to see Kaiya at the festival that celebrated love.

He met them halfway and scowled at Alexa's hopeful face. He hated disappointing her. "Heading to the Quinary?"

"Come with us? Please, Z?" She took his arm. "You haven't been to a festival since the quest."

"With good reason. You know how the guilds feel about me."

"An argument for attending." Greydon rubbed his chin. "They need to see you. If you're their leader, let them see you lead."

"Lead what?" Zander snorted. "A bunch of warriors getting drunk?"

Greydon leaned in. "It's Lash they see swaggering about, bragging how he's going to save the village. Father says he's gaining their confidence and placing doubt on your leadership."

Anger rose from Zander's gut. "It was your idea to have him be our liaison."

"Liaison, not leader. They need to see you."

He felt the wisdom even as he despised the reason. "Let's go then." He and Greydon hadn't talked again about Zander's favor, but they'd fallen back into being comfortable with each other—if comfortable meant Greydon not looking Zander in the eye.

Alexa walked between them, tucking her hands through their arms. As good as it felt to be with his sister and friend, Zander dreaded seeing the villagers. As they neared the market, shoppers crowded the booths, searching for trinkets and gifts only offered during celebrations. After the quiet of living at the stables, the din of the festival assaulted his ears. Shadow tucked into Zander's legs as if the noise bothered him, too.

"Hoy, there's Odo and Kaiya." Alexa tugged on his arm.

He knew Greydon would be happy to join the cousins, but Zander wasn't ready to see Kaiya. They hadn't talked since he'd asked the women to move to the healers. He was certain she was still angry with him, but then she turned and flashed a big smile. He checked behind him. Yep, it was for him. He let Alexa pull him to the wooden bench where they sat.

Clear quartz beads threaded through Kaiya's hair, which she had braided down the side and tied in back. When she turned her head, the sun sparkled in the beads. She'd lined her eyes, not as thick as Alexa wore hers, but enough to define her hazel eyes. She didn't look mad, she looked excited to see him.

Alexa tapped his arm. "Z, want a cider?"

"Um, sure." He squirmed. "Uh, nothing in it but cider, right?" He didn't want any of Alexa's potions added in. He had enough problems without adding in girl trouble.

She grinned and whispered, "No love potion for you." She nodded toward Kaiya. "You don't need it." She disappeared into the crowd.

Greydon and Odo moved to a stand selling roasted nuts, leaving Zander alone with Kaiya. He plopped down on the other end of the bench and glanced over at her. Still smiling—that was good. "So . . ."

"Let's not talk about it. I want to enjoy the festival and forget about war today."

Zander slid over next to her. He didn't want to fight. Maybe Alexa was right. It was good to be at the celebration.

Someone spat at his feet. Garrick, the guild master, stood in front of Zander, arms crossed, feet planted wide. "Surprised you had the guts to show yer face."

He stood, but Zander avoided looking the man in the eye. He didn't want the man's secrets. "What are you talking about?"

"You increased our tithe last month to support your little games." Garrick spat again. "You too shifty to look me in the face?"

Zander blanched. He'd known better than to trust Lash, and yet he'd let Greydon convince him. It would undermine his leadership if he tried to explain he hadn't given the order. He met the man's stare. "I think the coffers are level now. I'll see if we can reduce your duty to below the original commitment." He hoped the books were in order. He'd left that to Greydon.

Garrick grunted, but he dropped his arms. "I'm not the only one unhappy."

"I'll adjust everyone's contribution." And see that Lash wasn't taking a cut. It was time to deal with him. He couldn't wait for proof.

The guild master leaned in. "You better hope that invasion comes soon." Garrick sauntered away.

What the hell? Hope for war? Zander wanted to punch the smirk off his face.

Kaiya took his arm and guided him toward the music tent. "Find seats. You need more than cider."

In one corner of the tent, a Protector played a fiddle tucked under his chin. Next to him, Eva played a flute. Kaiya's father beat a complicated rhythm on the drum, and Merindah's mother tapped a tambourine against her leg. The center of the tent overflowed with drunken couples dancing to the lively music.

Zander stood at the tent flap and searched the crowd for one face. If Father was there, nothing would make Zander go in. When he didn't see him, Zander stepped inside. The music reverberated in his chest.

He found three empty seats at a small table shoved in a corner and waved at Kaiya. It was the first festival he'd attended since the quest. The first time he'd been old enough to drink. He knew most of the boys had sneaked mead before their quest, but with Father being a drunk, Zander had never been interested. Kaiya sat next to him and slid a tankard in front of him. Zander eyed the pint of black mead brewed for the festivals. The other warriors were having a good time. He deserved to forget about invasions and wars for a day. As Greydon had said, one pint wouldn't make him a drunk.

He tipped the mug up and choked at the bitter taste as Kaiya sipped her own pint, amused at his reaction. Why would anyone drink the stuff? But by the time the pint was empty, he understood. The only time he felt that relaxed was when he meditated, but even then, he carried the responsibility for the safety of the village. After the second pint, his worries had disappeared. After the third, he was tapping his foot to the music and roaring at the drunks stumbling around the tent.

Alexa joined them, and the disgusted look she gave him made him reconsider, but a fourth pint appeared in front of him and he drained it. Kaiya pulled him up, laughing, and dragged him to the dance floor. He must have looked panicked because she leaned in and said, "It's not that hard." There were enough people tipsy with drink to make him feel comfortable as he tried to imitate the dancers. When he stumbled and Kaiya threw her arms around him, he stayed with her, enjoying her warmth and the smell of lavender that drifted from her hair. She didn't seem to mind when he pulled her closer.

He whispered into her ear, "You're pretty."

She pulled away and pursed her lips. "That's what you think of me? That I'm pretty?"

Somewhere in his foggy mind he knew he was on dangerous ground, but he couldn't quite pinpoint why. "I thought girls wanted to be pretty."

Kaiya flipped her hair and batted her eyelashes. "Is that what you want? A pretty girl to cook for you and sew your clothes?"

Now he was confused. Is that what he wanted? He didn't think so, but he wasn't sure. "Uh, is that bad?"

He knew he was in trouble when tears glimmered in Kaiya's eyes. She rubbed them away. "I expected better of you, Zander. You're just like the others. At least Lash told me I was beautiful *and* strong."

Lash? Anger shot through him. He'd had enough of Lash. He turned from Kaiya and pushed his way through the crowd and out the door of the tent.

CHAPTER THIRTY

Alexa

Alarmed that Zander drank so much, Alexa steeled herself to intervene. She leaned forward to reach for his cup just as Kaiya pulled him off the bench and led him to dance. He deserved to have fun, but after they left, in the midst of the crowd, Alexa felt more alone than ever. She might be the only one in the tent not drinking. Unlike her brother, she preferred to stay clearheaded. She wouldn't make a fool of herself with Dharien. If Zeph was right, Dharien was helping Lash steal money from the warriors, and she didn't want to have anything to do with him. That's what her head said, but her heart whispered different thoughts, and she wasn't about to let mead make her do something stupid.

She glanced at her twin. Zander pushed his way through the crowd and disappeared out the tent. What happened to put that scowl on his face?

Kaiya plopped on the bench opposite to Alexa, tears in her eyes. "Your brother just ruined everything."

Uh, oh. She reached for Kaiya's hand. "What happened?"

"He said I was pretty."

Before Alexa could formulate a response, Kaiya said, "I'm more than that. Stars, I'm a warrior."

And then Alexa understood. Her twin was an idiot. "I'll talk to him."

"Don't bother. There're plenty of other men here."

"But none that hold your heart like my brother. Don't give up on him."

They sat morosely, Kaiya sipping at her mead, and Alexa chewing on her thumbnail. A throng near the entrance suddenly pushed outside. Shouts of "fight, fight," echoed from the side of the tent. A steady stream of people filed outside. One person pushed against the flow and searched the tent. When Dharien saw her, he strode to her table.

"Your brother's about to get the shit beat out of him."

Alexa and Kaiya jumped up and ran after Dharien as he pressed through the crowd. Shouts led them to a clearing behind the tent. Zander faced Lash with a dozen men circling them. Muffled music and laughter blended with the warriors' cheers. Alexa pushed through the circle, but a hand grabbed her shoulder and pulled her back.

"He doesn't need his sister saving him." Greydon leaned in. "This has been coming a long time. Let him handle it."

"He's drunk."

A grin lit Greydon's face. "So is Lash. It'll be a fair fight."

"What if he gets hurt?"

"All the better. Let the men see him as human. He holds himself apart too much."

Dharien held her arm. "Greydon's right. Let this play out."

Zander lunged at Lash and they crashed to the ground. The circle tightened as the men shouted, most for Zander, a few for Lash.

Lash threw sloppy punches as Zander straddled him, deflecting his fists. Zander connected with Lash's jaw and then flew backward when Lash shoved him off. They stumbled to their feet and locked arms. Lash headbutted Zander in the nose and blood spurted over both of them. Cheers rang out as the fistfight turned into wrestling.

It was only Dharien's tight grip that kept Alexa from running to help. She hated seeing Zander hurt.

Beside her, Kaiya jumped up and down. "Take him down, Zander! Punch him!"

Her encouragement seemed to energize Zander. He swept Lash's legs out from under him, and they crashed to the ground and rolled. Alexa lost sight of him as the circle opened to let them through. Dharien pulled her along for a better vantage point. She turned and pressed her face in Dharien's chest as Lash pummeled Zander's face. Then a punch from Zander coldcocked Lash, and he slumped on top of Zander. Zander rolled out from under him and crawled to the side. On hands and knees, he puked until he dry heaved.

Still, Dharien kept her from going to him. Over the shouts of the warriors, he pulled her close. "Let the men take care of him."

She watched, fascinated, as the men lifted Zander and half-carried, half-dragged him into the music tent. Lash lay passed out on the ground, forgotten.

Greydon appeared at her side. "This was the best thing that could have happened to Zander. Don't ruin it by making a fuss over him." He pointed at Kaiya. "That goes for you, too." To Dharien he said, "Brother, let's get drunk."

Dharien followed Greydon, but glanced back at Alexa. She couldn't decipher his look, and then he disappeared into the tent.

Later when Alexa and Kaiya looked in on the men, Zander was singing with the warriors, all of them drunk.

What was her brother thinking?

CHAPTER THIRTY-ONE

Zephyr

Disgusted, Zeph watched the warriors carry Zander into the tent. He hoped to never see Zander like that again. He'd discovered something Zander would be interested in, but now it would have to wait.

"Zander's a drunk like his father."

Zeph hadn't seen Elder Terrec until that moment. He tipped his head at Lash lying unconscious on the ground. "What about your son? Just as drunk."

"My son will pay for his ignorance." Terrec grabbed Zeph's arm and guided him to the church, deserted during the celebration. "I have an offer for you, Son."

"Don't call me that." Zeph pulled away from Terrec. "You've never been a father to me."

"Now, now, Son, you can't hold that against me." He smirked. "I can't be a father to all of the red-haired kids in the village."

Six kids with red hair lived in the shacks. Every one of their mothers either worked at Elder Terrec's manor or in the tavern with his mother. And every one of them, like himself before he joined the warriors, went to bed hungry. He turned. Zeph would go to hell before he'd listen to anything Terrec had to say.

"I'd hate to see anything happen to your mother."

Zeph froze. When he turned back, Terrec stood with arms

crossed over his chest and a sneer on his face. Zeph reached under his tunic and drew his knife.

"Good gods, boy! Put that away." When Zeph held his ground, Terrec stepped back and opened his coat. "Would you attack an unarmed man? I only want to talk."

"Then talk." Zeph didn't move. Let the man say his words and maybe he'd leave him alone.

Terrec stepped closer and lowered his voice. "You saw Zander. He's his father all over. A drunk and an embarrassment to the village. He's in over his head with this warrior training."

Zander *had* been struggling. Zeph wasn't sure he even wanted the responsibility. But Moira had chosen him.

"Look, all I'm suggesting is that someone else might be better suited to save the village."

Now Zeph sneered. "Like Lash?"

"Hells no! Not Lash." Terrec leaned in conspiratorially. "I have a firstborn no one knows of." He pointed to Zeph's hair. "A bastard, sure, but no red hair to give him away. He's trained as a Protector. He knows what he's doing, unlike your Zander."

As Zeph sifted through mental pictures of the Protectors, one stood out as always being around Elder Terrec. "Del."

"Smart lad." Terrec nodded. "Yes, Del." He motioned at a shadowy figure leaning against the church. Del stepped into the light and joined them.

Zeph could hardly believe it. Esteemed among the Protectors, Del also excelled as an archer. Zander had confided to Zeph that Del was the reason he'd once dreamed of becoming a Protector. If Del took over training the warriors, maybe the burden would be lifted from Zander.

"Del's ready to take over."

Nodding, Del said, "At first, I didn't believe the village was in danger, but now I do. The Protectors offered to join the warriors, but Zander's stubborn and refused us."

"Why would he listen to me?"

"You live with him. Plant some doubts about being ready in time."

Terrec rested his hand on Zeph's shoulder. "After all, the safety of the village is our concern, isn't it? Do we want that responsibility resting on a seventeen-year-old?"

If Del and the Protectors could help them prepare for war, why wouldn't Zander want that? And if Del was in charge, Zeph wouldn't be expected to act as an assassin. He took a deep breath. "I'll see what I can do."

Terrec smiled. "You do that, and I'll see that your mother is unharmed."

CHAPTER THIRTY-TWO

Zander

Zander woke the morning after the fight with a pounding head-ache, still clothed, draped crossways in his bed. He wasn't sure how he'd made it back to his room. How many pints had he drank after the fight with Lash? Each time he emptied a mug, another had appeared.

Shadow whined, wanting out. Zander rolled off the bed and clutched the foot post when the room spun. His gut ached as the roasted pork he barely remembered eating threatened to come up. Shadow shot out the door when he was able to open it. Thankfully, the warriors had the day off.

He wandered to the kitchen. Zeph sat at the small table and held out a slice of oat bread slathered with butter. Zander swallowed hard and shook his head.

"Cider first," he said. After he managed to sip most of the cup, he sat at the table with his head in his hands wondering how Father drank every day and still managed to work. After several silent min-utes, he looked up at the usually calm Zeph to find him fidgeting. "What is it?"

Zeph shrugged.

Zander wasn't in the mood for whatever it was Zeph needed to say. He held in a sigh. Might as well get it over with. Zeph probably had a message from Alexa. He did remember seeing her look of disgust in the music tent when he fell at her feet. It probably hadn't helped that he called her his pretty little sister. What was it about girls not liking to be pretty?

When Zeph drummed his fingers on the table, Zander reached out to stop him before his head split. "Say it, Zeph, before I go back to bed."

"You're still drunk."

"So I am. What is it?" Zeph's face hardened. Zander's stomach lurched. "Is something wrong with Alexa?" Relief flooded him when Zeph shook his head.

"Del offered to help train the warriors."

A spike of pain sliced through Zander's forehead. "Why would Del make that offer to you?"

Zeph's eyebrow shot up. "Because you were drunk?"

"Let it go, Zeph. It was the first time. And it's not likely to happen again." He rubbed his temples. Probably not anyway.

"Well? What do you think? He could help us get ready quicker."

Zeph wouldn't look Zander in the eye, but Zander's head wasn't clear enough to question him. "No. The Protectors will do their own part when we're invaded. And I don't trust Del. He's in Terrec's employ."

As if he expected Zander's response, Zeph nodded. "I found proof that Lash is stealing money."

"Too late. The guild master confirmed it."

Zeph slumped in his chair. Something else was wrong, but Zander couldn't think. He needed a few more hours of sleep. "Will you feed the horses? I'll muck the stalls later."

"I already did. It's past noon bells."

All right then. "Thanks." Zander stood slowly and all but crawled back to bed. He dropped on top of the covers, still clothed. His last thought was a question—why had Del talked to Zeph?

"Zander? Zander, wake up."

Still foggy, Zander rolled over. Greydon and Alexa stood over him. Alexa's eyes were red, and Greydon looked grim. He said, "We've got a problem."

"Lash is missing," Alexa blurted.

"Good riddance. That's what you woke me for?" Zander rolled back onto his stomach.

Greydon grabbed Zander's arm and hauled him upright. "He disappeared after the fight, and Terrec's blaming you. He's headed here now with the Protectors to arrest you."

"Arrest me? I was with the warriors all night and then here sleeping it off."

"Anyone here with you?"

Zander winced as he tried to stand. His head throbbed and his body ached like he'd been thrown from Helios and stomped on. "I don't know. Zeph?"

Alexa shook her head. "He slept at the bakery and didn't leave until mid-morning."

"Someone in the music tent overheard you say you were going to kill him." Greydon paced the small room. "Zander, this is serious."

"I didn't say that." At least he didn't think he said it. After the third pint, everything was a bit blurry. "Who brought me here? They can testify I was in no shape to leave, let alone search out Lash and kill him."

"I think I did, but I'm not sure." Greydon looked sheepish. "I woke up in our kitchen when the cooks showed at dawn."

So this was the aftermath of drinking. Alexa grabbed his arm and pain shot through his wrist. For the first time, he noticed his swollen, busted knuckles. He couldn't help feeling a great deal of satisfaction that they'd come from smashing Lash's face.

"You need to leave. Camp in the gulch until this blows over." Greydon slumped against the wall, looking as green as Zander felt.

"Hide? That would make me look guilty. I didn't kill Lash."

"Do you know that for sure?" Alexa leaned in. "Z, do you remember anything after you came home?"

Zander pulled away. "You think I killed him?"

"I saw the fight. You looked like you wanted to kill him."

The stable doors flew open. A Protector strode into Zander's room with Elder Terrec.

"Zander, son of Theron, I arrest you as a person of concern in the disappearance of Lash, son of Terrec," the Protector stated.

CHAPTER THIRTY-THREE

Zephyr

A Protector led Zander from the stable. Zander didn't even protest. Alexa was crying and Greydon looked grim. Zeph didn't believe Zander killed Lash. More likely, Elder Terrec hauled him home and hid him. And speaking of—Terrec walked back into the stable.

"I believe that's three times your friend has been in jail. Not much of a leader."

"You know he didn't kill Lash."

"Do I?" Terrec smirked. "He had motive and Lash is missing. And I need both of them out of the way."

"So you got what you wanted. Leave me alone." Zeph hated standing there with Terrec, but he suspected the scoundrel wasn't done with him yet.

"Now, Son, I just want you to think about some things." Terrec clasped his hands across his belly. "You think Zander's your friend, but Lash told me how Zander allows the warriors to pick on you."

Zeph started. Lash was the bully.

"In fact, Zander told Greydon he thought it would make you stronger. That you were too weak to be a warrior, and the only reason he let you join was because he felt sorry for you."

Heat rose from Zeph's chest to his face. He'd suspected Zander felt sorry for him, but he didn't think he'd talk about him to the others. He knew he didn't measure up to the other warriors. Why else would Zander have let him join unless he felt sorry for him? Sweat broke out on his forehead.

Dorothy brayed from her stall. He had a donkey for a patron. A jenny. Zander had barely held back his laughter when he found out.

Terrec placed his hand on Zeph's shoulder. "Del would respect you. He'd never let the others bully you. He knows you're his brother, his family."

Family—Zeph hadn't had much of that. He'd always wanted an older brother. And with Zander in jail, *someone* needed to continue their training. Why not Del?

"The warriors won't listen to me."

"They will if you say Zander wants it."

"But Greydon will know that's not true."

"I've bribed the jailer." Terrec looked smug. "You're the only one allowed to visit Zander. Go to him. Suggest Del. It doesn't matter if he agrees or doesn't. Tomorrow, you tell the warriors that Zander wants Del to take over while he's away."

"You want me to lie?"

Terrec grabbed Zeph's arm and hissed, "Your mother's safety depends on you, and you're worried about a little lie?"

Mother had struggled all his life just to feed him, and not done a very good job of it, but he knew she loved him. He'd never forgive himself if she was hurt because of him. Maybe it *would* be better if Zander weren't in charge. If he was in jail when they were invaded, it might even save Zander's life.

He sucked in a deep breath and nodded. "I'll do it."

An hour later, Zeph trudged down the alley to the jail. It stank. The jailer left him at the iron gate where Zander slumped on the other side with his head on his knees. A half-dozen men sprawled across the dirt floor. Most looked as if they'd been there awhile.

When Zander noticed Zeph, he stood and motioned him closer. "I need to talk to Elder Warrin. And Greydon."

"I'm the only one allowed to see you." Not a lie.

Zander ran his hands through his hair. "I didn't kill Lash. There's no proof."

"The warriors will have to train without you." He'd have to be careful how he brought up Del.

"I need to be there. Fulk can swear at them all he wants, but it won't make them work harder. And Greydon and I have to make plans."

"Can Greydon take over?"

"Stars, he'd hate that. I've got to get out of here."

"It could take weeks. You're accused of murder." He hesitated and then blurted, "Zander, what about Del?"

"No!" Zander slapped his hand against the bars. "No Protectors. They don't understand what we're doing."

Zeph's heart sank. He was going to have to lie. He hated liars.

CHAPTER THIRTY-FOUR

Alexa

After Zander's arrest, Alexa rushed home and flew up the stairs to her room. Mother was at the festival, and Father was asleep by the fire. She lit a single candle and set it in the middle of the floor on a black square of cloth. She arranged an assortment of crystals in a circle around the candle and sat cross-legged facing them.

With the basket of embroidery at her side, she chose the cloth she'd stitched of the village and gulch to use in her quest. Dirt smudged the edges and the center was frayed where she'd slit it to fit under her tunic. The scene remained static since she'd removed her signature after the quest. She threaded a needle with a single strand of black and stitched a likeness of Lash, changing thread to add his reddish blond hair and green eyes. Then she stitched her name and knotted it.

The scene came to life with the thirteen questers and Lash moving about the village. Zander's figure moved to the jail with the rest moving about the market on the final day of the festival. It was Lash's figure she followed, as he moved first to his father's estate and then down into the gulch. When he exited the far side of the gulch, the figure stopped at the edge of the embroidery and then disappeared off the cloth. Stars! He'd left the village property, and Alexa didn't know the area past the gulch. She couldn't stitch it. And without it, she couldn't prove Zander's innocence.

With the embroidery in her lap, she sat in a half-trance as the candle burned, wax dripping onto the floor. Images flitted through her mind as the past and the future mingled into one. Melina Odella's betrayal of Zander's trust when she stole his tokens. Her deception as Alexa's teacher. Her future treason of the village as she curses the warriors. Dharien hating Zander before the quest, Dharien becoming their friend, Dharien as Lash's accomplice. Discovering Zander as her other half, her twin. His rise to power as leader of the warriors. Zander . . .

Her door flew open. "What the hell's going on in here?"

Jerked from her visions, Alexa blinked. What *was* going on? A stitching of a battle scene she didn't remember doing lay in her lap. Smoke filled the room. The candle had melted into a puddle and caught the cloth on fire. Father threw a pint of mead on the flames. She ran to open the wood shutters across her window.

She moved through the motions of clearing the smoke and ignored Father's swearing as he stomped down the staircase. Three things she had seen for Melina Odella and three for Dharien. She'd missed the third for Zander. What was going to happen to her twin? She had to get him out of jail.

She aired out her room and accepted that the smell of smoke would remain until she could wash her bedding. She tucked the mysterious stitching into her bag and left for the festival.

She rushed through the congested streets, turning down one and then another, searching for Greydon. She caught sight of him at the leather stalls across the square.

"Hoy, Greydon!"

He pushed his way through the crowd, took her elbow, and guided her to a quiet spot behind the church. "We have to get Zander out of jail, but no one's allowed to visit him."

"Can't your father get him out?" Elder Warrin had bailed Zander out twice before the quest. "Zander has money."

"The judge won't speak with him."

"He didn't kill Lash."

"Of course he didn't!" Greydon rocked back on his heels. "How could you think that he did?"

"He was so angry. He's never been drunk like that, and he's trained to kill."

"Alexa." Greydon pierced her with his stare. "More than anyone, Zander will have a hard time in the war. Killing isn't in his nature."

He was right. Her twin had a gentle heart. How had Moira picked him to lead the warriors? She nodded. "You have to train the warriors until he gets out."

Greydon flushed. "I can't speak in front of that many people."

"They're your friends."

"Doesn't matter. I can't."

"How about Fulk?"

"We can break them into training groups, but no one can lead like Zander." Greydon ran his hands over his dreads. "We might make it a week without him, but after that, the men will lose their motivation."

"Then we'll get him out."

His eyes narrowed. "How do you plan to do that?"

"I don't know. Just keep it together for a week. I'll figure something out." Alexa wanted to show Greydon the stitching, but something kept her from bringing it out. She waved him away. "Go. Enjoy what's left of the festival."

As she watched Greydon move back into the crowd, her spirits sunk. She had no connections, no money, and no plan. There was no way she'd get Zander out of jail.

"Alexa?"

She twirled to find Merindah standing at the church door.

"I can get Zander out." Merindah lifted her chin. "But you may not like my way."

"I don't care what it is if it gets him out." Alexa followed Merindah into the church, hoping she didn't have to promise to come to church every week.

They wound through the back halls to the room behind the chapel. Father Chanse had his head bowed with his fingers spiked against his forehead, reciting words Alexa couldn't hear.

Merindah said softly, "Father?"

He looked up slowly. "Merindah?" He saw Alexa and frowned. "What is it?"

"Zander's in jail and they aren't letting anyone in to see him. He needs to be released. The fate of the village depends upon him."

Father Chanse hesitated. "God has spoken to you?"

"He has."

Alexa shrunk back. Merindah seemed to glow. Did God truly speak to her?

"Three things must happen: Zander training the warriors . . ." she touched Alexa's arm ". . . Alexa using her magic, and I must enter the cell." She smiled the smile of one in rapture. "If we all play our roles, we'll save the village and unite the tribes."

Alexa shivered. Merindah was mad. That was the only explanation that made sense. But if it got Zander out of jail, she didn't care.

CHAPTER THIRTY-FIVE

Zander

Zander lost count of how long he'd been in the cell. Days and nights blended into one. Sunlight didn't reach past the alley. All the meals were the same greasy, unidentified meat with rutabagas in a thin gruel. No one had been to see him since Zeph's visit the first day. He'd stopped pacing, stopped hoping he'd be released anytime soon. He looked around at the other prisoners. Men guilty of theft or, in the rare case, murder, they'd given up long before Zander was shoved in with them. Vacant eyes and listless bodies—would that be his fate?

Questions interrupted his sleep and squashed any chance to meditate. What were the warriors doing? Was Greydon continuing the training? As his head had cleared, he'd become certain of one thing. He hadn't killed Lash. So where was he? He dropped his head into grimy hands. He was going mad.

"Zander."

He jerked his head up. Father Chanse stood behind the bars. "You've been released to my custody."

"What? Why?" He scrambled to stand, but his wobbly legs betrayed him, and he sunk to his knees. Father Chanse was the last person he'd expected.

The jailer swung open the door. "Git yer ass out."

Father Chanse motioned Zander out. "I'll explain later. Come quickly." He turned and strode down the alley.

Zander hustled after him, anticipating what the sun would do to his eyes when they reached the end. But he needn't have worried. It was night. Father Chanse turned toward the church, not Elder Warrin's.

"I need to get to the warriors."

Father Chanse held up his hand. "The church first."

A sudden suspicion snaked into Zander's thoughts. Father Chanse had never liked him. He wouldn't save him. Was he to be condemned without a trial in the middle of the night? Who waited in the church for them? To his surprise, when they entered the common room, Merindah knelt at the front, and Melina Odella paced across the back.

The fortune-teller seemed equally surprised. "What's this? What's going on, Chanse?"

Merindah rose and seemed to float toward him. "Zander." She held out a hand and, although embarrassed at the dirt on his own, he clasped it almost as if he had no choice. Power ran between them and filled him with new strength. All of his doubts about leading the warriors disappeared. He stood taller and Merindah smiled. "God blesses you."

"What's going on?" Melina Odella's face twisted in rage. "You woke me in the middle of the night for this?" She spun and bolted for the door.

"Stop." Merindah's face turned hard. "You'll leave when dismissed."

Melina Odella whipped around. "You dare to order me?"

"You and Father must consecrate us. God and Fate together."

What the hell—was Merindah crazed? He didn't need to be consecrated. He didn't even know what that meant. He held up his hand.

"Zander?" Alexa ran to him from the back door and hugged him. She wrinkled her nose. "You stink."

Leave it to his sister to point out the obvious.

"Good, we're all here. Three working as one. We can begin the ceremony." Merindah walked up the aisle to the three lit candles on the altar.

Alexa whispered, "What's she talking about?"

Zander raised his eyebrows. "We're getting consecrated—whatever that means." He took her hand and joined Merindah.

She handed him and Alexa each a white candle. "Father? Fortune-teller?"

The priest and a reluctant Melina Odella stepped behind the altar. Father Chanse raised his hands toward the ceiling, palms out. "God be with you."

Zander chanted with Alexa and Merindah, "And also with you."

Stone-faced, Melina Odella spat, "Fate be with you."

"And also with you."

"Three as one. Day and night tethered by the anchor." Father Chanse closed his eyes. "Your will, our will, the will of God."

Night for Alexa, anchor for Merindah, day for him. Those were the words Melina Odella had given them at their Welcoming Ceremony for their quest a year ago. How could she have known? Then Melina Odella smiled, but it was a cruel smile, a knowing smile. Zander started to shake.

She held out her hands and began to chant, "Three as one, tie their fate. Tribes spurned, village burned. Warriors fall, invaders take, penance paid."

An invisible rope wrapped his body, tying him to Alexa and Merindah. The energy squeezed his chest, making it difficult to breathe. He struggled against the evil magic, but he had no defense.

Melina Odella clapped her hands, once, twice, three times. Wind blew open the door and swirled into the room, snuffing the candles. He couldn't move, he couldn't see, but he understood.

They hadn't been consecrated. They'd been cursed.

CHAPTER THIRTY-SIX

Alexa

When Melina Odella began her chant, Alexa felt the dark magic. A rope of energy surrounded her. It tightened, connecting her to Zander and Merindah.

Zander's eyes widened. Merindah's hand squeezed hers. They were helpless against the curse. Alexa alone could fight it. She pulled energy from deep within and pushed it out to envelop her. She sent it further to include Zander, and then Merindah.

She closed her eyes. The spell flew from Melina Odella's fingertips and rippled in the air, surrounding them. If she could find a weak spot, she might break it. As Melina Odella chanted "warriors fall," Alexa discovered a strand where the rope thinned. She forced her energy into the fiber and whispered, "warriors win." At "invaders take" she chanted, "invaders defeated." With "penance paid" Alexa's energy united with the curse. Merindah moved closer to whisper, "love atones."

Without reason, Alexa understood. Melina Odella's intent came from hatred for the village for thwarting her love for the priest. Alexa's flowed from her pure love for Zander and Merindah. Her energy wound deep into the curse. When Melina Odella clapped her hands, the energy bound itself to Alexa, Zander, and Merindah. It transformed into a living, breathing creature that could not be shaken. Two spells bound together. The question was—which would be stronger?

As the wind swept in and extinguished the candles, Alexa grabbed for Zander's hand. Merindah found a match and relit the candles. Melina Odella was gone, and an ashen faced priest grasped the table, trembling.

"Why would she curse us?" He fell to his knees. "Is this my fault? Am I to be the doom of the village?"

Serene, Merindah answered, "Alexa has given us hope. We may still win."

Zander stared at Alexa with a look she couldn't decipher. She leaned in to him. "I told you I had powers."

He muttered, "I felt your power. How did you get so strong? . . . Maybe I was wrong. The warriors need you."

She couldn't help her smile. They were in trouble, but if they could work together, they just might have a chance.

With dawn no more than an hour away, Zander wanted to leave for the stable. Alexa convinced him he needed sleep, food, and clean clothes before he saw the warriors again. She found sleeping mats and spread them on the floor of an empty classroom. Father Chanse retreated to his own room, as if still in shock. Alexa left Merindah kneeling in prayer.

As tired as she was, Alexa couldn't sleep. She envied her brother's snores, but the energy of the curse thrummed through her, leaving her on edge. She slipped out to join Merindah on her knees at the altar. It had been a while since she'd prayed, but Alexa found herself reciting a prayer from her childhood that had comforted her when she was frightened. They knelt together in silence for several minutes.

Merindah leaned to the side and touched shoulder to shoulder with Alexa. "Father Chanse was right. Day and night held by the anchor. We're tied together. We've always been tied together. I didn't understand until now."

"I still don't."

Merindah took her hand. "Zander is the day. He works openly, training warriors and preparing for war. You, as the night, work with the unseen, using power unknowable to others. My role is to hold the energy. This building holds both day and night in God and Moira. I'm the cornerstone."

Alexa shuddered. "You're truly going into the cell?" When Merindah nodded, Alexa whispered, "It's for the rest of your life. How will you stand it?"

For a moment Merindah's eyes saddened, but she replied softly, "It's the only way, my dear friend." She pulled Alexa in for a hug. "I've known my destiny since my time of magic."

That moment, the rising sun shone through a side window. Light surrounded Merindah like a halo. Sadness swept through Alexa. She would lose her best friend.

Reluctant to leave, Alexa said, "I need to wake Zander. He's anxious to get back to the warriors." She chewed the inside of her cheek. "From what I've heard, he's not going to be happy."

Merindah smiled. "Everything will be as it is. Tell him not to despair. His destiny is yet to be realized."

Alexa turned cold. She was afraid of that more than anything else.

CHAPTER THIRTY-SEVEN

Zephyr

It had been five days since Zeph had convinced Greydon and Fulk that Zander wanted Del to lead the warriors. Zeph had heard the men talking. Some of the older ones liked Del better than Zander. He had twelve years more experience than Zander, and those warriors felt better with a leader older than themselves.

But now, Zander walked up the trail to the stable, and Zeph's lie was about to be discovered. Regret soured his stomach. Zander had been his friend. That was all about to change. Regardless of what Puck wanted, Zander wouldn't tolerate a liar in the warriors.

Zeph saw the moment Zander realized Del was in charge. Zander slowed, but became deliberate with each step. His lips pressed together, and he threw his shoulders back. Zander stopped only to choose a blade before striding to where Del practiced hand-to-hand with the short blades against Paal. When Paal saw Zander, he stopped and stared.

With a sharp jerk of his head, Zander motioned Paal away. He faced Del and held up his blade. "What are you doing here?"

"The warriors need a leader, not a boy. When you became . . . indisposed, they agreed I was the best choice." Del sneered. "Ask them. I've done a better job."

Sweat wiggled down Zeph's back. Zander excelled with knives, but Del outweighed him by a good twenty pounds and most of that was muscle. If Zander was injured, it would be Zeph's fault. All because Zeph had been too much of a coward to defy Terrec.

Zander planted his feet in a stable, balanced stance. "We'll fight for the position."

A gleam appeared in Del's eyes, and he nodded. "Winner leads the warriors, loser crawls home to mama."

"You got it." Zander stared intently at Del. "Whenever you're ready."

Almost at once, the men formed a circle around them, and Zeph had to push through to stand next to Odo and Greydon. There was no way this would end well for Zander. At best, he'd lose the warriors; at worst, he'd lose his life.

Del lunged. Zander side-stepped before the blade sliced his chest. Zander thrust. Del twisted out of range. They set up across from each other. Zander's eyes never left Del's. When Del went one way, Zander went the other. When Del faked to the left, Zander moved where he shouldn't. He expended half the energy of Del. Del's frustration showed in ever more frantic attacks, but Zander remained calm. There must be something to that meditation stuff.

Then Del barreled forward and Zander tripped. It caught Del by surprise, but he slashed at Zander's face before they both fell. A thin line of blood swelled up across Zander's cheek. Zeph winced. That had to hurt. The warriors shouted, but not all yelled for Zander to get up. At least a dozen men cheered for Del's strike.

They both jumped to their feet and faced off. Blood dripped down Zander's cheek, Del flexed the hand he'd fallen on. Del stabbed, Zander stepped back. Zander rushed Del, and they locked blades. Shoving the blade up and off, Zander stared at Del and nodded. He pushed forward and Del stepped back, throwing them both off balance. They crashed to the ground, Del's blade inches from slicing Zander's neck. Zander lunged at Del, but he rolled to the left. Zander's blade sank into the earth.

More agile, Zander beat Del to his feet. As Del scrambled to rise, Zander kicked him back to the ground. He placed his boot across Del's back and held him down. When Del reached back and tried to stab him, Zander slashed at Del's hand, and the blade skidded across the dirt.

Zander looked up and grinned. He held up one hand for quiet and the warriors obeyed immediately. He sneered down at Del. "Ready to crawl home to mama?"

The Protector spat. "You cheated. An honorable fighter would never kick a man in the back."

Zander gave a final shove with his boot and turned to his men. "Good thing we're not honorable fighters then, isn't it? We're warriors." Blood dripped down his cheek, but he pumped his fist in the air. "This is why we can't depend on the Protectors to defend the village."

He motioned for Greydon to join him and said to the others, "Now, back to your practices. Remember, we fight to win."

Most of the warriors slapped each other on their backs and chattered as they returned to their groups, but as Del slunk away, Zander lost twelve men. The ones who stayed had witnessed their leader beat a Protector. Their loyalty would never be questioned. They were no longer second-rate warriors—they were training to be the best. But would the men who remained be enough to beat back an invasion? Zander may have won the fight, but the cost was lost men. He'd already alienated the women warriors. Zeph had to agree with Terrec. Zander didn't know what he was doing.

Zander looked Zeph's way as he talked with Greydon and Fulk. His eyebrows drew down. The other two men walked away, and Zander called out, "Zeph? I need to talk to you."

This was it. He was getting thrown out of the warriors.

CHAPTER THIRTY-EIGHT

Zander

High from his win over Del, a grin split Zander's face. He couldn't hide his satisfaction at having beaten a Protector. Even with his gift helping him see Del's every move, it wasn't as easy as he hoped it looked. Del thought he had a sure win, and his next move wasn't always the top thing on his mind. That man had secrets. Zander had almost dropped his blade when he saw that Terrec was Del's father, and that Terrec had ordered Del to attack Zander the night at the stable.

He'd used his gift to win, the same way he'd taken the championship in the wrestling tournament last year. Then, he'd earned a black panther omen for cheating. Moira had delivered it herself. He'd earn no more omens, but was it wrong to use a gift that way? It seemed a subtle difference between using it to win money and using it to reclaim what Moira had given him—leadership of the warriors. In war, he'd have to use every advantage to defeat the Odwans.

He wiped the blood from his cheek and studied Zeph, who looked like he'd swallowed a bug. He'd seen in Del's eyes that Terrec was also Zeph's father and that Zeph knew. And Greydon had told him about Zeph's lie. Just where did Zeph's loyalties lie?

He motioned for Zeph to join him. "Zeph? I need to talk to you."

Zeph stared at the ground, but came without hesitation. When he looked up, the tears were real, but with Zander's guard still down, what he saw in Zeph's eyes chilled him.

Before he could stop himself, Zander blurted, "Hell, Zeph! You know when someone's lying?"

Damn. How could he explain how he knew that? Could he trust Zeph? He was Terrec's son, and so far Lash and Del hadn't turned out to be so honorable.

He grabbed Zeph's shoulder. "Come with me. We need some privacy." He marched Zeph into the stable where Shadow practically attacked Zander. "Hoy, I missed you, too." After Shadow quit dancing circles around him, Zander sat with Zeph in the kitchen. So many thoughts flitted through his head, he couldn't choose where to begin. They sat for several minutes with Zeph staring miserably at the floor.

Zander took a deep breath. "You lied to Greydon. I told you I didn't want Del with the warriors."

When Zeph looked up at him, it didn't take Zander's gift to see the pain that wracked him. He softened. He'd give Zeph a chance to explain, but he'd better have a damn good reason.

"I–I . . ." Zeph swallowed hard. When he spoke again, Zander barely heard him. "Elder Terrec threatened my mother."

"He threatened your mother?" Zander leaped to his feet and began to pace. "I heard Terrec is your father. Is that true?" When he saw Zeph's startled eyes, he swore. He'd just lied, and Zeph could tell. Zander hadn't heard anything, he'd seen it in Del's eyes. He sat hard in the chair. "How can you tell when someone's lying?"

Zeph looked confused at the change in topic. "I see a black shimmer over their head. The bigger the lie, the bigger the shimmer." He looked away. "But if I share their blood, I see nothing. Lash is my half-brother. I can't tell when he lies."

Zander rubbed his neck. "Let me get this straight. You lied

about Del because Terrec wanted him in charge and threatened your mother?" Zeph nodded. "And you kept your favor a secret, why?"

"Not my favor. I've always had it."

No wonder Zeph was a strange one. "You didn't think it would be helpful for me to know about it?" Zeph's face turned impassive, and Zander continued. "Why didn't you tell me?"

Zeph exhaled a long breath. "For the same reason you don't share your favor. People don't like to think their secrets are seen or their lies known. Do they, Zander?"

So Zeph had guessed his secret. What was he to do with a boy who lied to protect his mother and had a gift that would be very handy? "It seems we've reached an impasse." Zander spread his hands out across the table. "What do we do now?"

Zeph hung his head. "I'll leave." He looked up with tear-filled eyes. "I won't tell your secret."

A knife twisted in Zander's gut, and he impulsively said, "You can stay." When Zeph's eyes lit, Zander held up one hand. "But you have to earn my trust back." After Zeph nodded, Zander said, "And from now on, if Terrec or anyone threatens your mother, you tell me, all right?"

Zeph nodded again. He whispered, "You're more like my family than Terrec or Del could ever be."

The knife twisted deeper. "Go muck out the stalls. I'll talk to Greydon and Fulk before you go back to training." When Zeph reached the door, Zander added, "Zeph? Most of the time I shield against a person's secrets. I only see them when I need to."

"I wish I could do that, but I don't know how to un-see the shimmer." He gave an impish grin. "You'd be surprised how often people lie."

With a start, Zander thought back. How many times had he lied around Zeph? He tried to be truthful, but sometimes a small lie was needed. Or maybe it wasn't. Maybe it was just easier. He'd be more careful of his words, especially around Zeph. It was an awful gift to have, but one that could be handy.

After Zeph left, Zander cleaned the cut on his cheek. Greydon had insisted on sending for a healer. His mind wandered to Kaiya. Would she find his new scar repulsive? Or did she care anymore?

Greydon appeared at the door. "Healer Eva's here with apprentice Cobie."

Cobie. Zander had hardly seen him since their quest. Eva, who was Mother's best friend, swept in and examined his face. "It's a nice clean cut. Knives will do that."

Zander tried not to grin at her disapproval, but the grin disappeared when she dabbed on a clear liquid that burned like fire. "Hells, Eva! That hurts."

Her droll response was, "Men who fight with knives can surely stand a little sting. You need stitches. Shall I call Lark to hold your hand?"

He reddened and muttered, "Leave Mother out of it." He rolled his eyes at Cobie's muffled laughter.

Then Eva threaded a needle, and Zander felt the blood drain from his face. "I need to sit." It didn't help when Eva and Cobie burst out laughing.

She handed the needle to Cobie. "Let's see how you do."

The next twenty minutes were almost unbearable. Cobie was slow and Eva kept stopping him to explain how to stitch without leaving a scar. More than once, Zander felt the room closing in. It was only sheer will that kept him from fainting. That and deep breathing.

Finally, he shouted, "I don't care about a damn scar. Just get it over with." When Eva took over and finished the final two stitches in about thirty seconds, Zander suspected she'd been teaching him something instead of Cobie.

"There you go, warrior. I'll check back in a week to take out the stitches." She gathered her supplies and threw them into a leather bag.

"Eva? Are you mad at me?"

"It's not you I'm angry at. It's the threat of war. Do you have any idea what the healers will be asked to do?" She dropped her voice. "I'm frightened, Zander. You're boys playing at war, and look at the injuries I've treated. If we're invaded, no one can imagine the toll on our village."

Zander stood and touched her shoulder. "And what will be the toll if we don't fight? Eva, I didn't choose this. I hate the thought of fighting as much as you."

"There's only four of us, and the apprentices will be hard pressed to be ready for field work."

"That's why I sent Kaiya and the other women to help you."

Eva looked puzzled. "Kaiya? She hasn't been to see me."

Lifting an eyebrow, Zander asked himself as much as Eva, "Then what have they been doing?"

CHAPTER THIRTY-NINE

Alexa

Clutching her cloak against the March wind, Alexa hurried to Elder Rowan's estate. She hadn't seen Kaiya since Zander and Lash had fought at the festival, and that was weeks ago. She'd been holed up in her room working at stitching scenes while in a trance. Sometimes it worked, sometimes it didn't. She carried five small squares. Each had taken days.

Within sight of the target field, Kaiya waved her to the group. "Hoy, Alexa. What magic do you have for us today? What else can we do to prove Zander wrong?"

Evidently Kaiya hadn't heard. "Zander spent a week in jail after the festival."

Kaiya looked suitably shocked. "What? Why?"

The women surrounded Alexa. "Lash is missing, and based on my embroidery, he's on the other side of the gulch. Terrec accused Zander of killing him. Del took over the warriors' training, and when Zander came back, some of the men left with Del. They're down to twenty men. It's not about showing Zander anymore. It's about saving the village."

"I've been so angry at being dismissed from the warriors, I'd forgotten why we're training." Kaiya slumped. "What can we do?"

"With God's help, we'll each play to our strengths." Merindah raised her hands, palms out. "I know His will."

Under her scarf, a knot formed in Alexa's throat. There was no way to argue with Merindah when she claimed her knowledge came from God.

A group of women and young girls from the village walked across the field toward the warriors. Alexa squinted. Mother was among them. She turned to Merindah. "What's going on?"

"If we're to win, we need everyone." Merindah cocked her head at Alexa. "This is how we unite the village."

The group drew closer. Every tribe and class was represented. If this worked, Merindah was brilliant. Or . . . Alexa hesitated . . . God was.

Two dozen women and a half-dozen girls surrounded them. In Alexa's mind, she stitched each one. Using the silver thread from Tshilaba, she imagined a shield that would reflect the light, making the women invisible. Unless they were unlucky and got in a cross fire, the enemy would never see them. What could go wrong with that?

After speaking with each woman and girl, Merindah and Alexa split them into two groups. Kaiya would teach them archery. Gia took a group to the side and handed each a sling.

Standing with Merindah, Alexa felt suddenly shy. Since the quest, she'd felt her calling had been higher than Merindah's and dismissed her friend as a religious fanatic. Now, she wondered if she'd been wrong. She sucked in a breath. "Merindah, I owe you an apology." When Merindah's eyes searched her own, Alexa continued. "I believed being a fortune-teller was more important than being a nun. I'm sorry."

Merindah took her hand. "Dear friend. I thought the same— that my calling was above your own. It was through prayer I saw my error. Our village is based on the two being equal."

"It's not equal now. Melina Odella is gone. I went to her cottage yesterday and found it deserted. She took her spell books and some of her potion ingredients."

Merindah's eyes widened. "Alexa, you must take her place."

"Equal with the priest?" Alexa started to shake. "I'm not ready. The Elders will never accept me."

"They have no choice." Merindah pulled her close. "I'll go now and tell the priest." She dropped Alexa's hands and strode down the path to the church.

Alexa stood blinking. She'd seen the power Merindah held over the priest, and Father Chanse would convince the elders.

The card of The Fool flashed in front of her. This was an unexpected opportunity. She could ignore it or leap into it.

Alexa was ready to jump.

CHAPTER FORTY

Zander

Zander strode to the practice arena to meet with Greydon, Fulk, and Dharien. With the loss of the men to Del, strategy had become a daily affair. Every man, every plan had to be precise. He began to rue dismissing the women.

If Kaiya hadn't joined the healers, then what was she doing? He knew her well enough to know she hadn't just quit. And she'd been too happy at the festival. Before he'd apparently insulted her by calling her pretty, that was.

His cheek throbbed and his head ached. Maybe he should have let Del have the warriors. He'd made so many mistakes, and he was beginning to think not trusting Alexa's magic was among them. The power she'd used to diffuse Melina Odella's curse had shocked him. If she could harness that for the warriors, they might have a chance.

He rubbed the back of his neck. Lash's disappearance haunted him. As drunk as he'd been that night, Zander knew he wasn't at fault, but where was he? Did Dharien know? Whose side was he on?

When he entered the arena, Greydon was speaking tersely, and Fulk was shaking his head. Greydon glanced up at Zander and then away. When Zander reached the table, Greydon wouldn't meet his eyes. Dharien stood grim, behind Greydon's chair.

Fulk crossed his arms over his chest and tipped back in his chair. "We have a problem."

"What now?" With the way Greydon stiffened, Zander braced for the worst.

"The ledgers are missing. The only one with access to them besides us was Lash." Greydon slapped his hand on the table. "This is my fault." He finally met Zander's eyes. "I should have listened to you." He bit his lip. "I resign my position. I'll stay on as a warrior, but I don't deserve your trust."

Zander exhaled a long breath. "On the walk over, I was counting all the mistakes I've made since becoming a leader." He clasped Greydon's shoulder. "According to your standards, I should have stepped down a long time ago." Greydon's astonished face made Zander laugh. "I need you, Greydon. Now more than ever." Next to him, Fulk nodded, and Zander continued, "Moira believes in us, even if we doubt. Will you stay?"

"What do we do about the missing accounts?"

Zander took that as a yes. He turned to Dharien. "Do you know where they are?"

Dharien shook his head, started to speak, and stopped. Zander wanted to believe him, but damn it, Dharien had been part of Lash's little covey. Still, he was Greydon's brother.

Zander said, "We start fresh then. I promised the guild master I'd lower the contributions. When Greydon set his mouth, Zander asked, "Is there more?"

"Paal told me the women are training at his father's estate. I was wrong. We need them."

So that's where they were. He looked down to hide his grin. No wonder Kaiya had seemed so smug. She meant to prove herself as a warrior without his help, and damn, if he didn't admire that. Understanding coursed through him. She wasn't just pretty. The next chance he had, he'd make it clear she was more than that. Much more.

"Are they there now?" At Greydon's nod, Zander stood. "Let's go get them."

Fulk snorted. "I'll leave that to you two. I've got warriors to train." When he walked out the door, he was chuckling.

A grin tugged at Greydon's mouth. "Alexa and Merindah are helping them. We're going to have to ask real nice."

Dharien looked up, interested. "Merindah says Alexa is key to our survival."

"I think she's right." Zander rubbed the back of his neck. "Maybe if we beg forgiveness?" Had it really come to that—that he'd beg the women to return? Damn right, he'd beg. He'd been obstinate for too long.

After saddling three bays, Zander, Greydon, and Dharien rode south and then east along the edge of the village. While Zander worried over war plans, the villagers went about their daily chores. He ached to think how an invasion would affect them. Within sight of Elder Rowan's land, Zander swore. "Hells, have they been recruiting?"

A group with slings faced him. A slew of stones flew through the air and pelted him. Star reared and Zander almost fell off, he was so surprised. Next to him, Lady turned in circles as Greydon struggled to bring her under control. Trailing behind, Dharien escaped the onslaught of stones.

At their laughter, the anger Zander had tamped down in his gut blasted through him. Moira had appointed him leader of the warriors and a bunch of women made fun of him? His sudden temper made Star panic and she bolted toward the women. Zander yanked Star to a stop just short of running over a young girl who tripped trying to get out of his way. Stars, his anger was so out of control he'd nearly run them over. When he saw the look of horror on Kaiya's face, he turned Star and galloped past an astonished Greydon.

What had he done? If he couldn't control a well-broken bay, he didn't deserve to be their leader. Maybe he'd give the mess back to Del.

He raced into the stable with a lathered Star and brushed her down as quickly as he could. He needed out, away from the pressure that was always waiting, always reminding him he wasn't good enough. Anger he'd ignored erupted and muddled his thoughts.

As he ran from the stable, he almost bumped into Greydon leading in Lady. He couldn't meet his friend's eyes. "If you need me, I'll be at the tavern." He rushed out before Greydon could reply and jogged to the village. He didn't know he was headed there until he'd said it, but it sounded like the perfect place to hide. One mug, he promised himself. Just enough to calm him and give him time to think.

He stood inside the door to the tavern, letting his eyes adjust to the dark. He strode to a table in the corner, darker still, and ordered a pint from the young woman who showed at his table. Rose was her name, Bindi's older sister by two years.

When she set the mug in front of him, she bent over and whispered, "Tonight the mead's on us." She nodded at the giggling serving girls standing at the counter. "And any one of us would be glad to help you home when you're done."

Zander felt a burn creep up his neck and onto his cheeks. But as he guzzled the drink and another replaced it, his shoulders relaxed, and he smiled at the girl who brought it. Midway through the third, someone scraped back a chair and sat opposite him. He glanced up and squinted.

"Father?"

His father took a long guzzle from his own mug. "I've been hearing good things about you."

He sat stunned. What could he have heard?

"It was about time you beat up that no-good son of Terrec's. All the villagers are talking about you finally acting like a man. Drinking with your men instead of hiding out on Warrin's estate during the celebrations."

Zander dropped his head into his hands. "I nearly rode down a group of women this afternoon."

"Don't go and ruin a good thing by being all pissy over it." Father leaned in. "I heard what you did. Having people fear you is the mark of a good leader. Word'll get around not to cross you. Them women were making fun of you. You can't have that."

"I didn't do it on purpose. I lost control of Star."

"You got their respect."

Zander looked up and his jaw dropped. "I act like a jerk and I get respect?"

Father grinned. "That's the way of it." He tipped up his mug, emptied it, and called for two more. "You've been playing at being a warrior. It's time to become one."

Just then, Greydon stepped through the door. He searched for Zander and, upon finding him, strode over, grabbing a mug on the way. "Those women were mad as hornets. I don't think they're coming back."

Zander clinked his mug against Greydon's and then Father's. "Here's to being a jerk. It's a hell of lot easier than being nice."

Together they downed their drinks in one long swallow and ordered another.

Kaiya would never forgive him now.

CHAPTER FORTY-ONE

Alexa

Alexa couldn't believe Zander had nearly trampled the women. Greydon had tried to apologize after Zander galloped off, but the women were having none of it. Kaiya, in particular, had been livid. After Alexa promised to talk to him, she left for the bakery.

Just outside Elder Rowan's land, Dharien stood holding the reins to his horse at the side of the road.

Startled, Alexa blurted, "What do you want?"

"Can we talk?"

He looked so unsure that, after a moment's hesitation, Alexa nodded.

"Zander came to apologize to the women. He was going to invite them back to training."

"He did a piss-poor job of it."

"Yeah, he did." Dharien ran his hand through his hair. "I don't know what happened."

Silence stretched between them. She started to ask about Lash, but didn't know if she wanted the truth. Her heart ached to believe Dharien had changed.

"I just wanted you to know." Dharien swung up on his bay. "Zander's a good leader." He urged the horse into the woods and trotted away.

Huh. That was a surprise. As he disappeared into the trees,

Alexa regretted not asking about Lash. She mulled over their short conversation the rest of the way home.

Mother returned shortly after Alexa. What a surprise it had been to see her pick up a bow. She was pretty good with it, too. Upstairs in her room, Alexa listened to Mother's high voice mixed with Father's low one as Mother told him about Zander's antics. Soon after, Father charged out of the house. Alexa wasn't sorry he'd left. She wanted to talk to Mother alone.

She shouldered the bag she'd packed that morning and slipped her arm through a basket of yarn. She glanced around the room she'd lived in for seventeen years. She'd spent most of those years wanting to be somewhere else. Now, the thought of leaving felt bittersweet. She'd move into Melina Odella's cottage so she'd be there when the villagers needed potions or spells. Even if Melina Odella returned, Alexa would not come back to the bakery. Not to live. She took a deep breath and walked resolutely down the stairs to the kitchen.

"Mother?"

Bright eyes turned sad when Mother saw Alexa's bag. "You're leaving?"

Alexa nodded. "Melina Odella has disappeared. I'm assuming her position."

Mother gasped. "As an equal with Father Chanse?"

"Yes." A shudder rolled through her. "I'm the only one who can."

Mother set her lips and began to gather rolls and loaves of bread from the front shelves—the ones meant for the elders' families. The best. She layered them in a basket before she held it out to Alexa. "You'll come home when you need more?"

Tears sprang to her eyes as she rushed to hug Mother. "I know I've been a disappointment to you."

Gentle hands held Alexa's cheeks. "Nonsense! I'm proud of you. I've known since you were small you'd never be a baker."

"What?" Alexa gasped.

"When you were five, Tshilaba read my future. She said you were meant for more." She wiped away a tear. "I thought if I ignored it, it wouldn't be so; but in my heart, I knew it to be true." She kissed Alexa's forehead. "Go and fulfill your destiny, my daughter."

Alexa didn't remember leaving or how she made it to the path leading to Melina Odella's cottage, but when she stumbled through the back door, it was as if her life had truly begun. She felt power swirl around her and settle into her bones. She was the fortune-teller. Moira, her only teacher.

After dropping her bags in the second bedroom—she couldn't think of staying in Melina Odella's—Alexa lit candles and wandered through the cottage. Melina Odella had taken many of the supplies, but some remained. She made a list of items to replace. Some she could buy at the market, some she would gather from the gulch.

As dusk settled in the woods surrounding the cottage, a knock startled her. Alexa pulled open the heavy front door to find Merindah and Father Chanse waiting outside. Five elders trailed behind them, wearing tribal dress in their familial colors. She stood aside and watched open-mouthed as they solemnly entered and stood in a semicircle in the divining room. Their embroidered robes brushed the floor. The beaded and feathered headdresses rose a foot above their heads.

Merindah pulled her to stand in front. "It's agreed. You're to take Melina Odella's place as Moira's mouthpiece."

Elders Warrin, in purple and gold, and Rowan, in green and gold, joined Elder Aherna, in her black and silver, and Elder Nhara, in her silver and red, in nodding their agreement. Elder Terrec, in blue and red, gave her shudders as he looked her up and down, as if appraising her worth like she was a prize goat.

Merindah continued. "This ceremony we do in secret. The ways of Moira are the ways of the night."

Father Chanse and Merindah moved to stand with the elders,

leaving Alexa to stare into their solemn faces. She'd never felt so exposed and alone. A quiet settled over the room as they waited.

A breeze rustled the silk panels that hung against the walls, and the sweet fragrance of frankincense filled the room. First as a shimmer, and then ghost-like, Moira appeared as the crone, withered and old. Her emerald eyes held each elder before she turned to Alexa. Alexa met her gaze and felt as though Moira's scrutiny flayed open her soul.

Moira held Alexa's chin. "You are my Chosen. Young as you are, your power is ready. When you falter, as you surely will, you may call upon my help."

Alexa swallowed. "Melina Odella cursed me. Can you lift it?"

Moira smiled, and it was as if the sun exploded into the room. "I could, but I shall not. It will be the first test of your powers. Break the binding, and then you'll be strong enough for war."

As Moira faded, it seemed foolish, but Alexa felt bereft.

"The will of Moira," the elders chanted.

Merindah hugged her and left with Father Chanse. As the elders filed out, the Queens and Kings of the cards appeared above their heads. The Queen of Cups, sensitive, but detached from the world, hovered over Elder Aherna. The upside down Queen of Wands flickered above Elder Nhara, signifying a hot temper and a tendency to controlling behavior. The King of Pentacles portrayed Elder Warrin as financially successful and strong minded. The family-oriented King of Cups shone on Elder Rowan.

The last to leave, Elder Terrec, looked smug. An upside down King of Swords followed him—the cruel bully.

CHAPTER FORTY-TWO

Zephyr

Every day of the past week, Zeph watched Zander head to the tavern after training and then stumble home with Greydon. And each morning, Zander woke bleary-eyed, but possessed. He pushed the men to exhaustion.

Zeph didn't much like him anymore. He'd lost the respect for Zander he'd given so easily. Zeph began to see no difference between Zander and Elder Terrec. Both thought of him as someone to use for their own gain.

Yesterday, he'd gone to see Alexa at the bakery and found she'd moved out. Lark said she was living in Melina Odella's cottage. He'd opened his heart to them and now neither Zander nor Alexa gave any thought to him. He wouldn't let them hurt him again.

He led Dorothy from her stall and headed to quester class at the Quinary. When he arrived, he was shocked to see Alexa standing with Father Chanse. He wanted to ignore her, but Dorothy had other ideas. The donkey headed straight to Alexa and nuzzled her shoulder.

Alexa absentmindedly rubbed Dorothy's nose. She looked up as if surprised to see him. "Zeph?"

He felt his cheeks heat. "I'm in the class," he mumbled.

She took hold of Dorothy's halter and led them both to the side. "Melina Odella has taken a break."

A black mist hovered over her. Why the lie?

"She asked me to take her place."

Another lie.

Alexa didn't seem to notice that Zeph didn't respond. She smoothed her hair. "I'm worried about Zander. I hear he's been drinking every night." She searched his eyes. "Is it true?"

He nodded, but didn't feel inclined to elaborate. Like Zander, she only used him for information. He thought back to the times he'd run messages for her. He'd been so desperate for a friend that he'd done everything she and Zander had asked. As soon as he quit, they'd both forget him. He meant nothing to them. Nothing.

"Will you take him a message?" Alexa dug in her bag for paper.

It took all his courage, but Zeph said, "No. You'll have to take it yourself." He tugged on Dorothy's lead and joined the other questers. If felt good to say no—and it also felt awful.

After class, back at the stable, Zeph packed his few belongings. He'd avoided Geno and any more assassin lessons. If he left now he wouldn't have to admit to Zander he didn't have the mettle to kill. At the last moment, he grabbed the bow that Zander had given him and a quiver of arrows. It was too small for anyone else. He stepped outside and the scent of venison roasting on the outdoor spit made his stomach growl. He should have waited until after the noon meal. He'd miss the food.

Dorothy meandered behind him. Although he headed toward his old house, Zeph wasn't sure it was his destination. Mother didn't seem to miss him. Luckily for Dorothy, there were plenty of dried grasses and green sprouts. She, at least, wouldn't go hungry. Zeph couldn't say for sure where he'd find food, but he'd spent most of his life with a growling stomach. He'd survive.

The farther he walked along Elder Warrin's estate, the slower his steps became. Zander and Alexa were the closest thing he'd had to feeling like he belonged to a family. The bow came from Zander. His questing clothes were a gift from Zander's mother. He reached in his pocket and pulled out the embroidery Alexa had given him. Helios raced around the cloth. Zeph stifled a cry. He'd miss that war horse.

He came to the fence that ran between Elder Warrin's estate and Elder Terrec's. Another fence separated the village land. Once he stepped off Elder Warrin's land, Zeph knew he wouldn't return. He stood for several minutes, undecided.

Dorothy stuck her head in his back and pushed him forward. Not toward the village, but onto Elder Terrec's land.

Toward his father.

CHAPTER FORTY-THREE

Zander

Zander rubbed at eyes gritty with lack of sleep. He wasn't sure what time he and Greydon had stumbled home, but he was pretty sure the east sky was lightening. Shadow whined and shot out the door as soon as Zander opened it. He heard Fulk rattling around in the kitchen and winced. He remembered now that Fulk had said something about needing to talk when Zander had lurched into the stable. He sat up on the edge of the bed and dropped his aching head into his hands.

Greydon had convinced Zander to give the men a day off for the May Day Festival. That's why they'd stayed out so late. And something about a table full of women laughing at everything he said. He'd discovered he was a lot funnier when he was drunk. He rubbed the back of his neck. The women were fun, but they weren't Kaiya. Bindi's sister had told him Kaiya was furious with him. He had a feeling his time at the tavern had more to do with that than anything else he'd done.

He groaned as his head pounded. He'd become the one thing he hated about Father—a drunk. Anger shot through his gut. He was seventeen. He deserved to act it. Moira asked too much. The elders should be the ones worried about protecting the village instead of a ragtag group of men barely past their quest. Guilt replaced the anger. Left up to the elders and Protectors, the Odwans wouldn't get much of a fight. Puck's Gulch was founded on peace. His resolve hardened, even as his head pounded. He stood, a bit unsteady. Might as well face Fulk and get it over with.

He dragged himself into the kitchen and poured a mug of hot cider from the kettle sitting on the wood stove. Maybe it would clear his head. He sneaked a look at Fulk. The man looked thoughtful as he drank his own cider—spiced with a bit of cinnamon from the smell that drifted over. "You wanted to talk?"

Fulk set his cup down and thrummed his fingers against the table. "Do you want to lead the warriors or be a drunk?"

The marshal never did mince words. Zander set his own cup on the table. He let down his guard and searched Fulk's eyes. The only secret he held was personal, and Zander wished he hadn't seen it. "Why can't I do both? Do you have any complaints about how I'm training the men?"

Fulk grunted. "You stay out all night and train hard all day. You may think you're invincible, but trust me, you're not."

Zander started to speak, but Fulk interrupted him. "I was young once. I know how it feels to have a pint of mead in your hand and women hanging on your every word. And if these were regular times, I'd be all for you being a young man with no worries." He leaned in. "But it isn't. I know you aren't in any shape for this, but there's something you need to see." He scraped his chair back and rose.

Zander's stomach heaved as he followed Fulk down the hall to the tack room. The iron bolt was locked, and he had a bad feeling about whatever was behind the heavy door. When Fulk swung open the door, a man lay unmoving on the dirt floor, bound hand and foot, with a purple bruise across his forehead. Fulk strode in and pulled off a headscarf, revealing a shock of red. Zander had never seen the man, which meant one thing—he was an Odwan.

"Caught him sniffing around the edges of the manor late last night. I'd have sent for you then, but figured you'd be useless."

He'd been drunk while a spy sneaked around the training grounds. He owed Fulk for many things, but this he couldn't repay. "Did he speak?"

Fulk grunted. "He hasn't been awake since I hit him."

The man rolled to his side and groaned. When he opened his eyes, fear was quickly replaced with a sneer. "The boy warrior."

He recognized Zander, which meant he'd been watching for more than a night. Zander had a sudden memory of a man drinking in the corner of the tavern the past three nights. His gut had tried to warn him, but he hadn't listened, distracted by the mead and women. He squatted down next to the man. "So, you know who I am. Who are you?"

The man spit at him. "I'm the one who'll soon be sitting at your table with your women."

An image of Kaiya flashed in Zander's mind. If the Odwans took over their village what would happen to her? Or to Alexa? He stood and kicked the man in the groin. One way or another, the man would talk. "We'll see if you'll cooperate after a few more hours in the dark."

He motioned to Fulk and they backed out of the tack room. Fulk threw the bolt across the shut door. In the kitchen, Zander rubbed his tight neck. "Does anyone else know he's here?"

Fulk shook his head.

"Where's Zeph?"

"See what a cloudy head does for you?" Fulk snorted. "The boy moved out yesterday. Left without a word, with that donkey of his trailing behind."

Where could Zeph have gone? A nagging feeling in his gut told him he should be worried, but Zander had something he needed to do first. He'd find Zeph later.

He swallowed the rest of the cider, not caring it was cold, and turned to Fulk. "Give the man some bread and plenty of mead, but don't untie him. Maybe his tongue will loosen. I'm going into the gulch for a few hours to get myself sorted out. Tell no one except Greydon." After he recovered from his hangover and returned from the gulch, Zander would use his favor on the spy. This was why Moira insisted he keep it. He'd see the man's secrets.

"Watch yourself. He may not be the only spy roaming around."

"I'll take Shadow and my knives."

"And Zander?"

He hesitated at the door.

"You have to break Helios. The men laugh behind your back that you can't ride him. Not only to show your strength . . . you're going to need him soon."

Shame reddened his neck. "After I return." He all but ran to his room.

CHAPTER FORTY-FOUR

Zephyr

Zeph and Dorothy had taken but a few steps toward his father's estate when Del rode up. All the Protectors had horses, and Del rode a white palfrey. She was a fine horse, but didn't come close to Helios's size or beauty.

Del and Lash. Zeph had two half-brothers, and if his father hadn't been bragging, maybe every red-haired kid in the shacks was a blood relation to Zeph. What did that mean? Blood relation. He'd wanted a brother for as long as he could remember, but now it felt too late.

"So little brother." Del's smile looked real. "You've seen the wisdom of Father's plan?"

"What plan?"

"He didn't share it with you? No matter. You've done the first smart thing in your life. You left the warriors and their deluded leader behind."

Zeph stared at Del. He'd seen so many people lie, and now, for the first time, he couldn't rely on his gift. He wouldn't know if Del spoke the truth.

"Let's find a spot for your donkey in Father's stable."

"Her name's Dorothy."

Del didn't try to hide his smile. "Dorothy? You got a girl patron?" Chuckling, he turned his horse and headed toward the estate.

As if planted in the ground he stood on, Zeph waited. Then, Dorothy nudged him, and Zeph took a step toward the family he'd never known.

He followed Del along a winding path that straightened when it went between sectioned fields. Men that Zeph recognized from the shack houses worked the first segment with plows pulled behind mules. In the next field, women in ragged clothes planted seeds by hand. One had a squalling baby wrapped on her back. She'd been pregnant when Zeph had moved out of his mother's house. And in the last field on his right, boys not much older than Zeph used pitchforks to spread manure across the newly opened ground. Three of the boys had red hair like Zeph's. Likely, also bastard sons of Terrec's.

With a start, Zeph understood this was his fate. He hadn't thought past the quest. He hadn't realized his life would follow those who lived with him in the shacks, working for an elder and kept poor.

Anger burned in his gut. It wasn't fair to have no choice in where you worked. No hope for a better life. He muttered, "Damn Moira. This is the life she sentenced these people to?"

He stopped and Dorothy stuck her head under his arm. He pulled her close and leaned his head against hers. "Dorothy, how do you fit into this? Will you be forced to pull a plow? Maybe it would be better to die in the quest." He let his tears fall. "I thought I'd make a difference with my life."

A young woman with long silver hair and emerald eyes appeared in front of Zeph. Moira wiped away a tear on Zeph's cheek. "And you can. You have a choice to make, Zephyr."

"A choice?"

Moira's laugh filled him with foolish hope.

"You may choose who to claim as family." Moira disappeared. Where she'd stood, a white rock appeared.

Zeph crouched over the stone. It sparkled as if tiny diamonds were embedded across the surface. Mesmerized by the light, past scenes flashed in his memories. Lash locking him in the shed. Del taking over the warriors. Terrec threatening Zeph's mother. Alexa bringing him a sugar biscuit. Zander inviting him to live in the stable.

A cloud floated across the sun and the sparkle faded, releasing Zeph from the visions. He picked it up and dropped it in the empty leather pouch he carried for tokens and omens. He made his choice.

He stood and stared across the field at Elder Terrec's house. With Dorothy at his side, he took one step and then another toward his blood family.

CHAPTER FORTY-FIVE

Zander

Zander washed with cold water. It helped clear his head. After dressing, he slid a knife into each boot and attached one at his belt. He slung the bow over his shoulder and the quiver across his chest to hang at his side. Outside, he whistled for Shadow.

The coyote danced in circles around him. Zander had a lot to feel guilty about, but neglecting Shadow was one thing he could fix. "Come on, boy."

They hiked across Elder Warrin's land to Elder Terrec's border. He skirted along the village land until he got to the gulch. Spring rains made the way down treacherous. He slid for a foot or two, grimacing at the mud caking on his boots. As he hiked lower into the shadows, the warmth of the sun disappeared behind the steep walls of the gulch, and he shivered.

At the bottom, snowmelt had engorged the usually small stream, making it impossible to cross. He followed it downstream until he reached a fallen cottonwood lying across the water. Shadow ran the length of the trunk and jumped off past the stream. Zander followed more slowly, stepping over and ducking under tangled branches. He reeked of stale mead. Disgusted to be reminded of all the times Father stunk in the mornings, Zander swore to stop going out.

He hadn't meditated for a long while. And now that he thought about it, since he'd started drinking, Moira had stayed away from his dreams. It hadn't been so long ago that he'd have thought of that as a good thing. But now, he needed her. Had he lost her favor? And where was Puck?

He wended through the mud until he reached the oak Moira had led him to in his dream the last night of the quest. So much had happened since the day he'd chosen their futures. He laid a horse blanket on the soft ground and plopped down to sit cross-legged. What if he'd chosen differently? Alexa would still be a fortune-teller and Merindah a nun, but the others would be in apprenticeships now instead of acting as warriors and healers. Kaiya, so strong, would likely have been sent by Moira to work in an elder's kitchen alongside her mother. It would have killed the spirit he loved in her. He realized with a start that he did love her, and he'd been acting like an ass. As soon as he got himself straightened out, he'd make it up to her and hope she'd forgive him.

He whistled for Shadow, who'd taken off to explore. The coyote ran up, muddy, tail wagging. Zander scratched Shadow's head. "I need you to keep watch."

Shadow circled once before lying down at Zander's side, alert and watchful.

After setting his bow within easy reach and tucking a knife under his thigh, Zander inhaled a deep breath of musty forest air. Already, his shoulders were beginning to relax. He scanned the gulch. Birds he'd startled returned to the tree and settled above him, and they were as good as a second lookout.

He closed his eyes and steadied his breathing. In for five counts, hold for six, and out for seven. He imagined the earth's energy filling him and realized how empty he was. The energy came in through his legs and traveled up his chest, into his arms and head. For the first time in weeks, his head was freed from the obsessive worries that sent him to the tavern each night. His breath slowed and with it, his sense of time.

And then, with eyes closed and body relaxed, Zander felt Moira's energy, calm but focused, surround him. Her words came into his head without actual sound.

"I've waited for you."

"I need your help. I've lost men and all the women. I've been a jerk."

Her laughter filled his soul. "Defender of all, you've learned much for your age."

He resisted opening his eyes for fear of losing contact. "It's not enough. We've caught an Odwan spy. We're not ready."

"The spy will be of no help to you."

Zander opened his eyes. Moira sat facing him, emerald eyes sparkling, long silver hair floating down around her unlined face. She was ancient as the earth itself, but she looked young. For a moment, her gaze enraptured him. He shook his head to break the spell. "Can you stop them from coming?"

"I cannot."

He felt suddenly desperate. "Do we have any chance of winning?"

She stared at him for several minutes. "Don't despair. This is only a small moment in time."

"What does that mean?" His calm disappeared as a rush of adrenaline raced through his body. "It's not small to me. The lives of everyone I care about are in danger."

Moira reached out and touched his knee. "Lives will be lost. It is the way of war." Her eyes saddened. "Many wars have I witnessed. Sometimes it is too much to bear."

He'd never thought of Moira feeling pain. What must it be like to live forever?

She brightened. "And then comes a boy and a girl who bring me hope."

Her talk confused him. "Me and Alexa?"

"Who else?" Her smile spread and she seemed to glow.

"Help us, Moira. Help me save the village."

Predictably, Puck chose that moment to moan, "Unite the tribes. Save the village."

She lifted her hands and held them out at her side. "The ghost is correct."

Tired of riddles, Zander felt his anger rise. "I don't know what he means."

"You're not using all your resources."

He leapt to his feet. "What resources?"

"Your twin knows. You have one week."

And then Moira disappeared.

Zander kicked at a root of the tree. "Moira, come back! I need help." He knelt next to Shadow and buried his face in the coyote's fur. "I can't do this alone."

CHAPTER FORTY-SIX

Zander

After clearing the tumbling thoughts from his head and recovering his calm, Zander spent an hour in meditation. He'd taken to drinking to hide his fears. When he meditated, he faced them. He would need the stillness if he hoped to ride Helios.

He stood and stretched. "Shadow, let's go home." He glanced across the gulch and glimpsed a flash of red through the trees. Stepping behind the oak, he signaled Shadow to quiet.

Then he heard voices. He peeked around the trunk. Del and Lash picked their way down the north side of the gulch. Very much alive, Lash swore when he slipped and fell on his backside in the mud. They followed the stream away from Zander, and a third person fell into line behind them. Zeph. Three brothers.

Zeph had joined Zander's enemies. He bent over, hands on knees, as if he'd been punched in the gut. When his breathing evened, he followed.

As they climbed up the south side of the gulch, Zander trailed behind. Del and Lash seemed unconcerned with being seen, talking loud enough to scare off all the birds from the trees they passed under. Zander heard his name and then laughter.

Zeph appeared nervous, looking right and left. Once, he stopped and turned. Zander ducked behind a fir tree just in time.

As the trio reached the rim, Puck's ghost moaned, "Beware—the assassin moves among us."

Zeph jerked to a stop, but Del and Lash seemed deaf to the warning. They disappeared over the top.

They couldn't hear Puck. Zander held back a laugh.

It was long moments before Zeph moved again, looking determined. Whatever Zeph had planned, he was going through with it. Zander just hoped the assassin wasn't coming after *him*.

When the three turned onto the path to Elder Terrec's land, Zander didn't follow. He had other things to do—like interrogate a prisoner, ride Helios, and find his twin. He jogged on to Elder Warrin's land. Ahead, he glimpsed Greydon and Odo. Oblivious to Zander, they held hands. He remembered then that Odo had walked back from the tavern with them that morning.

Shadow yipped a greeting. Greydon turned and grinned. Odo blushed and dropped his hand, but Greydon leaned in and said something that made Odo stare at Zander in surprise. He waved then and took Greydon's hand as they waited for Zander to catch up.

"Hoy. I need your help." Zander jogged to meet them. "Odo, can you find Alexa and Kaiya and bring them here?" When Odo nodded, Zander turned to Greydon. "I need Father Chanse to ring the gathering bells in two hours. Can you do that?"

"What's going on? Is there news of the invasion?" Greydon glanced worriedly at Odo. "The men are all at the May Day festival."

"I have information from Moira. It's not today, but we don't have much time. And I have something you need to see."

When they found Fulk, he looked grim. He nodded to the open door of the tack room. "I checked on him an hour ago."

The man lay limp. Feet still bound, his hands were free, his face pale.

Greydon gasped. "Is he dead?"

"I cut the ropes on his hands so he could feed himself. I ain't no nursemaid. He must have carried poison."

Zander rocked back on his heels. The first casualty of the war. How many more would die on both sides? And for what? The control of a small village founded on peace. For a second, he wondered if it was worth the lives it would cost the village. If they peacefully surrendered, maybe it wouldn't be so bad. Then he thought of Alexa and Kaiya. What would happen to the women? And as leader of the warriors, he'd likely be executed. He'd fight for Kaiya and Alexa and his mother. His chance of dying seemed pretty equal either way.

"I got him drunk enough to get some information." Fulk looked pleased despite his dead prisoner. "The Odwans have been driven out of their lands by the Kharoks. They were a small tribe before the war, and now they only number around a hundred men with twice that in women and children. They want land, and ours, being already settled, looks damn attractive to them."

Zander rubbed the back of his neck. "Why didn't they ask to join us rather than fight?"

"After a lifetime of war, they've forgotten how to make peace. The only way they know is to take what they want."

Such a waste of lives this war would be. After Greydon and Odo left to follow his instructions, Zander turned to Fulk. "What do we do with the body?"

"When you see the Father, ask him to come out and bless it. Then we'll bury him. It's only the first of the dead." Fulk ran his hands through his hair. "I never thought this would happen. There's going to be a war."

Zander met the marshal's eyes and saw fear where he'd never seen it. If Fulk was afraid, what would that mean for the others? "It's time I rode Helios."

Resolve replaced the fear in Fulk's eyes. "Hells, yeah. I'll get him saddled."

While Fulk saddled Helios, Zander brought his energy into his core. The calm he'd found in the gulch flowed through his bones and filled him. He'd never be more ready.

Fulk stood expectantly, holding Helios's reins. Zander matched his grin and stepped to Helios's side. The horse raised his head and nickered. Zander placed a hand on Helios's neck and let his calm seep into the horse.

As if surprised, Helios stared into Zander's eyes. Zander let down his guard and allowed the connection, inwardly cursing himself for not trying it before. Helios had his own secret. He'd been mistreated as a foal by a man with black hair. Zander reminded him of that man.

While staring into Helios's eyes, Zander laid both hands on the horse's face and took the fear into himself. He sent it into the ground and replaced the fear with love. All the tension in Helios dissolved, and he lowered his head. When Zander mounted, Helios remained calm. Zander took the reins from Fulk and urged Helios to the outside ring. When the horse showed no signs of panic, Zander motioned for Fulk to open the gate.

Helios and Zander moved as one to the field. Zander gently shook the reins. Helios responded by moving into a canter. He pranced along the practice field, past the path to the manor, and on to the border between the village land and Elder Warrin's newly sprouted fields. Not once did Helios try to throw Zander.

Lulled by the three-beat gait, Zander realized it was fear that sent him to the tavern all those nights; fear of not being a strong enough leader, that he couldn't save the village. It was Helios's fear that made him throw Zander time after time. And Zander wondered then, what were the Odwans afraid of? And how could he use that to win?

He turned Helios back toward the stable and saw in the distance a small group waiting for him. When he came closer, Greydon and

Odo stood with Alexa, Kaiya, and Merindah. Fulk leaned against the stable door looking as proud as Zander had ever seen him.

Zander brought Helios to stand in front of them and dismounted. He whispered to the horse, "Well done, friend," before handing the reins to Fulk. "Keep him saddled. I'll ride to the Quinary."

Kaiya ran to him and threw her arms around him. Surprised, but happy, he hugged her back.

"Kaiya, I'm sorry. I've been an ass," he whispered into her hair.

She pulled back and held him at arm's length. "You *have* been an ass, and we'll discuss it later. For now, we need to work together."

He looked over her shoulder to where Alexa stood off from the group with a frown on her face.

CHAPTER FORTY-SEVEN

Alexa

When Zander rode up on Helios, Alexa had nearly burst with pride. Then Kaiya ran to him and wrapped him in a hug, when Alexa knew Kaiya was still furious with him. Alexa should have been the first to congratulate him. They were twins. That bond was stronger than anything Kaiya could have with him.

When Zander's eyes met hers, her frown deepened. He'd ridden Helios without her help. Now, he'd never accept her magic.

Zander wrapped one arm around Kaiya's shoulder and headed toward her. She composed herself and pushed her feelings aside until she saw the King and Queen of Wands cards superimpose over the two. Tears sprang to her eyes. Zander and Kaiya were destined for each other. Where did that leave her?

"Alexa, what's wrong?" Zander touched her arm. "Kaiya tells me you've taken Melina Odella's place. What's going on?"

Kaiya had even robbed her of the chance to tell the news she'd longed to share with Zander. She stood stiff and miserable. "If you cared about anything but drinking and war, you might know."

At Alexa's words, Kaiya looked shocked, but Zander seemed ashamed, which made Alexa ashamed. She closed her eyes and took a breath to calm herself. "You need our help."

"Yes!" He seemed excited. "I've talked with Moira. I understand now. It's going to take all of us."

She'd been warning him for months, and one talk with Moira made him a believer? She fought her anger. If he'd listened, they could have done so much more to prepare.

He motioned for the others to join them. "Greydon, did Father Chanse agree?" When Greydon nodded, Zander glanced at the sky. "We've not much time. Tell me what you've been doing."

Alexa and Kaiya took turns explaining how they'd trained the women to shoot and sling rocks.

"You'd be proud of Mother. She's one of the best with the bow." Alexa's surprise had matched Mother's when she consistently hit the mark.

"Use the women as archers?" Zander shook his head as if he couldn't believe it. "Gia's teaching the others to use a sling?"

"Even the young girls can hit a target." Kaiya said, practically dancing with pride. "I told you women could fight."

Zander pulled Kaiya in to his side and held her. Alexa shouldn't have felt jealous, but she did. She'd had only a little over a year with her twin. Now, she was losing him. She caught the puzzled look Zander gave her and dropped her head until she regained her composure. Zander guarded against seeing others' secrets, but she couldn't take the chance of him seeing that one. She fingered the garnet brooch she wore on her tunic and the energy brought order to the chaos swirling in her head. Merindah slipped her arm through Alexa's. Gratitude filled Alexa for the support.

"Merindah's been helping with spells for the embroidery."

Her twin rocked back on his heels as he studied her. "You still plan to use magic?"

Stubbornly, she met his gaze and nodded.

"Moira said I needed to use all my resources." He grinned and rubbed the back of his neck. "I guess magic is one of them." He suddenly became serious. "She said we have one week."

A week? Only Merindah's hold on Alexa kept her from falling to her knees. She whispered, "Can we be ready?"

"We have to be." Zander came to her then and hugged her close. To her alone, he said, "Only together can we win this war. Our names—together we defend all. Together we'll save the village."

In his ear, she replied, "First, we unite the village."

He pulled away, determination on his face. "That starts today."

A series of bells rang from the church. Three peals, a pause, three more, a pause, and repeated. Warning bells calling all the villagers to the Quinary.

Alexa's heart thumped until she saw Zander's grin. "Is this what you asked of Father Chanse?"

"Come as quickly as you can," Zander said. Then he grinned. "Your brother is about to make the speech of his life."

Fulk brought Helios. Zander mounted and turned the horse in a circle. His grin disappeared. "I almost forgot. Beware of Zeph. He may be working for Terrec now."

With that, he galloped off, leaving a trail of dust. His words twisted in her gut like the stab of a knife. Zeph, gentle Zeph, couldn't possibly have conspired against them. Could he?

CHAPTER FORTY-EIGHT

Zander

Helios flew toward the Quinary, and Zander considered his words. This speech would either bring the tribes of the village together or split them wide apart. United they could win. He couldn't think of what would happen if they divided into sides.

He reached the market where confused celebrators made their way to the Quinary. Some ambled, obviously drunk, and some ran, glancing back and forth, trying to find the danger. Zander had only heard warning bells once, when he was ten, and a pack of wild boars ran through the village.

As the villagers became aware of Helios, they parted. Zander rode into the Quinary, confident and calm. Helios snorted and pawed at the ground until Zander sent energy through his hands placed on either side of the horse's neck. Those standing close fell quiet when they saw Zander astride the majestic war horse. Father Chance, red-faced and sweating, joined Zander under the Quinary roof and stood to the right of Helios.

Zander peered out among the villagers. He absorbed their energy, bringing their fear, excitement, and confusion into himself and releasing it into the sky. Members from each of the tribes mingled and pushed to move closer. The Raskan traders, who came twice a year for festivals, hung at the back of the crowd, interested but wary.

Tshilaba's eyes met Zander's from the back. With a single nod, her energy gave him strength. He had a vision of Alexa traveling with the fortune-teller. He shook his head. He needed to stay focused. Later, he'd consider what that meant.

It wasn't until Zander saw Alexa that he raised his hand. From astride Helios, Zander felt a quiet ripple out to the edges of the crowd. It was then he found his words.

"Our village was founded on peace, and yet we find ourselves at war." He turned Helios in a circle to meet the stares of all the crowd. He motioned for his twin. "Alexa, come forward and join Father Chanse."

She walked purposefully to the Quinary and stood to the left of Helios.

He continued. "We have God and Fate leading us through Father Chanse and Fortune-teller Alexa. As a reminder of our tribal roots, I call Greydon to represent the Chahda tribe, Merindah the Dakta, and Kaiya the Yapi." He noticed Kaiya's surprise, but she hid it quickly and joined the others to each stand at a supporting post of the Quinary.

Zander moved Helios to stand at the fourth post, representing the Kharok tribe. He needed an Odwan besides the priest. His eyes were drawn to the back of the crowd where Zeph stood alone. Zander heard his voice before his heart told him Zeph was not a traitor. "Zephyr, come forward to represent the Odwa tribe."

The crowd mumbled, turning to search for the boy as he picked his way up to the Quinary. Zeph blinked back tears as he walked past Helios to the final post. He stood with the bow Zander had made for him on his shoulder, a quiver of arrows slung across his back. Zander wondered briefly why he'd forgotten his own bow at the stable.

Zander held up his hand for quiet. "Once, you may have expected the elders or at least those past their teen years to stand here, but it is the seven of us who are called by Moira. We have pledged to protect you." He waited for his words to settle. "Moira came to me this morning. We have one week before we're attacked."

Shouts broke out in protest, until a voice boomed from the back. "Don't believe this nonsense." Elder Terrec pushed his way to the front and addressed the frantic crowd. "Calm down. We're not being invaded. This is a boy who's played you for fools while you supported his little games of fancy." He faced Zander, but didn't look him in the eye. "Get down off that horse."

"I have information yet to share." The crowd slowly quieted. When Zander held their attention, he said, "We've captured a spy." Gasps echoed across the crowd. "He confirmed the Odwans plan to attack."

Standing next to Zander, Terrec turned a deep shade of red as rage twisted his face. "Even if that's true, they only number a hundred men. We've ten times that."

How did Terrec know their numbers? Zander dismounted to stand at Helios's side. "It's true we outnumber them, but they've lived their lives at war." He hesitated. He had knowledge that might frighten the villagers more than bring them to his side. "I've consulted with Tshilaba. The Raskans travel through Odwan territory. She says the Odwans have bows that shoot four times as far as ours and deliver three arrows in the time it takes us to shoot one." He started to rub his thigh and stopped. It made him look weak. "They wear an armor that protects their chest. Whatever Elder Terrec has told you, this will not be an easy victory."

What would happen next was now out of his hands. Either the villagers would align with Terrec or himself. The people looked back and forth between Zander and Terrec.

Terrec stared into the crowd and nodded.

A hooded figure, hidden among the villagers, raised a bow, arrow nocked and aimed at Zander. The crowd pushed away in a panic and left a clear path for the arrow. "Let's end this now," the man shouted. Zander watched as Lash released the arrow.

CHAPTER FORTY-NINE

Zephyr

Horrified, Zeph watched Lash draw his bow. Without a thought, he slid his bow off his shoulder, grabbed an arrow, and released his shot as he raced to stand in front of Zander. He felt no surprise and no regret when Lash's arrow pierced the right side of his chest.

As he fell at Zander's feet, Zeph watched Lash crumple. His arrow had flown true, straight to Lash's heart. He was Puck's assassin, after all.

Zander knelt to hold him, and Zeph whispered, "I saw you in the gulch. I was spying. I'd never help Lash. You're more my brother than he could ever be." He coughed and blood trickled from his mouth. "Thank you for trusting me to stand with you."

Zander placed his hand around the arrow in Zeph's chest. "Hold on, Zeph. You can't die."

But Zeph knew he would die. Even now, his heart slowed as blood poured from his wound. He shivered and wondered how he could be cold when just minutes before, he'd been hot with excitement.

"Zeph!" Alexa hovered over him. She looked to the sky. "Moira! You can't let him die. Not like this. Not so young."

A velvety nose rubbed his cheek. Dorothy. He reached out to touch his patron. "We didn't even get to quest," he whispered. He understood then why he'd received no tokens, no omens.

His pulse slowed until he thought it must be minutes between each beat of his heart. "Alexa?" he rasped, "Will you take Dorothy?" She nodded and broke down sobbing. "Don't give up, Zeph. Eva's here now."

He felt more than saw Eva shake her head as she laid a blanket around the arrow to cover him. He was so cold, his teeth chattered. And then, the pain left.

Beside him, Moira and another presence he knew as God lifted him. He stared down at his body on the ground.

Zander and Alexa sobbed over him as Greydon, Kaiya, and Merindah knelt beside them. Another group huddled over Lash. Zeph observed curiously as Lash's spirit drifted up and over to where Zeph hovered. Together, they watched Elder Terrec crumple as he realized Lash had died.

Lash turned to Zeph. "We're free of the bastard."

Zeph could only nod.

It was then Moira spoke. "Well done. You played your parts as I expected. Your reward now is peace." She turned to Zeph. "Light-bearer, you have one final task. I'll let you know when you're needed."

And then Zeph was transported to an entirely different place. He found it beautiful.

CHAPTER FIFTY

Zander

Eva felt for Zeph's pulse and shook her head. Zander felt as though his heart was torn asunder.

At that moment, Dorothy began to bray, crying pitifully as she shook her head back and forth.

Alexa broke down, and Dharien appeared out of the crowd to take her in his arms.

When Zander bowed his head into his hands, Kaiya wrapped her arms around him. What would his life be like without Zeph? Zander cursed himself for his suspicions. He should have known Zeph would never betray him. He'd never told Zeph he loved him.

Zeph's mother broke through the crowd, frantic and pale. She threw herself over Zeph's body and wailed. She looked up at Zander and choked out, "My boy would be alive if it weren't for your warmongering."

He accepted her accusation in silence. Zeph *would* be alive if Zander hadn't allowed him to join the warriors. And when the war was over, there would be many more deaths to haunt him. He raised his face to the sky and gasped, "I can't bear it!"

"Zander," Kaiya whispered beside him, "you won't do this alone. We'll help you."

He searched the grief-stricken faces surrounding him. His friends. And he realized that this was only the beginning. He stood and faced the stunned villagers. Their fear assaulted him, and he almost dropped to his knees. He drew strength from the five oaks supporting the Quinary. Five tribes, one people.

With Zeph's body at his feet, Zander controlled his breath, in and out, and waited for silence before he began. "This is only the beginning of heartache, but we can't win a war if we're torn apart."

Alexa moved to his left, still crying. Merindah stood to his right, somber. He took their hands and felt their energy combine with his own.

"God and Fate brought our ancestors to this gulch as Puck led them in search of peace. Today that peace is threatened. We can pretend all is well and, when the invaders come, give in to them and hope they'll be merciful." He stopped to take a deep breath. "Or we can stand together and fight for the village we love."

Murmurs broke out over the crowd. Half the people nodded their heads and half cast angry glances between Zander and Lash's body. It seemed Terrec had been recruiting.

"There will be more deaths. There will be injuries. I can't promise we'll win."

Helios towered behind Zander, his breath hot against Zander's head. Shadow squeezed between Zander and Alexa to sit at Zander's feet as Dorothy pushed her head under Alexa's arm. Merindah's sparrow patron, Angel, landed on her shoulder.

One by one, the warriors, male and female, came to stand behind Zander. The women who trained with Alexa joined them. To Zander's surprise, Father strode to the Quinary, fist raised, and stood next to Lark. Last came the healers, led by Eva, tears in her eyes, but chin up.

It was what the villagers needed to convince them.

Elder Warrin spoke first. "I stand with Zander. Moira chose him to lead us."

The crowd began to chant, "Zander, Zander."

Zander let the energy fill him. For now, they supported him. When they learned they would all be needed to fight, they might hold regrets. He held up his hand and the chants faded. "We've not much time. Meet back here in two hours."

He knelt next to Zeph's body and whispered, "Thank you, little brother. Your sacrifice will not be in vain. We'll save the village and unite the tribes." He placed his hand on Zeph's motionless chest. "I promise there will be no more hungry children."

Father Chanse knelt beside Zander and bowed his head. He lifted Zeph's body and carried him to the church, Zeph's mother weeping beside him. There would be a service. There was time to honor his courage even in the midst of war plans.

Dharien and Paal carried Lash's body to the church. Zander knew Lash hated him, but to try to kill him was shocking. Were there others who wished him dead? Maybe he'd been remiss to not use his gift. He hated seeing secrets, but if it was necessary for his safety, he'd do it.

After the villagers dispersed, Zander turned to address the group still standing under the Quinary. He dropped his guard and searched each face. He found only love and respect. He'd had their support even when he'd been trying to shoulder the responsibility alone.

His voice broke. "My friends. You have trusted me from the beginning. Thank you. We each have our part to play." He couldn't help but feel it was a complex game they were involved in. Moira had spun the wheel of fortune, and there was no turning back from their destinies. "I waited too late to tell Zeph, but I want you to know that whatever happens, I love each of you. I can't do this alone. You are all important. Go home and prepare for war. Come back in two hours."

They waited in line to shake his hand, give him a hug, or simply say thanks. Humbled at their affection, Zander fought back tears.

He almost lost it when Father and Mother stood together in front of him, and Alexa joined them.

"We're proud of you, our children," Father said.

Mother mused, "I wonder if we'd named you differently, we could have saved you from this burden."

"It's not a burden, Mother." Alexa grabbed Mother's arm. "It's an honor."

Zander swallowed. Alexa sometimes saw things more clearly than he did. She was right.

Moira honored them with this responsibility.

CHAPTER FIFTY-ONE

Alexa

Zeph was dead.

Alexa couldn't process it. The others had left, but she didn't feel like making the trek to Melina Odella's cottage. She'd have to pass Zeph's home and know that she'd never see him again. Instead, she'd found herself slumped on a bench under one of the trees supporting the Quinary, holding her head in her hands. She'd taken Zeph for granted and missed so many opportunities to tell him how much his friendship meant to her.

The bench shifted, and Dharien put his arm around her. He looked as miserable as she felt. "I'm so sorry, Alexa. I know Zeph was your friend."

"What about Lash?" Her words came out harsh and bitter. "Wasn't he your friend?"

"No," Dharien's voice was low and tortured. "He wasn't. I pretended to be his friend because I knew he'd cause problems. But I swear I didn't know he'd try to kill Zander."

"If it wasn't for Zeph, Zander would be dead." Alexa started to shake.

He pulled her into his chest, and she sobbed. When the tears slowed, she stayed tucked in his arms. Some conversations were safer when you didn't look at the person you were talking with.

"Dharien? I–I . . ."

His arms tightened around her. "Whatever it is, you can say it, Alexa."

Her heart thudded. "I thought you'd changed after the quest, and then when I heard you were helping Lash steal from the merchants, I thought you hadn't. I'm so mixed up, I don't know what to believe."

"I didn't help him steal. I knew about it, but if I'd told Zander, he would have kicked Lash out, and then I wouldn't know what he planned." Dharien rested his chin on her head. "Terrec's up to something. Lash almost told me before he disappeared. I saw him once after that." When she tensed, he added, "It was after Zander got out of jail, I swear, Alexa." She relaxed and he went on. "Lash said I needed to be ready to switch sides. I thought he was deluded, but now I'm not so sure. I'll tell Zander to be careful."

"It's a little late, don't you think?"

He stiffened. "Alexa, if I'd had any idea Lash would try to kill Zander, I would've warned him. I swear it."

"I believe you. I hate this." She sighed. "Two people are dead, and the war hasn't even started." How many more would she lose?

"It won't be easy." Dharien played with the ends of Alexa's scarf. "You don't need this. The scar doesn't matter. You're beautiful." He hesitated. "I know this isn't the best time, but Zander's right. We don't know what's going to happen. I need to tell you something."

She pulled away, wondering what could be so important. When she saw his eyes, she knew what he'd say.

"Alexa . . . I love you. Whatever happens in the next week, I want you to know that." He stared at the ground. "You hate your scar, and mine is worse. I know you can't love me, but . . ."

She placed her hand on the jagged scar on his cheek. Every doubt she'd had about him flew away. "I do love you." She leaned forward and kissed the scar. "This reminds me every day of how brave you were in the quest."

He pulled her in and held her against his heart where it thumped as hard as Alexa's. He kissed the top of her head. "Thank you for believing in me," he whispered. "I need to find Greydon and Zander. It's past time I was honest with them."

He held her another few seconds and then rose and walked briskly away. As he stepped off the Quinary platform, the Knight of Cups card hovered over his head. Romance. But there could be none until they won the war. It would have to wait.

She stayed on the bench. Zeph was dead. Dharien loved her. The two things twisted round and round in her head until she was sure she'd never think of one without thinking of the other.

A flash from the side of the church drew her attention. Frowning, she stood and haltingly walked toward it. What was it? Another flash. She walked faster and caught a glimpse of someone she hadn't expected.

Melina Odella.

Alexa ran, but the fortune-teller disappeared. Alexa halted at the back of the church and glanced from side to side. Melina Odella reappeared next to Elder Nhara's gate, where she slid open the bolt and dashed behind the wooden planks. By the time Alexa slipped past the open door, she was just able to glimpse the back of Melina Odella's black robe before she rushed out of sight on the twisty path. Alexa reached the turn as Melina Odella disappeared once more around a bend.

She sped up, rounded the turn, and skidded to a stop when she found herself face-to-face with Melina Odella, Elder Nhara, and the old woman Alexa had seen with her teacher in the Yapi alley. The village bells rang, summoning the villagers to Zander's meeting. It seemed she'd be late.

Melina Odella held up her hand and muttered words Alexa couldn't hear. The Elder and old woman opened their hands and funneled energy to the fortune-teller. The spell hit Alexa's chest and immobilized her as invisible ropes tethered her to the ground.

As unprepared as she was, Alexa managed to utter her own spell. It was the one she'd copied from Melina Odella's book when she wasn't looking. Not exactly a spell, but an antispell.

Undetectable to Melina Odella, the ropes loosened, and Alexa had access to her magic. The situation was dire, but now Alexa had hope.

When the magic settled and Melina Odella thought she was safe, she snarled at Alexa, "Who's stronger now? You think I didn't know you hid your power? You believe you're smarter than me? Without my teachings, you're nothing but a second-rate, tag-along nobody, unworthy of being anything more than a baker."

Magic swirled through Alexa and gave the words power. They wound into her mind and released fears she'd buried deep. Mother always busy. Father a drunk. The mistakes she'd made using her embroidery. Almost killing Kaiya and Zander with her spells. Feeling too young for the position of village fortune-teller. Zeph's death—if she hadn't befriended him, he'd never have joined the warriors.

She dropped to her knees, head bent.

Melina Odella's ragged laugh rang through the air. "Finally, you understand your position."

In that space of hopelessness, a light began to shine behind the brooch Zander gave Alexa on her birthday. The garnet pulsed against her heart and pushed away the evil, protecting her. The quartz stones transmuted the dark energy and rendered it harmless, while the gold amplified both stones' effects. Her thoughts cleared, and she understood the difference between her and Melina Odella. Alexa had her family, she had friends. She knew true love.

She experienced that love as a red flame. The garnet fed it, and Alexa let it fill her until the fire consumed her. The vastness of her soul opened and silver energy surrounded her.

Alexa stood and lifted her arms. The red mixed with the silver and spread in a circle around her.

The sneer on Melina Odella's face turned to fear. She backed away and whispered, "No, you cannot be this strong."

Elder Nhara gasped. "You promised you could control her." She spun and ran.

Almost gleeful, the old woman clapped her hands together. "I warned you she was powerful. Kill her now, Melina Odella, and allow her energy to disperse and strengthen us." Was the old woman also a fortune-teller? Confusion turned to resolve, and words flowed from Alexa without conscious thought. "You deserted your calling, but it's not too late for repentance."

Melina Odella shook her head. "I cursed you and Zander. You'll fail and all will die!"

The curse from the consecration wound up around Alexa's arms and chest. With a shake of her hands, it released, and she sent it into the earth at her feet. A small smile crossed her face. She'd broken it. The village had a chance.

"You have no power over me, Melina Odella. Moira's strength lies within me now."

The fortune-teller pointed her hands at Alexa and began to mutter.

Even then, Alexa couldn't hate her teacher. She saw herself in Melina Odella. Not so long ago, she'd have done anything for Zander. She'd cheated, she'd put his safety over the other questers, she'd tried to control his future without his permission. Alexa had already hidden away in Melina Odella's cottage. If she didn't make changes, she'd turn bitter and cold like her teacher. No matter her future, she wouldn't let that happen.

Alexa expanded her energy until it included her teacher. She sent love, acceptance, and forgiveness in a three-strand rope connecting her heart to Melina Odella's.

Melina Odella collapsed, screaming, "No, I don't want it."

Alexa knelt next to her. "I give it freely. You can accept or refuse, but you can't make me take it away."

Confusion washed across Melina Odella's face, and then her eyes hardened. "I refuse. Leave me."

A mist rose from the ground, disorienting Alexa. When it dissolved a few seconds later, Melina Odella and the old woman were gone.

CHAPTER FIFTY-TWO

Zander

During the two-hour break, Zander met with Greydon, Fulk, and Geno. The villagers needed time to absorb the news, and he needed a plan. Back at the Quinary, the villagers, with grim faces, trailed in to surround him.

Behind them, the Raskans were packing their wagons. Earlier, Tshilaba had come to explain why her tribe was leaving.

"This isn't our war," she'd said, and Zander understood. Out of the six tribes, the Raskans were the one who'd never been at war. "It's not our way," she'd added. "We don't know how to fight." Then she'd hugged him and asked him to tell Alexa goodbye and that she'd see her soon. The problem with talking to fortune-tellers was their reticence. He had no idea what she meant. It would be six months before the Raskans returned to Puck's Gulch.

Dharien's confession had been a surprise. He'd interrupted the strategy meeting with his suspicions that Terrec was helping the enemy. Greydon's relief that Dharien wasn't against them was evident. His brother wasn't a traitor.

But two traitors did remain—Terrec and Melina Odella. He'd sent Protectors to arrest Terrec, but he wasn't at his estate. Lash's body had been taken to the church. It galled Zander that he lay next to Zeph. In two days, there'd be a service for both. Terrec had to show up sometime.

At the Quinary, the villagers waited nervously for his instructions. Kaiya and Merindah spoke quietly with the group of women they'd been training. Greydon and Dharien stood with a group of elders. It was good to have their support. All but Terrec and Elder Nhara were in attendance.

He squinted, looking for Alexa. He needed her to explain how magic would help. Dorothy rubbed her back against one of the oaks supporting the Quinary, but Alexa wasn't with her.

When the murmurings grew louder, Zander raised his hand. He'd have to start without her. Before he could speak, a wave of disorientation swept through him. He grabbed at Shadow to steady him as magic swirled around him.

Merindah ran to his side and whispered, "Did you feel the unbinding? Alexa has broken Melina Odella's curse."

If Alexa was with the fortune-teller, was she in danger? Helplessness washed through him. Events were running out of control. He took a moment to compose himself before he turned to the startled villagers. "Any who can shoot, go stand with Greydon."

It took awhile to separate the confused villagers into groups, sending some with Fulk, some with Geno, the women with Kaiya. And there were still plenty he didn't know what to do with. As he stood contemplating how to use the willing, but feeble elderly, Zander felt Alexa's energy. At a collective gasp from the villagers, he spun in time to see her step up onto the Quinary platform. Silver light surrounded her, and from the looks on the others' faces, he wasn't the only one to see it.

She walked slowly toward him, hands held out at her side. The silver faded until it was just Alexa standing before him.

To Zander and Merindah, Alexa whispered, "I've come from Melina Odella. She no longer has any power over us."

"What about your vision? Will she curse the village?" Merindah asked.

Alexa laughed, deep in her chest. "Oh, she'll try, and I'll stop her."
Zander grasped her hand and pulled her to stand next to him.
"The villagers need to know what you can do."

She faced the crowd. "Melina Odella intends to curse us."
Startled gasps filtered through the crowd.

"She's a traitor. If you see her, she's not to be trusted." Alexa
opened her energy and the silver shone again. "I will stop her."

Merindah joined their hands, and the three stood linked in a
triangle, back-to-back. She cried out with the fervor of one consumed with conviction, "God will fight with us, but the outcome is
not assured. It's time for me to assume my destiny as the anchoress."

Zander felt an energy build, starting in his chest and flowing
outward toward his hands. As golden light engulfed him, the silver
returned to Alexa, and copper pulsed around Merindah.

The villagers stepped back. Many shielded their eyes.

Father Chanse stepped forward and said, "Don't be afraid. These
three are consecrated by God. I attest to their favor. Our hope lies
with their powers. I urge you to release your fears and follow their
leadership. Unite, my friends, unite!"

When Merindah and Alexa loosened from his hands, the energy faded, but Zander felt it deep within. He tested it and found
he could bring it forth at will. He formed a ball of gold energy and
held it in his palm.

Alexa whispered, "Gold, the masculine energy of the day, and
silver, the feminine energy of the night, combine with the copper
of the anchoress. Together, we cannot be stopped."

His sister had truly become the fortune-teller.

"I'll be at Melina Odella's cottage." Alexa spun and strode away.
Dorothy followed, moving faster than Zander had ever seen her.

He rubbed the back of his neck. He had one week to prepare
for war.

CHAPTER FIFTY-THREE

Alexa

Uttering long pathetic brays, the small gray donkey trailed behind Alexa. Dorothy missed Zeph. So did Alexa. Was Dorothy now her patron?

She slowed at the shack houses where Zeph had lived. Small faces peered out the doors. Did they know of Zeph's death? They must recognize Dorothy. Another hurt toppled into her heart. She hadn't followed through on her pledge to bring them food. Determined, she quickened her pace to the fortune-teller's cottage. She had time to honor her promise.

She led Dorothy to the back garden with a strict warning. "Don't eat the plants behind the brick wall." At Dorothy's plaintive cry, Alexa hesitated. Poor baby. She spent a few minutes brushing the donkey's back and sides. Satisfied Dorothy would be all right, Alexa shut the gate and walked to the front door, feeling an unaccounted dread as she drew closer.

The moment Alexa stepped through the door, Melina Odella's angry energy swirled at her feet. She stilled for a moment, sending her energy through each room to confirm the fortune-teller was gone. Alexa followed the anger into the stockroom and found broken glass littering the floor. She gagged at the odor of the pooling liquids.

She replaced the unbroken bottles on the shelves and swept

away the glass, careful not to touch the herbs that had mixed. She sprinkled cornmeal on the soupy spots on the floor. After the shelves were in order, she discovered the foxglove and aconite jars were gone. Alexa rubbed the carved foxglove pendant that Merindah had given her for her birthday. Foxglove could be used to heal or to kill. Aconite, known as the queen of all poisons, had only one use.

To calm her mind, Alexa went to the kitchen. One week until war. She tied on a soft green apron and opened cabinet after cabinet searching for ingredients. The kitchen was surprisingly well stocked.

She hefted a large kettle of water onto the wood stove and threw kindling on the coals. After cutting up the two rabbits left earlier by Zander, she dropped the pieces into the boiling water. She added cubes of potatoes and carrots from the basement along with fresh basil and spring peas.

As the aroma filled the kitchen, she turned to another task. She measured out flour, baking soda, and salt. She cut in lard and stirred in goat's milk until the ingredients stuck together. She dumped the dough out on a floured counter and began to knead it. With each turn, her sorrow eased. Maybe baking was how Mother survived when Father left with Zander. It was a revelation that doing something she'd hated for so many years could be soothing.

She rolled the dough into a one-inch thick slab and cut circles with a metal ring. After arranging them in rows on a shallow, earthenware tray, Alexa sprinkled sugar across the top. By the time four dozen biscuits sat cooling on the counter, the stew was tender. Alexa stirred in a little flour to thicken it and pulled it to a cool spot on the stove top.

Good, hearty food for hungry children. How would she get it to them? She remembered seeing a small wood cart with peeling green paint buried in the corner of the shed holding pots and chunks of wood. After digging it out, she hauled it into the yard and brought Dorothy out through the gate.

"Think you can pull a cart, Dorothy?"

The donkey raised her head and stepped backward.

"It's to honor Zeph."

Her ears twitched at Zeph's name.

"Come on, girl. Let's get you hitched up."

Dorothy shifted from side to side, but she allowed Alexa to harness her and strap the cart behind. Alexa led her to the front door. "Wait here."

Wearing heavy gloves, she returned carrying the pot of stew and settled it in the corner of the cart. Next she brought out stacks of tin cups, spoons, and a ladle. Last, she tied two baskets of still-warm biscuits to the side of the cart. She stood in front of Dorothy and laid her forehead against the donkey's long nose.

"We'll miss him together." She turned and walked the path to the shacks. Dorothy ambled behind her as if she'd always pulled a cart. Alexa knocked at a door of the first house in the row.

A girl who looked to be twelve stared out with a frown wrinkling her dirty face. "What are you doing with Dorothy?" She sniffed. "I saw Zeph save your brother. He better protect us from those invaders."

"He will." A pressure built in Alexa's chest until she found it hard to breathe. If they beat the Odwans, Zander would next fight to protect these children from the inequality in Puck's Gulch. "Zeph gave me Dorothy. We brought food."

"Food?"

"For all the children who live here."

The girl stepped out of the house, stuck her fingers in her mouth, and whistled two long calls. Kids poured out of the shacks and ran to stand in front of the girl. "The fortune-teller brought us food."

It seemed odd to be called the fortune-teller in that way. To these kids, she was interchangeable with Melina Odella. The fortune-teller, they called her.

A small red-haired boy tugged at Alexa's arm. "That other fortune-teller used to bring us ham slices and apple bread. What do you got?"

The other kids jumped up and down while Alexa stood shocked. Melina Odella fed them? She shook her head. "Come around to the cart. I have rabbit stew and sugar biscuits."

Still reeling from that news, Alexa ladled stew into the cups and gave each child a spoon. When the cups were empty, she handed out the still-warm biscuits. Most of the kids raced away, yelling their thanks, but the little boy who had tugged her arm stayed.

"Are you Zander's sister?"

Alexa nodded. "What's your name?"

"Milo." He stared up at her and shifted from one foot to the other. "When I grow up, I'm going to be just like your brother. I'm going to be a hero, too." Then he spun and ran.

Alexa stared after him until he disappeared into one of the shacks. "I hope you get the chance," she whispered.

Filled with love, Alexa led Dorothy back to the cottage. She'd do everything she could to see that Milo got that chance.

With a lighter heart, Alexa carried her basket of embroidery to the front room. She cut squares of cloth and threaded her needle. Drifting in and out of a trance state, she stitched late into the night.

CHAPTER FIFTY-FOUR

Zander

Two days after Zeph's death, Zander woke, bleary-eyed from another late-night strategy session with Fulk, Greydon, and Dharien. At least he had a clear mind, unlike after the late nights at the tavern. He stumbled to the small kitchen and poured a cold cup of cider, too tired to build up the fire. He glanced around the room. He missed Zeph's quiet presence.

The boy had been his shadow for months. When Puck demanded Zeph become an assassin, Zander had thought the ghost wrong—Zeph was too young, he didn't have time to learn, but Zeph had been determined. Zander had given in, thinking it wouldn't hurt to train him.

He scratched the back of his head. Did Puck know Zeph would save Zander's life? And if he did, couldn't he have just warned Zander? Zeph might still be alive. And what about Moira? She gave Zeph a jenny, knowing Dorothy would go to Alexa. He couldn't begin to think about how God fit into all this.

"Let it go, Zander." Fulk leaned against the door. "I know what you're thinking. You can't change what happened. The boy did a brave thing."

"Two dead." He set down the cup. "How many more will we mourn?"

Fulk's face hardened. "As many as it takes to win." He moved to the stove and tossed a handful of splinters onto the embers. "You scouting the gulch this morning?"

"Greydon will be here in a few minutes. Kaiya and Yarra are meeting us at the gulch." He rubbed his aching thigh. Not a good day for it to act up. "We'll be back for Zeph's service this afternoon."

The stable door opened and shut with a click. Greydon appeared, looking as distraught as Zander felt. He handed Zander and Fulk biscuits tucked with ham. "The cook insisted. Said you can't fight a war if you don't eat."

His stomach protested, but Zander took a small bite and found himself ravenous. When was the last time he'd eaten?

"You be careful in the gulch. Another spy might be skulking about," Fulk said.

"This is really happening, isn't it?" Greydon blanched. "With all our training, I don't know if I can kill someone."

Fulk held Greydon at the shoulders. "Kill or be killed. Remember that."

"Let's get Lady and Helios saddled." Zander strode from the kitchen before Fulk could see the same reluctance on his face. Zander hadn't had time to take Helios into the gulch. He needed the experience before the invasion.

After they had the horses ready, Zander loaded his knives, hung a quiver across his front, and grabbed a bow. He hesitated. With the Odwans' bows, they could shoot without him seeing them. He went back into the kitchen and rustled around in the cookware. He pulled out four flat cast iron trays used to bake biscuits. He handed one to Greydon. "Shove this under your tunic."

"Huh?" Greydon stared at Zander like he'd lost his senses, but he pushed the pan between his tunic and undershirt and tightened his belt to keep it from slipping out. "It's heavy."

"It could save your life." Zander turned to Fulk, who nodded his approval. "Go to market and buy every tray you can find. And see if the smiths can make more."

Zander led the horses out of the stable. He and Greydon mounted and cantered toward the gulch with Shadow loping alongside. The gulch ran along the whole north side of the village. It was a lot of ground to patrol, but Zander was relieved to see the Protectors lined up every twenty yards with bows drawn. The Protectors nodded at Zander and resumed their watch. Behind the tavern, Kaiya and Yarra were waiting for them atop Elder Rowan's horses.

"Hoy," Zander guided Helios next to Kaiya's horse. He handed her and Yarra each a pan. "Stick it under your tunic."

Without a word, Kaiya opened her tunic. She laid the pan against her undershirt and tied her tunic back around it. She squirmed in the saddle as she moved the pan up and down. "It's not very comfortable."

"It could deflect an arrow." Zander couldn't take his eyes off her. The fire in her eyes, her excitement. He didn't want her in danger, but it was what she wanted. If he truly cared for her, he needed to accept her decision to fight, but he'd do everything he could to protect her.

As the four horses picked their way down into the gulch, Yarra asked, "What are we doing?"

"Planning our defense," Greydon answered. "The Protectors will stand at the top of the gulch. The old and young will supply them with arrows."

"Halfway down, we'll set up the catapults," said Zander. "The smiths' guilds have saved their scrap iron and nails. We'll lob them across the gulch." It was a desperate measure, as it would ruin the far side of the gulch. "We're searching for the best spots for the archers and the women with slings." He winced, thinking of Mother with a bow, taking her place among the skilled archers.

Puck's ghost moaned across the gulch. "Save the village."

All four horses came to a stop. Zander glanced at Kaiya and Yarra. "Did you hear him?"

They nodded. Kaiya shivered. "He gives me the creeps."

Yarra's wide eyes showed her fear.

He held up his hand and thought for a minute as the others stared. "Tshilaba says the Odwans are superstitious." He cocked his head at the sky. "Puck? Will the Odwans hear you?"

"I choose who hears and who does not."

Huh, that was a surprise. "Will you help? Make the Odwans hear you?"

"I will. Call when I'm needed." Puck's voice faded away. "All you had to do was ask."

Astonished, Zander sat back in the saddle. "All I had to do was ask?"

Greydon snorted. "If we had an army of ghosts, we could win without loosing a single arrow."

An army of ghosts! "That's it. That's what we're missing." Zander's excitement caused Helios to prance.

Greydon's jaw dropped. "You're mad."

Was he mad? Maybe it took madness to win a war. How could he use Puck?

"Zander's right," Yarra said. "We can make a fake ghost army. Every quester this year except Zeph was given a bird patron. Father Chance taught the birds to carry messages to their questers. If we hide them in the trees and have the birds drop things as Puck moans, it'll spook the Odwans."

"We can roll up long strips of canvas and tie them in the trees where we expect the Odwans to come in. Korble's smart. She can untie them when Puck moans and it'll startle the Odwans even more." Kaiya practically danced in the saddle.

"Let's do it," Zander said.

A ghost army. It might give them enough time to take the advantage.

CHAPTER FIFTY-FIVE

Alexa

Alexa and Father Chanse had agreed. With war looming, the service today would lay to rest Zeph and Lash, bless the questers, and consecrate Merindah before she entered the cell. Well, Alexa hadn't agreed on the consecration.

She stood at the front altar with Father Chanse. Her black skirt with white embroidery swirling in moving patterns was meant as a reminder to the villagers of her magic.

The villagers packed into the sanctuary as the noon bells rang. She scanned the crowd. Elder Terrec hadn't been seen since he'd disappeared after Lash's death. If he showed today, he'd be arrested after the service.

Dorothy brayed outside the front doors. Alexa hated leaving her, but Father Chanse insisted the church was no place for a donkey. He was right, but Dorothy somehow knew the service was for Zeph and had tried her best to nose her way inside.

On the right side of the center aisle, flanked by the other two nuns, Merindah sat on the front bench. Her plain brown dress contrasted with Alexa's finery, but now Alexa understood their differences, down to their clothing, were vital to their roles. Eyes closed, she serenely clasped her hands in her lap. On the left side, the six questers sat in contrast, fidgeting. Their patrons perched on their shoulders or on their knees. Normally, patrons didn't attend the blessing, but after Alexa learned of Zander's plans, she'd convinced Father Chanse the birds needed blessing, too. At least if a bird dropped a poo, the smell wouldn't fill the room, unlike with Dorothy.

She tried not to think about the two wooden caskets on the scaffold behind her. Zander and Dharien, standing across the back wall with the other warriors, gave her courage. Together they'd get through it.

As the bells ended, the sanctuary quieted. Father Chanse stepped forward to stand slightly in front of Alexa. "Friends. We gather today in a time of fear and sorrow. We honor our dead and consecrate our living." His eyes roved across the villagers. "At our altar, we have the child of an elder and the child of a servant."

Zeph's mother burst into sobs. Alexa's mother moved to her side and held her, her own tears flowing. Alexa's eyes filled with tears as well, but she choked back her grief.

Father Chanse continued. "Our society has elevated the elders and placed their worth above the others, so much so that our children, such as Zephyr, have little hope of any life better than working long, hard hours and going to bed hungry in shacks that the winter wind blows through."

The elders, in their tribal finery, squirmed in their seats. Except for Elder Warrin. He pursed his lips and looked intently at the priest before nodding.

"And yet, in these fearful times, Zephyr found hope in the warriors that gave him friendship and respect. He willingly made the choice to put the safety of the village above himself when he saved Zander's life. Today, we honor his sacrifice and bless the life he lived in courage."

He allowed a minute of silence before he continued.

"Lash, the first son of an elder, never lacked for any material thing. Only two years past his quest, and still under the influence of his father, Lash committed an act we cannot understand." He rubbed his forehead. "I knew of the abuse of his father. Not to excuse Lash's actions, for each one of us makes our choices, but the craving for a parent's love is strong. Today, we lay his body to rest and hope his soul is at peace. I ask that you not judge him, as that is now beyond our earthly concern." Father Chanse stood tall, and his voice became stronger. "For too long we've turned a blind eye to injustice. If we survive this invasion, changes will be made. Our children will not be hungry, they will not be abused. I give you my word."

From the back, the warriors cheered. Bewildered for only a few seconds, the villagers joined in. Dorothy brayed from outside. The Elders sat thoughtful before slowly clapping. Alexa nodded her approval. No one should oppose taking care of children.

For the first time, Alexa felt grateful to be on the council. She no longer saw it as a drudgery, but an honor. She would be a part of the change. Working with Father Chanse, they would unite the tribes and find a way to help the poor. She glanced at Zander, whose face was shining, and at Dharien, who looked back at her with such love she couldn't help but grin. They would all do it together. In Zeph's memory, they'd make a new society.

Father Chanse held up his hands until it was again quiet. "Now, we bless the questers. Come forward."

The questers trailed to the front and stood in a line between Father Chanse and Alexa. Their birds settled on shoulders or arms. Alexa felt their nervousness. In a normal year, the fear of not surviving was real enough, but now, knowing they would participate in a war, their fear rolled off them in waves.

Alexa stood behind the first teen. She placed her hand on his shoulder and said, "This year, your omens will be used against our enemy, and your patron will be a vital part of our strategy. May you fight with honor as your fate still lies in Moira's hands." She choked back a sob before adding, "May you have the courage of Zephyr."

With each quester, Alexa repeated the words. Through her

palms, she sent energy into the teens, replacing their fear with strength. They stood tall, filled with pride.

Father Chanse concluded the ceremony with a prayer. "We ask blessings upon each young person standing here. May their good deeds and courage save not only them, but our village. Amen."

After the service, Alexa followed Merindah from the front of the church to the northern wall. The bricklayers had finished the cell except for the narrow door, which would be bricked in after Merindah entered. A small window, the squint, opened into the sanctuary so Merindah could attend services. An outside window allowed for people to seek her advice and prayers. A third window in the back wall would be used to bring in food and water and remove waste. Altogether it was a seven-foot square that held a cot, a table and chair, and a lantern. A woven yellow prayer mat covered what little was left of the floor.

Merindah's serenity unnerved Alexa. She held tight to Merindah's hand. "Please don't go in," she pleaded for the hundredth time. "You don't have to do this." The biscuit she'd eaten for breakfast revolted in her stomach, and she fought the urge to vomit.

The bells rang. Two short, one long, two short, one long. The call to gather.

"It's not too late. There're other ways to help." Tears brimmed her eyes. "Please, Merindah."

Merindah took both of Alexa's hands. It wasn't in Alexa's imagination that her friend glowed. Merindah's calm seeped into Alexa and dulled the panic. Fates, there was no talking her out of it.

"As surely as you've been called by Moira to be the fortune-teller, I've been called by God to be the anchoress. You risk much and yet, you won't give up your favor. I won't give up mine. The cost to both of us will be great, and yet if we don't follow our destiny, the loss will be greater than we could bear." She closed her eyes. "Feel it, Alexa. Feel it in your soul."

A small flame ignited behind Alexa's heart and burned away her fear. The truth of Merindah's words became clear. There was a choice, but the consequence of choosing the other was too great. She pulled Merindah into her arms and hugged her, not wanting to let her go. They would never hug again. She wanted to apologize for all the times she'd doubted Merindah's calling, for her arrogance at believing her own work was more important, and for the time she'd wasted being angry with the best friend she'd ever known. But when she looked in Merindah's eyes, she knew she'd already been forgiven.

At the last council meeting, Alexa had asked Father Chanse why he allowed Merindah to make this sacrifice. He'd answered so strangely that Alexa had walked out dumbfounded. His words repeated in her head.

Merindah hasn't been of this world since her quest.

She knew it to be true, but she didn't have to like it.

Father Chanse held up his hand. "It is time."

Holding back a sob, Alexa moved away from Merindah and joined Zander and Kaiya at the side of the church. Dorothy nudged her from behind, and although it was another reminder of loss, the donkey's presence comforted her.

Merindah's patron sparrow landed on her shoulder, her fate tied to her owner's. Alexa had laughed when Merindah named the sparrow Angel—gift from God. So many things Alexa didn't understand a year ago were becoming clear.

Appearing at her side, Dharien took her hand and leaned in to whisper, "Even those who die in this war will make no greater sacrifice."

She leaned into him. Was that true? She stared at Merindah's shining face. Her friend did not see it as sacrifice. She believed it an honor. Alexa chose that moment to trust her friend's decision.

Alexa wasn't losing her. She'd still be able to talk with her. It wasn't bad, it was just different. She answered Dharien with the only truth she knew. "She is love."

He pulled her in tighter and nodded against her head. "We can all learn from her."

Silence fell when Father Chanse turned to Merindah. "In our darkest hour, God sends light. You anchor us to the source of our power. God hold you, God keep you, God receive you. Amen."

Merindah lifted her head. "His will be mine."

"Do you accept this call as the anchoress of Puck's Gulch, entering the cell of your own free will?"

She stared out across the villagers. "I do."

"Knowing you will spend your life serving the village in the name of God?"

"I do."

"So be it."

"So be it," murmured the villagers.

Alexa's heart seized when Merindah disappeared into the shadow of the cell. She held tight to Dharien's hand to keep from running after her.

The brick layers moved in as the priest stepped back. The slap of mortar on top of the first row of bricks jarred Alexa from her thoughts. She began to shake, and only Dharien's arms held her upright. Surely someone would call an end to this madness. Father Chanse? God? Moira? But no one protested, and with each layer, the finality seeped into her bones.

Out of the one hole left, Merindah's eyes sought Alexa's. It was not joy, but sadness that Alexa saw in those eyes. She stepped forward, but Dharien held her back as the final brick was wedged into place.

The bells rang, slow and steady. God's will had been done.

CHAPTER FIFTY-SIX

War Begins

Zander

Five days had passed since Merindah entered the cell. Alone in the stable, Zander paced. Four scouts roamed the gulch. The Protectors rotated guarding the edge with the catapults loaded and primed below them.

The warriors gathered in the dining hall, waiting for Zander. He'd been anxious since he woke. Couldn't Moira pay him a visit and tell him when the Odwans would arrive? He closed his eyes and counted his breaths.

Greydon popped into the stable. "Hey, Z? You've got some restless warriors out there."

"Five minutes. Send Kaiya to me." When he'd stilled his mind, an idea had formed at the edges of his awareness.

"Not a time for romance, my friend." Greydon said, and ducked as Zander threw a bridle at him. Greydon laughed as he left the stable, but Kaiya showed up a minute later, breathless from running, clutching a dozen rolled up canvas ribbons.

"Alexa spelled them. When they unroll, they'll twist and flutter. It won't last long, but maybe it'll spook the Odwans."

"Good. Any extra time will help." He took her hand. He had to be careful how he worded his request. "I have a special assignment for you and Odo."

Her eyes narrowed, and she tried to pull away, but Zander held tight. "Hear me out. You two are the strongest climbers we have. Once the invasion begins, if you can cross the gulch and climb the rock walls behind, I want you to take a message. The Odwan women don't fight. Tshilaba says they're sick of war, but they'll defend their children and elders." He pulled her into his chest and wrapped his arms around her. "It's not a safe mission. If they shoot, you'll be outnumbered." He whispered the message for the Odwans.

When he felt Kaiya soften, he knew she'd agreed. She reached her arms around his neck and hugged him. "You're a good man, Zander, Son of Theron." She kissed his cheek. "You'd better stay alive. I have plans for you when this is over."

His cheeks burned. "I intend to," he said. He reluctantly pulled away. His five minutes were up.

Kaiya studied him. "You're afraid."

"I'd be a fool if I weren't. The village will fall if I can't protect them."

"You have more courage than anyone I know, but you don't fight alone, Zander. The warriors would follow you into hell if you asked them."

"I hate everything about this." He dropped his head into his hands. Kaiya was strong and beautiful. How would the invasion change her? "Even if we win, how do we recover from this?"

"Together. We do it together." Kaiya leaned in and pulled his hands away from his face. "I'll send Korble to tie the ribbons. The questers' birds can unfurl them." She placed her hand against his chest. "Now, you have a speech to make," she teased. "It better be good."

"It will be." He grasped her hand, and together they walked

to the stone outbuilding and entered the hall to face the anxious warriors. Kaiya joined the women. The muttering ended as Zander marched to the front. Gratified to see the men who'd left with Del standing along the back wall, he took a moment to acknowledge each man and woman. How many would die? Be wounded? The weight of his task twisted his gut. He sucked in a deep breath.

"A year ago, we were weak and unsure. We fumbled our blades, we dropped our knives. Our muscles ached, and our bodies screamed to quit. But our will was strong. We swung the blades and picked up the knives. We shot arrows until we were seeing targets in our dreams. Today we stand together as true warriors, ready to defend our village. I won't lie. You'll have moments when you'll want to run. It's how you react to that feeling that will show your true courage."

The men and women sat taller and more than a few eyes shone at Zander's words.

"I've driven you hard, and we haven't always agreed." A few nods and smiles greeted him. "Although the Protectors have their roles, we warriors are the key to our defense. My friends, we are ready. Fight smart, fight with heart. Fight to protect everything you love. Puck's Gulch will remain free. We will defeat the Odwans!" He added, "May you have the courage of Zephyr."

The warriors stood as one and roared. Fists pumped the air. They chanted, "Puck's Gulch! Puck's Gulch!"

And then the bells began to ring.

Zander shouted above the din. "Go! To your places. Save Puck's Gulch!"

CHAPTER FIFTY-SEVEN

Alexa

The bells! The Odwans had entered the gulch. Alexa tied a bag of crystals and herbs to her belt. She grabbed her basket of embroidery squares and sprinted to the Quinary, thankful she'd traded her skirt for trousers. The bloodstone beads, the warrior's stone, she'd braided into her hair clacked against the tiger eye beads used for grounding. When she drew near, she expected chaos, but instead found quiet determination.

Kaiya had the women off to one side, and Alexa headed there first. Bindi distributed quivers of arrows while Kaiya explained their positions in the gulch. Father stood at the back with Mother. Both heads bent, they spoke in low voices, and then Father kissed her and quickly strode away.

"Father?" she called after him.

He jerked to a stop and rubbed his eyes before looking at her.

"What will you be doing?" she asked.

"Zander gave me a scimitar."

Alexa blanched. "Hand-to-hand fighting? Will it come to that?"

"If it does, I'm ready."

She tied an embroidery around his neck. "This reflects the light and makes you harder to see."

"You stitched one for your mother?"

Alexa nodded.

He gave her a quick hug. "Use your magic to protect your brother," he said, and was gone.

Clutching her basket, Alexa joined the women. She hugged Kaiya and tied a square cloth around her wrist. The scene depicted Kaiya, bow drawn and aimed at a black X. Silver thread surrounded her to deflect the Odwans' eyes.

She tied similar cloths around each woman's wrist, leaving Mother for last. Alexa's chest tightened as she tied the cloth and gave Mother a hard hug. No words could convey how she felt. She said a quick, "I love you," and turned to the grim women.

"My magic protects, but it's not invincible. Be brave, not reckless." She searched each face before she added, "May you have the courage of Zephyr." She spun and ran to catch Father Chanse.

Dressed in the clothes of a field worker, Father Chanse led frightened but determined questers away from the Quinary. Pouches bulging with metal scraps were slung across their chests.

"Father Chanse? I have protection for the questers."

He helped her tie a spelled cloth to each quester, and then said, "Find Melina Odella. Convince her to help us."

"I'm going to try," Alexa replied as the questers headed down into the gulch.

Next, Alexa caught Gia's group. Boys and girls, armed with slings, marched to where the bricklayers' guild had built crenellations for the shooters to hide behind. She spent a few minutes spelling the piled stones to fly fast and true.

She approached the Protectors with the offer of a magic cloth, but one after another, insisted she give them to the ones going into the gulch. Before leaving, she said, "May you have the courage of Zephyr."

In the middle of the Quinary, Zander coordinated the groups. Pride filled her as he stood, confident, with a bow across his chest and a sword hanging at his side. He didn't hesitate as he answered questions and directed the troops. The amulet she'd embroidered for him lay against his chest. He glanced in her direction and caught her eye. It lasted only a second, but understanding passed between them. Their roles would not bring them together until later.

Next to Zander, Shadow stood alert, the hair on his back standing on end. Alexa had done the right thing when she sacrificed her patron to save Shadow. She'd stitched the collar he wore to carry messages. Woven with turquoise for safety and imbued with a spell for speed, she hoped it would help him survive. The mounted warriors surrounded Zander, wearing their magical cloths tied at their chests, like Zander.

She handed out the remainder of the cloths to the villagers going into the gulch. One cloth remained. The battle scene she'd stitched under trance lay in the bottom of her basket. Satisfied she'd done all she could to protect the fighters, Alexa turned toward the church. She needed to see Merindah.

Ahead of her, Eva and the healers carried boxes of supplies to the church, where the temporary hospital was set up.

Alexa sped up and slipped her arm through Eva's. "There are herbs and salves in my storeroom. Go there if you need supplies."

"Will you stand with Zander?" Eva's face wrinkled with worry.

"Not just yet. I need to find Melina Odella."

At the church door, Eva pulled Alexa in for a fierce hug and kissed her forehead, before releasing her. "Go. Do your magic and end this war." Without waiting for a response, Eva disappeared into the church.

Stunned, Alexa stood for a few minutes leaning against the stone wall. Eva believed in her. *Do your magic,* she'd said. Alexa sucked in a deep breath. That's what she'd do. Right after she talked with Merindah. She marched to the side of the church.

"Merindah?" Alexa peered into the shadowed cell and repressed a shudder. How did Merindah tolerate such a small space?

Her friend knelt on the woven rug. It took a few seconds before she stood and faced Alexa. "The war begins." At the small window, she searched Alexa's eyes. "Is Zander ready?"

"He's sending everyone to their places." Alexa reached through the rectangle window for Merindah's hand. "I need your help. I must stop Melina Odella before she curses the village. I don't understand her anger."

"Don't you?" Merindah's voice was gentle, but accusing. "Father Chanse drank the love potion you intended for yourself and Paal. There were consequences to your mistake. He believed he was in love with Melina Odella."

Alexa pulled her hand away. "You think this is my fault?"

"No, it's not your fault what Melina Odella does. You asked why she was angry." Merindah's voice softened. "When Father Chanse and Melina Odella quested together, they were in love. They planned to betroth after the quest and marry after their apprenticeships. After Moira told Chanse he'd be a priest, he accepted that they couldn't be together. Melina Odella never did. Father Chanse confessed to me his shame at how he kissed Melina Odella after drinking the potion."

Horrified at what the priest would think of her, Alexa exclaimed, "You didn't tell him about the potion?"

"He said he forced the cup from you. He blames only himself."

"Melina Odella was angry when it happened, but the spell has dissipated. It no longer affects him." It couldn't still be potent. If the spell still had a hold on Father Chanse, then Dharien might also be influenced.

"No, but it gave her hope, Alexa. And hope crushed is a hard thing to overcome. It grew into hate."

Melina Odella's hatred *was* her fault. This information might prove helpful, but she'd come for another reason. She handed a pair of scissors through the window. "I need a piece of your hair and your blessing."

If Merindah was surprised, she hid it. Her hair had grown enough that she snipped several strands and handed them to Alexa. "My prayers are for you and Zander. If either of you fail, the village will fall."

A weight settled in Alexa's gut, but determination flowed in her blood. She wouldn't fail. She tucked Merindah's hair in a small leather pouch at her waist. It held locks of her own hair, along with Zander's. Then she pulled out the embroidery and handed it through the window to Merindah. "You can follow the fight. Each of last year's questers are stitched on the cloth. I added Father Chanse, so you'll know if he's safe." Alexa turned to leave before Merindah could see her tears.

"Wait." Merindah untied the knot on her prayer beads and motioned for Alexa to lean her head against the window. She deftly wove seven amethyst beads into Alexa's hair. "These will unite us. My prayers will fly true to you. Blessings to you, Alexa."

"Thank you, my friend. Stay safe."

A shadow crossed Merindah's face. "What can happen in a brick cell?"

Alexa turned before Merindah could see her tears. She yanked her hood up and pulled it low over her forehead. From her sewing bag, she withdrew the calcite stone Melina Odella gave her for her birthday. Melina Odella had not cleansed it before she gave it to Alexa, and it still pulsed with the fortune-teller's energy. Alexa would use it to find her. She clutched her bag of stones and herbs, and raced for the gulch.

CHAPTER FIFTY-EIGHT

Zander

The scouts estimated it would be two hours before the Odwans hit the gulch. Astride Helios, Zander led the two dozen mounted warriors. Greydon rode behind him, Fulk and Geno at the rear. They left the Protectors on the rim and trotted toward the eager youngsters huddling behind brick walls with slings. It was still a game for them. Zander's chest tightened—he didn't want even one of these children to die.

When he approached, the kids chanted, "Zander, Zander."

A red-haired boy raced out from the others and yelled, "I'm going to be a hero like you!"

Zander pulled on the reins to bring Helios to a halt. "What's your name?"

The boy stuttered, "M-M-Milo."

"Milo." Zander ran his tongue over his chipped tooth. When he was Milo's age he'd worshiped the Protectors because one man— Del—had been kind to him. And yet, it was Del who'd attacked him late that night at the stable. The boy thought Zander was a hero, but who would he become in the years after this?

Greydon cleared his throat. They didn't have time to chat with young boys, but Zander felt it worth another minute.

"Milo, a hero isn't always the one getting the glory. You knew

Zeph?" When the boy nodded, Zander said, "Zeph is *my* hero. Even before he saved my life, Zeph was honorable and brave and true to his word. That's a hero for you to become."

At Milo's thoughtful look, Zander kicked his heels against Helios. He urged him down into the gulch, past the catapults, loaded and attended by hard-muscled metal smiths. Elders and peasants alike made up the next line of defense, bows ready and faces tense. The newly trained women turned and watched him pass.

Mother lifted her hand. "May you have the courage of Zephyr."

"May you have the courage of Zephyr," the others cried out.

For a moment, Zander wished Mother and Alexa and Kaiya were far away from the danger. He wished the peace of the village was not about to be destroyed. Then he mentally kicked himself. Wishes belonged to children like Milo. This was reality, and each person had chosen their role. He glanced across the mixed groups. The invasion had accomplished Puck's dream. The tribes had united. If he survived, Zander would see that it lasted.

Out of old habit, Zander reached for the red heart he'd worn before the quest. Instead, he found the stitched cloth Alexa had given him for protection. She'd said it would deflect an arrow. He had to trust it wouldn't have unintended consequences. He stopped at the stream running through the middle of the gulch and held up his hand. Shadow paused next to Helios. Before the warriors spread out across the bottom, he gave them final instructions.

"We fight to defend our freedom, but I offer refuge to any Odwan who wishes to surrender." He stared at the men and women who surrounded him. "May Moira and God bless you. Go now and protect our village."

Silently, they turned their horses and headed to their appointed positions.

Before he left for his post on the far left, Fulk said, "I'm proud to fight under your leadership. Whatever happens, know that you're the only one who could bring the village together." He pulled the reins to Tipper and sped away.

Greydon guided Lady to face Zander and Helios. "So it begins. We fight united, my friend."

"It's the only way we have a chance," Zander replied. They faced the upward slope of the north side of the gulch. Thick brush and old trees impeded their sight. Sound would be their first alert to intruders. Shadow stood, ears twitching, ready to follow orders.

Zander strained to hear anything out of the ordinary. When he could stand the silence no longer, Zander called, "Puck?" A breeze surrounded him.

"Yes?" the ghost moaned.

"You know the plan?"

"Yes." The air cleared.

A crow cawed, and Zander searched the sky. He'd sent Kaiya away from the upcoming fight, but not away from danger. If she ran into trouble, she was to send Korble. Relieved to see the crow flying away from him, Zander shifted in the saddle. Helios shied sideways until Zander pulled him back to a stand. He stilled his emotions, and the horse calmed.

As if reading his mind, Greydon asked, "Where'd you send Kaiya? I thought she was going to fight with us."

"Not Kaiya alone. I sent Odo with her."

"What the hell? Where'd you send them? Odo didn't tell me."

"They might be safer than here. Our enemies camp above the east bluffs. Once the fighters leave, it'll be women, children, and elderly left. I sent Kaiya with an offer of peace. If we can beat back the invasion, I want them to know we'll welcome them into the village if they're willing. If we can convince the women, I hope they can convince the men who survive."

Greydon stared out across the gulch. "Did you think to ask anyone else before you made that offer?"

"Father Chanse agreed with me. Whom should I ask? The Council?"

"Maybe the Elders whose land you're giving away?"

"We have to do something with them. There will be dead and injured on both sides. We can't turn them away."

"Stars, Zander! Your soft heart will plague us for years after this."

Greydon's words stung. Father had often said the same of Zander. He never meant it as a compliment. "Not if we make the changes Puck wants. If we parcel out the Elders' land, we have plenty for our people and them. The Raskans say the Odwans are known for their metalwork and a fermented drink they call ale." He glanced sideways at Greydon. "Maybe the day will come when we can enjoy a drink without using it to hide from our troubles."

"Maybe so." Greydon allowed Lady to graze. "I can't believe you sent Odo without telling me." He scowled. "I hate this waiting."

Helios's ears twitched and Zander leaned forward. Far off, but approaching rapidly, Zander heard what sounded like a herd of boars crashing through the forest. Shouts drifted down from the village edge, but Zander couldn't distinguish the words. Arrows flew over his head toward the opposite side.

He urged Helios across the stream. Finding an open spot where he could see up the side, Zander gasped. "What the hell is that?"

Coming down the opposite side, a phalanx ten men wide fought to stay together in the heavy brush. Shields protected them in front and above. A picket of ten-foot spears with heads that looked like sword blades rose above the front line.

This was it. All the training, all the work was for this moment. Adrenaline rushed through him, and Zander reached for an arrow. He sent a shot rushing toward the phalanx. His aim was true, but useless. The arrow stuck in the shields but did no harm. He had to find a way to break the formation.

An arrow thudded into the tree next to him. Zander fought to keep Helios under control as he pushed down his rising panic. A foot closer and he would have been hit.

Lady reared as an arrow grazed her flank. Greydon nearly fell, but recovered in time to pull her behind a tree and avoid the rain of arrows. Greydon slumped on Lady's back. "We've lost. There's no way to defend against them."

"It's time for Puck and the questers." Zander yelled to his warriors. "Hold up. Save your arrows!"

Shouts rang up and down the gulch repeating the orders as the warriors scrambled to find cover.

"Puck? Now!"

A sudden wind swept across the tops of the trees.

The phalanx continued its slow descent. Arrows flew from behind the wall. The Odwans must be shooting blind and hoping they hit something by sheer luck.

He felt a coward, but Zander hid behind trees as he encouraged the others to move out of the line of fire. He hated waiting, hated feeling powerless.

Wind whipped up the north side of the gulch. Puck moaned, "You disturb the spirits. Leave the gulch!"

The phalanx halted.

"The spirits are angry. Leave, leave, leave . . ." his voice trailed off.

From the trees, the questers' birds dived at the Odwans and dropped bits of metal. Wave after wave of bolts and stones fell from the sky.

The phalanx resumed marching down the gulch. Patrons swooped over their heads and released the canvas strips. The narrow ribbons unfurled to the ground, rustling as they swayed in the breeze. Alexa's spell held. It was as if the phalanx hit an invisible wall. Swears came from behind the formation. Puck loosed a blood-curdling scream, and the men scrambled to retreat.

The questers tossed down omens. Razorback boars raced

squealing after the Odwans. Peacocks pecked at their feet, while hornets buzzed around the men's heads, stinging anywhere they found exposed flesh. Scorpions landed on their shoulders, but it was the snake omens that caused the most panic. Screams echoed down the gulch as adders hissed and struck.

"Archers! Now!" Zander yelled. Arrows flew true toward the Odwans. Frantic to retreat, three men ran into the traps that Greydon had set. They flew feet first into the air and swung from ropes tied high in the trees.

Zander aimed and hit a man in the back. His stomach lurched as the man fell face forward and didn't move. It felt cowardly to shoot as they retreated, but the words he'd repeated to the warriors drifted through his head.

We fight any way we can to save our village.

CHAPTER FIFTY-NINE

Alexa

As she approached the gulch, Alexa slowed. Doubt rose without warning. Could she truly prevent Melina Odella from cursing the village? Was she too late? Under her scarf, the carved wooden heart and foxglove pendant pulsed against her skin, reminders of Zander's and Merindah's love.

The calcite stone vibrated, guiding her toward the west side. She reached the edge as Kaiya and Odo disappeared over the embankment.

"Hoy!" She ran to catch them and slid in loose leaves at the edge. When she regained her footing, the cousins stood six feet below her, faces lit with excitement. Bows slung over their shoulders, the embroidered band of protection tied across their wrists.

"Zander sent us on a special mission." Kaiya rocked from toe to heel. "We're headed west to where the cliffs meet the gulch. The Odwans won't come down there. It's too tight for more than a single-file path."

"I'm searching for Melina Odella." She held out the pulsing stone. "It's leading me this way, too."

"Follow us. We'll protect you." Kaiya sprinted along an overgrown path.

Alexa struggled to pay attention to the stone and keep up. Shouts echoed from the gulch. The Odwans were invading.

Odo nocked an arrow.

Alexa pushed them forward. "Go. Do what Zander asked."

Kaiya hesitated only a second before she spun and ran. "Find the fortune-teller," she yelled over her shoulder. "Don't let her curse the village."

Where the cousins went straight, Alexa turned left into the rocky cliffs. She picked her way over boulders. In the steep canyon, Alexa lost her sense of direction, forced to rely on the stone's guidance. Far from the gulch, the only sounds were the rocks she slipped against and a lone crow cawing as it circled above her. She slid down a boulder and blood beaded on her scraped palm. She pressed it against her side until the sting faded.

As she stepped out around a boulder, a wave of energy knocked her back. Alexa quickly gathered her own energy and wrapped it around her. She built a solid wall before she stepped back out in the open. She drew out a labradorite stone and used its vibration to deflect the energy Melina Odella threw at her.

"Melina Odella," she called. A ball of energy blasted toward her. It dissipated harmlessly into the air. Like Zander, she hoped for peace without bloodshed. She hid behind a boulder and removed an embroidery from her pocket. An image of Melina Odella and her patron wolf, Sheba, stood in the center. Coils of rope encircled them. Alexa tied the last stitch on her name and felt the energy come alive.

Stitching in one hand, labradorite in the other, Alexa stepped out to face her mentor.

Standing between two large boulders, Melina Odella, anger warring with fear across her face, struggled against the invisible ropes. The silver-haired wolf stood at her side, snarling, hackles raised.

"Use your power to save the village." Alexa stepped closer. "You love Father Chanse. Why would you hurt him?"

"Chanse made his choice," Melina Odella snarled, "and it wasn't me." She began to mutter.

Melina Odella broke the bindings, and a bolt of energy blasted bits of stone around Alexa. A shard ricocheted and cut her cheek. Blood trickled down her chin. She gathered her power and sent it streaking toward the fortune-teller.

Melina Odella held up her hand and deflected it upward where it sheared off a limb of a twisted pine. It crashed down behind the fortune-teller. "You can't defeat me, Alexa. I've been gathering power for twenty years."

Leaning against the rock, Alexa tried to steady her breath. She was no match for her teacher's experience, but if she kept Melina Odella distracted, it might give Zander time. Alexa searched for power in the stones surrounding her. An energy of a different sort flowed into her. Merindah's prayers! She pulled it into her body. Alexa stepped out. "I'm not alone, Melina Odella."

She gathered the strands of hair from her pouch and tossed them into the air, while chanting, "Day, night, anchor, unite!" The hair swirled and grew into a tornado that twisted and curved toward Melina Odella, flattening the sage and brush in its path.

A second before it hit, Melina Odella threw out both hands and sent the twister back toward Alexa. A cruel smile lit her face.

For the first time, Alexa felt her teacher would delight in killing her. She ducked between two boulders. The twister passed, throwing up shards and sticks. She closed her eyes against the dust and waited for it to settle. A grimy film covered her. She spat out a mouthful of grit.

It would take more than that to defeat her. She reached for the black and white stone that saved Zander in the quest.

CHAPTER SIXTY

Zephyr

Zeph watched Zander and Alexa from above. He didn't understand how, but he was aware of both scenes even as they occurred together. Wherever he put his attention, Zeph was there.

He focused back and forth. First on Zander's fear of the Odwans' phalanx and then on Alexa as she fought Melina Odella. He saw all of it and felt helpless. Moira had said he had a task, but he hadn't seen her since the day he died.

Soon after their deaths, Lash had left Zeph, dissipating into the ether. Or maybe Zeph had left Lash. He wasn't sure, but for the first time in his life, Zeph felt at peace. And yet he was anxious for his friends. It was confusing.

For now, all he could do was watch and wait for Moira's instructions. She'd said she'd let him know. He had to trust her—and hope he didn't become a ghost like Puck, wandering the gulch for hundreds of years.

He tossed his sparkling white stone from hand to hand. Moira had given it to him for a reason, but how could he help from where he was now? She and Melina Odella had called him light-bearer. The waiting tortured him. His friends were in danger.

A flash caught the corner of Zeph's awareness. He turned his attention away from Zander, away from Alexa, to a small gray donkey.

Dorothy was picking her way through the cliffs and heading straight toward the fight between Alexa and Melina Odella.

CHAPTER SIXTY-ONE

Zander

As the Odwans retreated, Zander rubbed the back of his neck. From the jubilant faces of the warriors, they thought they'd won. They were uninjured, unlike the half-dozen Odwan bodies lying on the other side of the gulch.

Only Greydon understood the retreat was merely a momentary reprieve. He stood next to Zander, solemn and shaken. He and Zander had seen the phalanx better than the rest. If the Odwans made it past Puck, the warriors would find it near impossible to defeat them.

Fulk and Geno returned from checking the bodies. Fulk spat, "All dead."

A cheer rose from the warriors, but Zander held up his hand. "We don't celebrate death." He filled his lungs and exhaled slowly. "The Odwans won't quit this easily."

The warriors' jabber ended as fear replaced jubilance. How could they have believed it was over?

Grim, Fulk cocked his head at the three swinging upside down from the trees still holding bows. "What do we do with them?"

The first prisoners. "If they'll drop their bows, cut them down and take them to Elder Warrin's estate. Lock them in the tack room. And search them for hidden weapons and poison."

Before Fulk could comply, Puck's ghost drifted in to coalesce over Zander. "Fire, fire," he moaned.

A tendril of smoke swirled above Zander. Moments later, the cackle of flames swept down from across the upper eastern gully. The Odwans were burning the gulch.

Frantic, the priest yelled, "Get the questers out of the trees!"

Zander wrote a quick note. *Fire. Get water.* He tied it to Shadow's collar. "Go! Take this to a Protector." He turned to Greydon. "Take Dharien and Bindi west. Paal? You and Rosa come with me. Fulk, take Jarl and Yarra, and get the middle questers."

Zander pulled a cloth from his pocket and tied it over his nose and mouth. He guided Helios toward the flames. The horse skittered and turned away. Zander slid from his back and placed a hand on each side of Helios's head. Zander opened his mind to the war horse and sent an image of the questers caught in the fire. When Zander felt Helios's understanding, he remounted.

Helios raced toward the danger with Paal and Rosa behind.

Field workers, used to hard labor, were digging a trench down the side of the gulch. If the trees didn't catch fire, the turned earth might halt the blaze. At the top, men and youngsters carried buckets of water to send tumbling down the trench.

"Dam the stream and flood the bottom," Zander yelled as he rode past.

Sweat dripped down Zander's chest from the heat. Even with the cloth over his nose, the air burned his throat. When he entered a patch of dense smoke, he hollered for the questers, "Cam? Bo?"

Faint cries responded from his left. He urged Helios across the stream. A sparrow swooped down and guided Zander to a large cottonwood tree. Two boys crouched on the bottom limb as smoke drifted into the upper branches.

"Jump!"

After they hit the ground, Zander boosted the boys to sit behind Paal and Rosa. He slapped the horses' rumps. "Go!"

"What about you?" Paal shouted over the roar of the flames.

"Give me a minute. I'll be right behind you."

As Paal's horse disappeared through the smoke, headed to safety, Zander fought the urge to follow. Instead, he turned Helios and rode into the fire.

The heat almost drove him back, but he wound around until he found a spot he could get through. As he'd turned to find the boys, he'd felt an energy he recognized from his past.

A few more paces, and he spotted a flash of gold hunkered in the hollow of a dead tree. A tree that would burst into flames in minutes.

During Zander's time of magic, he'd earned a mountain lion token for throwing two hares to a mama lion instead of shooting her. That token had saved Alexa's life in the quest.

That same lion stood now with a cub in her mouth. Another lay at her feet. The mother couldn't save both cubs and was frozen in indecision.

Zander crept up to the lion. She dropped the cub behind her and snarled, protecting her young.

He didn't have much time before the tree caught fire. Zander dropped his shield and linked mind-to-mind with the cat as he'd done before the quest. Her fear roiled through him. He absorbed it and returned images of taking her cubs to safety.

He inched forward on hands and knees, vulnerable if she decided to lunge.

She growled, but allowed Zander to reach in and cradle a cub. He tucked one and then the other between his jacket and shirt as they mewled. He sent an image of riding out of the fire and whispered, "Come, mother. Follow me."

As he mounted Helios, the tree exploded into flames. Helios

needed no urging to race toward safety. Mama lion loped next to them.

Helios waded across the muddy trench. The mountain lion leaped gracefully over it.

Zander reached the warriors and shouted to Greydon, "Are the questers safe?" When Greydon nodded, Zander continued riding west, aware of the amazed faces of the warriors at the sight of a mountain lion traveling beside him. He continued to the mouth of the canyon before he halted.

The lion led Zander to a small cave. Zander laid one and then the other cub next to their mother. The twins, a male and a female, snuggled into their mother's side.

Zander's breath hitched. They'd be safe. It was a small compensation for the man he'd killed.

CHAPTER SIXTY-TWO
Alexa

Pressed against a granite boulder, Alexa held tight to the black and white stone. How could she use it? Surrounded by boulders, she'd trapped herself. The high walls of the canyon cast shadows across the bottom. This fight needed to end before dark or she'd be stuck in the canyon overnight.

She cocked her head at a sound in the canyon mouth. Braying echoed through the rocks. She peeked around the corner. A spot of gray picked its way through the rock strewn path.

Dorothy.

Alexa had left her at the cottage. How and why did she follow Alexa? Alexa snapped her head back as a ball of energy raced toward her and crashed into the wall behind her. Heat filled the enclosure. Melina Odella had Alexa cornered and was moving closer. Alexa held out the stone. Its vibration cleared the negative energy that had accumulated in the cave-like enclosure.

Wave after wave hurtled toward Alexa. Her energy shield frayed at the edges. She couldn't hold it strong for much longer against Melina Odella's attack. She didn't expect an easy fight, but Melina Odella's strength surprised her. So many things her teacher had hidden from her.

Alexa stepped out, palms facing her teacher. "Melina Odella, you don't have to do this. The village needs you."

"When did they ever care about me? All they wanted was potions and spells. I hate them."

"What about the children? You must care about them."

For a moment, Melina Odella's face softened. Then her eyes glittered. "Why should I? They grow up and forget that I kept them from starving. Not one ever comes back to thank me. I don't care about any of them." She spun and pushed a ball of energy at Dorothy.

Not Dorothy. Alexa watched the energy sail toward the donkey, who'd stopped to munch at a rare patch of grass between the stones.

The ball of energy sheared up and away to dissipate in the air above Dorothy. Melina Odella sent another and another. Dorothy ambled toward Alexa, unharmed.

Dorothy almost reached Alexa when Melina Odella conjured a black cloud of angry hornets and pushed it over Alexa.

Panicked, Alexa flailed. Welts rose on her arms and face as the hornets stung again and again. One eyelid swelled from a sting.

Dorothy's nose touched Alexa's arm, and the cloud streaked away. The donkey's immunity to Melina Odella's magic extended to her? Alexa caught her breath, gathered her energy, and sent it flying toward Melina Odella like a lightning bolt.

Seconds before it hit, Melina Odella wound her fingers through Sheba's thick coat. The energy shot around her and set fire to a bush. The fortune-teller sneered, "It seems our patrons have an ability I wasn't aware of. I call stalemate."

What now? They both possessed weapons of magic, not swords or bows. Alexa hadn't planned on needing anything else.

With one hand rooted firmly on Sheba, Melina Odella strode toward Alexa.

Alexa faced her teacher. Did she come to talk? They could still work together to protect the village.

Melina Odella stopped two feet in front of Alexa and sneered. She fumbled in her pocket with one hand, the other firmly on Sheba.

Before Alexa realized what she held, Melina Odella splashed the liquid from a brown vial across Alexa's face.

"Aconite," Melina Odella spat. She cocked her head, and a slow smile spread across her face. "There's no antidote."

Alexa opened her mouth to scream, but numbness spread across her face and silenced her. Her heart beat erratically as the poison absorbed into her bloodstream. She dropped to her knees and clutched at Dorothy. Poison wasn't magic. The donkey couldn't help.

"You're a stupid girl. Moira should have never chosen you." Melina Odella grabbed Alexa's scarf. "I don't have time to wait." She jerked, tightening the scarf around Alexa's neck.

Gasping, Alexa fell to the ground between Dorothy's feet. At the edge of death, in that moment of in-between, Moira appeared as a shimmer with long silver hair and emerald eyes soft with love.

Rage contorted Melina Odella's face. "You come to save her?"

Moira ignored Melina Odella, speaking only to Alexa. "If you give up, fear wins."

"It's too late. I'm dying." Alexa shivered. "I'm not strong enough."

"The scarf has blocked your power. Release your fears. That scar has nothing to do with who you are. Alexa, find your love."

Behind her heart, where her soul resided, a tiny silver spark ignited. She tended it with love. Zander, Mother and Father, Dharien, Merindah, Kaiya.

Zephyr.

Their love fed the flame until it consumed her and spilled into her aura. Clutching Dorothy, Alexa stood. She unwrapped the scarf and dropped it. She rubbed the red heart at her neck and felt the silver energy grow brighter.

Melina Odella gasped. Unable to withstand the light, she faltered and turned to the side.

"Will you stop now, Melina Odella? Help the village?"

The fortune-teller shook her head. "I will not!"

Tears flowed down Alexa's cheeks as she yanked the foxglove pendant from her neck. She laid it in her palm, where it turned to powder. At her command, particles of poison drifted toward her teacher. The card of Death hovered over her.

Eyes frantic, Melina Odella stood rooted, held by a power stronger than Alexa's. The powder swirled above her head while she tried to hold her breath and struggled to move.

Was there no other way? Alexa fought the urge to call back the powder, and then the fear in Melina Odella's eyes made her reach out. She couldn't kill her.

Her teacher expelled the breath she'd desperately tried to hold and breathed in the foxglove. Within seconds, she crumpled to the ground.

Sheba howled once and lay over the body.

Their bodies dissolved into dust and swirled away. They were gone.

CHAPTER SIXTY-THREE

Zander

Shadows crisscrossed the forest floor as Zander rode into the circle of warriors. Greydon lifted an eyebrow, but said nothing of the mountain lion.

Fulk glanced at Zander and then returned his scowl to the three prisoners. They sat back to back, hands and feet tied. Heads down, they refused to speak.

Near the stream, Father Chanse stood with the questers, quietly reassuring them. Clothing scorched, they slumped, exhausted. Their patrons nested in their arms.

The fire burning on the opposite side of the gulch would keep the Odwans from coming down that way. Red embers glowed from the east.

Zander gathered what energy he could find from the surrounding trees. It was weak, as if the trees mourned those lost in the flames. Somewhat renewed, Zander strode to the prisoners. He knelt, let down his guard, and gazed into one of the men's eyes. The Odwan stared back defiantly, but in his heart, he was terrified. Not for himself, but for his wife and child. Zander turned to the other two prisoners and, using his gift, saw the same fears.

A jolt of understanding hit him. He looked like the Kharok, the tribe that forced the Odwans from their home. He motioned for

Father Chanse. With his red hair, he looked Odwan, and he was a priest. The prisoners might respond to him.

He whispered to Father Chanse, "Tell them we won't harm them if they don't fight. Tell them . . ." Zander's throat closed. "Tell them we won't harm their women or children."

Father Chanse repeated the message. The men glanced from Father Chanse to Zander. He nodded to affirm the message. "We won't harm you if you don't fight." Fulk marched them up the side of the gulch as dark settled over the camp.

Zander turned to the warriors who surrounded him. "Bindi? With your favor of seeing in the dark, take the first watch."

"I'll stand with her." Paal joined Bindi, and they melted into the darkness.

"I have an idea," said Yarra. "It involves the questers."

Zander motioned her to follow him. He rubbed his thigh. It ached, and probably wouldn't get any better. "Greydon, Dharien—join us."

As he led them to a circle of tree stumps, children climbed down into the gulch, laden with baskets of dried meat, bread, and cider. As soon as they made the delivery, they scrambled back up. Zander welcomed the comfort of good, hardy food, even with his stomach in knots. His energy grounded in the normalcy of eating, restoring his calm, but a gnawing fear swirled in his gut. Where was Alexa? And Kaiya and Odo should have been back.

The other warriors lit torches and settled in small groups, talking in low voices as they ate. Eva moved among them, checking for injuries and calming nerves with her presence.

Zander sat with Greydon, Dharien, and Yarra. "What's your idea?"

"Send the questers up the west side of the canyon," Yarra began. "They're nimble enough to climb onto the rock ledge and wait for the Odwans. They have plenty of omens left." She smirked. "Their bad behavior is paying off. Once the Odwans cross over the edge, the questers can toss omens down after them. They're already spooked."

"No." Zander didn't want to risk them. "It's too dangerous. They're too young."

"Zander," Dharien interrupted. "They're only a year younger than we are. If not for the Odwans, they'd be questing right now. The quest is hardly safe."

Zander hesitated. Dharien spoke true, and yet . . . he slapped at a mosquito. Damn. They needed every advantage.

Dharien grinned as he rubbed the jagged scar on his cheek. "Two of them have black panther omens. That ought to create some mayhem."

"Better the Odwans than the questers," Zander conceded. He hated sending them into more danger. "Dharien, go convince Father Chanse. He won't like it."

As he left, Bindi called, "Someone's coming up the stream from the west."

Next to him, Greydon swore, "Hells, I hope it's Odo and Kaiya." It wasn't. Elder Terrec, along with three burly Odwans and Del, emerged from the dark into the light of the torches. Clothed in chest shields and carrying bows and swords, Terrec and the men sneered. "What did you think of my troops?"

"*Your* troops?" Zander spat as he jumped to his feet. Greydon, Yarra, and Bindi drew their bows behind him.

Terrec laughed, a rumbling, gloating sound. "How else did you think the Odwans could invade?" He tossed the missing money journal at Zander's feet. "And with your cash to buy weapons, we're well prepared to win."

Zander held back from rushing the traitor. "I suppose they've agreed to your leadership?"

"Of course. Things will change in Puck's Gulch." He scowled. "And not your foolish plan of unity."

"I won't let you." Zander planted his feet and drew his sword.

"Surrender, and we'll spare the warriors' lives." Terrec snickered. "Except yours. We can't have the esteemed leader free to plot against us. It's a small sacrifice. Your life to save all. You want to be a hero? Now's the time, boy."

If it meant the other's safety, Zander would consider it, but Terrec was bluffing. The warriors held the advantage.

"You're too smug, Terrec." Greydon raised his bow. "We have no casualties, while a half-dozen Odwans are dead and three are prisoners."

"Three men who were quick to spill their guts for clemency," Zander added. It was a lie, but Terrec reacted as Zander hoped.

Terrec's face contorted and his already red complexion turned blotchy. "Three men who will die," he snarled. "I tolerate no cowards."

From behind Terrec, Dharien raised his bow. "I say we kill him now."

The warriors chanted. "Kill him, kill him."

Del turned and trained his bow on Dharien.

Zander raised his hand. Terrec wouldn't surrender. He glanced at Del's stony face. No sympathy there. Maybe the war-weary men with them would listen. He looked to them. "We offer peace. Join our village, and we'll accept you as our own."

They crossed their arms and shook their heads. He looked back at Terrec. For once, the elder met his gaze, and in his eyes Zander discovered a secret that gutted him. Zander had to end the war and surrender. Before he could step forward and lay down his bow, a second secret rose: the warriors would be killed, and so would anyone else, male or female, who Terrec felt threatened his leadership. Any decision Zander made was wrong. Someone he loved would die.

He shouted at Dharien, "Stop!"

"Zander! Watch out!" Bindi yelled.

A knife flew from the shadows. It stabbed into Zander's injured thigh. He fell to his knees, gasping at the pain.

Terrec and his men backed away. "You have until dawn to decide," Terrec snarled. He turned and receded into the dark with his men.

Greydon knelt at Zander's side. With one smooth pull, he yanked out the knife and pressed a cloth against the wound. "Why didn't you let us shoot him? Five against the warriors? We would have taken them easily."

Zander choked out, "They have Kaiya and Odo. They'll be killed if Terrec doesn't return."

CHAPTER SIXTY-FOUR

Alexa

The crescent moon fell behind the west rim of the canyon. Night fell, so black Alexa couldn't see more than a few feet in front of her. She slumped against Dorothy. She'd killed Melina Odella. Zander had a chance. Should she stay in the canyon? There was no body to bury, but didn't her mentor deserve some sort of memorial at her passing?

She lifted her hands and spoke to the heavens. "Receive Melina Odella's spirit." She hesitated. "I forgive you, my teacher. May you be at peace." She wasn't good with words like Merindah. "So be it."

Dorothy nudged Alexa's arm and lowered her head. Alexa wove her fingers through the donkey's mane and pulled herself onto her back. She rode out of the canyon, jostling on Dorothy's back as the donkey picked her way out.

She'd killed Melina Odella.

Alexa leaned down against Dorothy's neck and sobbed. Did this happen because of the love potion Alexa had asked Melina Odella to concoct on that hopeful day over a year ago? Merindah spoke true. Melina Odella's hatred began the day Father Chanse drank the potion. Breaking out of the canyon, Alexa urged Dorothy to continue along the stream at the bottom of the gulch. Another hour and they'd reach Zander. No sounds broke the quiet. Her thoughts tumbled around one thing—she'd killed Melina Odella.

Next to the donkey, Moira appeared as the crone. For a few minutes, she walked in silence. Alexa took comfort from her presence. She had questions but not the courage to ask. Did she want to know why this happened? What was done, was done.

As if she knew Alexa's thoughts, Moira said, "Alexa, take responsibility for your actions, but only your own. Dharien and Melina Odella made their choices of their own free will."

"But I used the love potion."

Musical laughter filled the stillness and bounced off the canyon walls. "Magic is strong, but not powerful enough to make one fall in love. It was merely effective in the idea of it."

Confused, Alexa blurted, "They didn't know I poured a love potion in the cups."

"Didn't they?"

"No. I told no one." Alexa searched her memory. Not even Merindah knew her plan.

"There was one other who knew."

"Melina Odella?" Alexa frowned, trying to sort out Moira's accusation.

Silence from Moira.

"Why?"

"In confiding to the priest, the fortune-teller gave him an excuse to act on his feelings without assuming the consequence. He kissed her because he desired it, and then he regretted it. But still, he could place the blame on you."

"What about Dharien? He didn't know."

"He'd gone to Melina Odella for the same potion you requested. She told him what he needed to do, to convince you he loved you."

Dharien knew the potion was in the cup? "Dharien's reaction to my confession in the quest was false?"

"He didn't know you intended it for Paal. He was crushed by your confession."

Alexa reeled. Was everything she believed about Dharien based on lies? Did he love her now, or was that another lie?

Moira touched Alexa's arm. "Not everything is as it seems. Search your heart for truth. For too long, you've allowed your mind to rule."

Alexa closed her eyes and thought of Dharien. Before the quest, his love was self-serving and possessive. Their fight with the panthers changed him. She realized then the moment he shifted. It was when she'd lain, blood coursing from her neck, at the edge of death. Was this why they fought the panthers? To change their hearts? After the quest, she'd told him she forgave him, but had she? She'd been so quick to believe he'd helped Lash. Her heart nearly broke as she imagined his pain. As soon as the war ended, she'd make things right.

When Alexa opened her eyes, Moira said, "I give you one warning. Be careful how you use the omens. Dark magic is attracted to light." And with that, Moira disappeared.

Dark was attracted to light—what did Moira mean?

Dorothy halted and Alexa bumped against her neck. The crunch of footsteps and men's voices drifted toward her. She was too exhausted to do more than cower against Dorothy. When five torches bobbled into sight, curiosity overcame her fear, and she urged Dorothy to inch forward. Five men came into view. Terrec and Del were with Odwans? She shrunk back, heart pounding. Terrec had disappeared to help the Odwans! She'd been reckless to move so close.

What an evil, evil man he was. So callous he'd sacrifice his fellow villagers—for what? More power? What had he promised the Odwans if they won? How could a person be so heartless? She thought of Zeph. How did his gentle soul come from one so vile?

A sob escaped her and she jerked upright. If Terrec heard her ...

But some kind of luck must have been with her. They turned and hiked up a steep trail without noticing her. Alexa released a long breath. A half-hour later, she rode up on the warriors.

Dharien spun and aimed his bow at her. "Stars! Alexa?" He ran to catch her as she slid from Dorothy's back. "You're stung!" He carried her to where Zander slouched on a fallen tree, looking grave. Equally grim, Greydon sat next to him.

"Alexa!" Zander jumped to his feet and stumbled. A bloody rag encircled his thigh. "Thank the fates, you're safe."

Seeming unwilling to put her down, Dharien held her. His warmth and strength renewed her. She wished more than anything she could stay in his arms, but she needed to share what happened in the canyon.

Alexa whispered into his neck, "We need to talk later, but now I have news."

He sat her at her feet and put his hands on each side of her face. Tenderly, he kissed her, leaving her weak in a different way.

He released her, but held her eyes. "I love you."

She touched the scar on his cheek and leaned in for another kiss.

Greydon coughed. Zander cocked an amused eyebrow, and Alexa blushed.

Father Chanse interrupted them. "Did you find Melina Odella?"

She jolted from the kiss that had transported her somewhere else back to the reality of what she'd done. She faced the priest and summoned her last bit of courage. "I found her in the canyon. She . . . she tried to kill me." At his horrified look, she took his arm. "I gave her every reason to change her mind. I'm sorry, Father. She's dead."

Father Chanse rocked back on his heels. "How?"

"I killed her." Dharien caught Alexa as she slumped. "She would have cursed the village."

"This is my fault." Father Chanse fell to his knees and dropped his head in his hands. "I chose the village over her. What have I done?"

Alexa knelt next to him and repeated Moira's words. "Melina Odella made her choices with free will. You cannot blame yourself."

"It *is* my fault. I'll live forever with my shame." He stumbled to his feet and pushed her away as he rushed out of the circle of light.

"You killed Melina Odella?" Dharien stared as if he'd never seen her.

"You've trained to kill. I did what I had to do." The horror in his eyes chilled her. To hide her discomfort, she turned to Zander. "Did Kaiya and Odo make it back?"

Standing next to him, Greydon's face flashed in anger. "The Odwans captured them."

"No!" She fell against Dharien. "How . . ."

"Quiet," Zander whispered. "I saw it in Terrec's eyes. If I tell the warriors, I'll have to disclose my favor. I'd rather they didn't know." Zander fiddled with his bow and glanced at Greydon. "We'll rescue them unharmed. I promise it."

A flash of understanding at Greydon's distress hit Alexa. The two most important warriors were distracted by love. She couldn't let them do something foolish. "You're needed here. I'll go."

"Alexa, no." Dharien stood in front of her. "You defeated the fortune-teller with magic. These are a hundred men with bows and swords."

She drew herself up and felt her power stir. Dharien didn't understand, and how could he? He thought of her as the girl who needed protecting in the quest. She was the fortune-teller, chosen by Moira. Silver energy rose and surrounded her, lighting the night.

Dharien stumbled back a step, but he stubbornly said, "Light won't rescue them."

She raised her hand and pushed the energy toward a tree twenty feet away. A crack split the air and the tree toppled. His eyes widened, and he threw his arms up to protect against the flying twigs. She regretted scaring him, but she didn't regret her power. This was who she was.

The warriors, jolted from sleep, jumped to their feet and grabbed their bows.

Zander's belly-laugh drew confused looks. "Go back to sleep. We have magic on our side. The next battle will be the last." He took Alexa's arm and guided her to a circle of downed logs. "We need a plan."

After a short discussion, they agreed that Alexa would leave at first light. If the Odwans were spooked by Puck's ghost, they should be terrified of magic.

He hadn't looked her in the eye since the tree demonstration, but Dharien insisted on accompanying her. "Even with your magic, an arrow can take you down. You need someone with a bow to watch out for you."

She nodded her agreement. She didn't need him, but she'd like having him with her. And if, after witnessing her power, he still claimed to love her, she'd believe it was real. Nearing midnight, Alexa yawned. "What do we do now?"

"We wait," was Zander's terse response. "And try to sleep."

The others left to find spots to sleep, but Dharien slid down against a log and patted the ground. "Rest with me." Alexa sat next to Dharien, and he cradled her in his arms. "Aren't you afraid?" he asked.

"Aren't you?"

He jerked away and then sighed and pulled her closer. "Of course. But I have a bow and a sword."

"And I have magic."

"I'm afraid I'll lose you."

She searched his eyes. "I don't think we can win without magic. Zander needs me."

"What about me? I need you."

"We'll figure this out after the fighting is over. I promise." Alexa reached up and kissed him. "I don't intend to die."

Warm and safe in Dharien's arms, she slept. Dorothy stood behind them, head drooping, as exhausted as Alexa.

Alexa woke when an owl landed on her knee. The glow of dawn reached down into the gulch. She should have left an hour ago! With shaking fingers, she untied the message on the quester's bird's leg and unrolled it. *Omens didn't work. Odwans coming. Two panthers loose.*

Dharien rubbed his eyes. "What happened?"

"We're late!" She jumped up and raced to find Zander. His look of shock shamed her.

"I thought you'd left."

"I got word from the questers. The Odwans are coming."

"Alert the others," Zander shouted to Greydon.

Alexa grabbed Zander's arm. "There're two black panthers loose."

"Damn, I hope they stay on the Odwans' side."

The sound of marching rumbled through the brush. Alexa and Zander ran to the stream and stared down the gulch. The phalanx moved steadily forward, shields protecting them, and spears extended.

Bruised and bloody, hands tied at their backs, Kaiya and Odo were being frog-marched ahead of the enemy.

CHAPTER SIXTY-FIVE

Zander

"Hold fire, hold fire," Zander yelled.

The phalanx stopped thirty feet away. Fire raced through Zander's veins. A purple welt marred Kaiya's cheek. A cut above her eye dripped blood. Odo's left eye was swollen shut. Oh, gods, what had Terrec done?

On the left side of the phalanx, Terrec and Del broke from the group and stepped forward. Terrec lowered a shield and sneered. "Your answer, Zander. Do you surrender?"

Beside him, Greydon grabbed Zander's arm. "We have to surrender."

If giving up saved Kaiya, he'd do it, but Terrec couldn't be trusted. "If we surrender, he'll kill them anyway." Zander sought Kaiya's eyes. Her look of love gutted him, and then she shook her head. She knew he couldn't surrender.

Her bravery astounded him. He'd sent her into danger and still she loved him, still she put the safety of the village before her own life. He had to stall Terrec. None of the options were acceptable.

"I have an idea." Alexa pushed between Zander and Greydon. "Be ready to rescue Kaiya and Odo."

"Ah, the fortune-teller wannabe," Terrec taunted. "Your little spells are useless against real weapons. Leave the fighting to the men."

Beside Zander, Alexa's energy vibrated. She held her hands out toward the phalanx and pushed. The spear shafts splintered into jagged pieces.

"Go! Go now!" she hissed.

He and Greydon raced for the phalanx. Zander flipped a knife from his sheath.

"Archers!" Terrec yelled as he raced to rejoin the Odwans.

Arrows flew from the back of the line. One hit Zander's chest and bounced away, leaving him unharmed. Alexa's magic cloth had worked.

Answering arrows from the warriors flew overhead. Dharien called the orders. "Nock, draw, release."

Zander cut the ropes holding Kaiya and caught her as she fell. An Odwan reached out from behind the shield and slashed blindly. Zander drew his sword and ran it between the shields. He felt it slide into a body. He twisted the blade and pulled it out, bloody. His gut wrenched.

Greydon and Odo pulled aside the shields and fought the front men. Kaiya grabbed Zander's knife and stabbed a man in the heart before he could smash a shield down on Zander's head.

Then the warriors rushed down the gulch, whooping and hollering, swords drawn, to fight next to Zander.

Standing above the brawl, Alexa snapped the Odwans' arrows as they flew. A sword glanced away from Zander as if hitting an invisible shield. Zander caught sight of Alexa standing, eyebrows drawn, mouth tight. Zander deflected a sword thrust and cut the man down with his sword. Magic helped, but Terrec was right—the war would be won by men with bows and swords.

No, not by men alone. The women had come down into the gulch and shot arrow after arrow into the Odwans' flank. Mother's determined face was among them.

His father appeared next to Zander, swinging a scimitar in one hand and a long butcher knife in the other. As he slashed an Odwan's chest, he grinned at Zander. "Not gonna let you have all the fun."

Across from Zander, an arrow pierced Fulk's chest. The burly marshal made a final stab and killed a man before he dropped.

Not Fulk! Zander had no time for grief. Back-to-back with Kaiya, Zander fought with her as a team—he with a sword, she with a long knife. Blood soaked his sleeve from a slice across his forearm.

Behind Zander, Helios joined the fray. He reared and kicked at the Odwans. Their shields meant nothing to the war horse. He back-kicked man after man.

Suddenly, Kaiya screamed. She sprinted for an Odwan with his sword raised to strike Bindi.

Helpless, Zander watched Bindi fall and Kaiya kill the man who'd stabbed her.

CHAPTER SIXTY-SIX

Alexa

Fulk and Bindi lay unmoving as the battle surrounded them. Ignoring the chaos, Eva and Cobie, wearing the green tunics of healers, darted in and pulled them to the side.

Her energy depleted, Alexa sagged against a tree. Her stones had crumbled as she'd drained all their energy. Despair racked her—she hadn't done enough to protect them. She gathered what little energy remained in the garnet brooch. A crack split the air as it gave up its final charge. When she thought she'd collapse, Dorothy pressed her nose under Alexa's arm and filled her with fresh power.

Even with Dorothy's added help, Alexa had to choose between firing at the Odwans or protecting the warriors. She chose to protect, but there were many, and she had to be careful or she would end up protecting the Odwans as well. When Father joined Zander, he was another to watch over. She shielded Zander and Kaiya, Greydon and Odo, and those fighting in the worst of the battle. Dharien plunged down the ditch to join in the hand-to-hand fighting, and she included him.

The omens the questers had tossed caught up to the fight. Feral pigs attacked at random, snakes struck, and hornets buzzed in the air, not discriminating between the warriors and the Odwans. Alexa's left hand held the protective shield, while her right sent bolts of energy to dissipate the omens.

Moira had warned Alexa. If only she'd stopped the questers from releasing them. Her comfort in Dharien's arms had come at a steep price. Indulging in her regret, Alexa's attention faltered. An Odwan raised his sword and swung at Zander. She threw out her hand—too late.

Father lunged to protect Zander. The sword intended for her twin sliced their father from neck to gut. Zander struck down the Odwan and dropped to his knees next to Father while Greydon protected him. Zander lifted stricken eyes to Alexa and shook his head. Then he stood and, with an impossible strength, blindly swung his sword with a vengeance Alexa shared. He struck down Odwan after Odwan.

"Halt!" Terrec's shout echoed through the fight. He held Elder Warrin with a knife at his throat. Two elders stood: one triumphant, the other's life in peril.

Alexa gasped and turned in a furious circle. Somehow, during the fighting, the Odwans had enclosed the warriors from all sides. A wild fear swept across Zander's face, and he lifted his sword in what Alexa knew would be a fatal move.

"Wait!" she yelled.

She struggled to find power, any power, but even with Dorothy's help, she was depleted.

"Stars, be damned!" She'd forgotten Moira's promise. "Moira?" she cried out, desperate for help. "I need you!"

At her cry, Terrec slit Elder Warrin's throat.

CHAPTER SIXTY-SEVEN

Zephyr

Moira appeared next to Zeph. "Now, Zephyr. Use the stone." Heartbroken and frantic to help, Zeph cried, "I don't know how!"

If he didn't act now, he'd fail the ones he loved, and he didn't know what to do.

Moira smiled.

An unexpected peace filled him. He held the stone, glittering with diamonds, to his chest. He was the light-bearer. All his love—for Zander and Alexa, for the warriors, for the village—he sent into the stone. It began to glow, and he directed it to Alexa and Zander.

Alexa's silver aura surrounded her. Zander's gold energy encircled him. Their energy grew, but it wasn't enough. He would fail them, after all.

And then, Merindah's spirit joined him. "You don't do this alone, Zephyr."

"Merindah? What are you doing here? You died?"

"I've always known it was my fate. This is my task, as it is yours."

Merindah placed her hand over his on the stone. The energy surged. Copper mixed with diamond and filled Alexa and Zander until the glow was so strong, everyone standing near averted their eyes.

God gently took Merindah's hand. "You've earned your reward."

They faded.

Moira took their place. Her smile filled Zeph with warmth.

"Zephyr, whisper of wind, light-bearer. Because of your love, Zander and Alexa have a chance to save the village."

"Am I done? Will I never see Zander or Alexa again?" Longing overwhelmed him. "Or Dorothy?" He suddenly didn't want to go.

"Gentle boy, you will be a part of their lives yet again." She held out her hand. "But for now, come with me and rest."

Zeph took her hand. The battle below was gone. The pain was gone. Only the diamond stone remained. Its brilliance grew until Zeph became the light.

CHAPTER SIXTY-EIGHT

Alexa

Zeph's love bloomed in Alexa's heart. Silver energy flowed in and around her. Below her, Zander glowed with gold.

She felt Merindah's death and stumbled. Energy shot through her like a taut band snapping. Tears streamed down her face as copper energy blended with her own.

She walked down the side of the gulch toward her twin.

Silence filled the gulch. Confused, the Odwans and warriors separated and created a path to her twin. Zander grasped her outstretched hand and jerked as their energy joined.

Awed faces from both sides surrounded them. Fulk, Bindi, Father, Elder Warrin and others, dead and wounded, lay scattered among the living.

Clear and strong, Zander's voice rang out. "Enough. We offer sanctuary to all those who embrace peace. No Odwan will be turned away who pledges to put down his weapon and join us, united to work together." He stared at Terrec. "We made that offer to Terrec last night. Did he tell you?"

Odwans glanced back and forth between Zander and Terrec, as if they doubted her twin's sincerity. But right before them, Terrec had slit a man's throat without reason—did that not shock them?

Dharien's father lay at Terrec's feet, bloodied and lifeless. At the corner of her vision, Dharien and Greydon's grief-stricken faces broke her heart. She'd attend to Dharien's pain later. This war had to end now.

She met Terrec's eyes and then the eyes of the Odwans around him. "As a council member, I attest his offer is true."

Del appeared at Terrec's side. "Father, enough. You promised an easy win, not this bloodbath." He glanced at the warriors and the weary villagers. "These are innocent people. I won't be a part of this anymore."

"You bastard traitor," Terrec spat.

An Odwan grabbed Elder Terrec and knocked the knife away. He twisted Terrec's arms behind his back. "Is this true?" he grunted. "They offered us shelter?"

Terrec snarled, "You believe him over me?"

"Your own son has deserted you." The man tightened his hold on Terrec. "We lost men with families. We're sick of war." He shoved the unarmed Terrec away from him. "You lied. You're worse than the Kharoks."

Terrec returned the man's stare. "You're pathetic. You're afraid of boys?"

Dharien stepped forward and aimed his bow at Terrec. "You murdered my father!" Blinking back tears, he loosed the arrow.

It flew true. Terrec crumpled, shot through the neck where the armor didn't cover.

One by one, the Odwans dropped their weapons and kneeled, as if dazed.

Healers moved silently among the fallen, tending to both sides. The war was over, but the cost had been great, and all because one man wanted more power.

Shocked warriors gathered around Elder Warrin's body, comforting Dharien and Greydon as they bent over their father, weapons abandoned. Exhausted, Alexa buried her head in Zander's chest. He seemed as unable to move as she. There was no joy in the victory, only relief it was over.

Snarls drew her attention. Two black panthers stalked toward her and Zander. Confused, Alexa froze. Were they now to die? Had Moira only delayed their punishment from the quest?

Light attracts dark.

The panthers crouched to pounce.

Accepting her fate, Alexa waited for the strike, but it wasn't her they took down. Dharien jumped in front of her, and the panthers slammed him to the ground. One tore at his shoulder, while the other ripped open his stomach.

In a blur, Odo stabbed one with his sword. Kaiya shot the second.

Alexa fell to the ground next to Dharien. Blood soaked him. She yanked the wooden heart from her neck and pressed it against his heart, but no magic flowed. She'd used everything in the fight.

Eva pressed a cloth against Dharien's mangled stomach, but the blood spurted from the sides.

"Don't leave me, Dharien. Please don't leave me!" Clutching his hand, she screamed at the sky, "Moira! Help him."

Greydon knelt on the other side of Dharien and clasped his other hand. "I can't bear to lose you too, brother." Odo stood behind him, one hand on Greydon's shoulder. Zander and Kaiya stood shoulder to shoulder.

Dharien gasped, "I'm paying for my past mistakes. I shouldn't have survived the quest."

"You changed. You don't deserve to die." Alexa sobbed. "I need you." This was her fault. She didn't get to the questers in time to stop them from using their omens.

Dharien's breathing slowed and his eyes glazed. "I see Father. I'm going to be all right."

"But I won't be." Alexa's heart ripped apart. "Don't leave. I love you, Dharien."

He squeezed her hand. "I always loved you." He glanced at Greydon and the others. "I love all of you."

He smiled, and then he was gone.

CHAPTER SIXTY-NINE

Zander

Zander thought he couldn't hurt worse than when Zeph died, but he was wrong. Each one—Fulk, Bindi, Elder Warrin, Dharien, and Father, who'd died to save him, created a unique pain. As the wounded were carried on litters up the steep gulch, Zander sat frozen next to his father's covered body. Mother sat with him, her hair tied back in a knot, sporting a long scrape down the side of her face. She'd killed. How would that change her? Mother held Father's hand. "He loved you both so much," she mumbled, choking on tears.

Leaning against his shoulder, Alexa wept openly. What scars did they carry now that the fighting was over? He put his arm around her. She'd lost a father and Dharien.

He glanced at Kaiya as she helped Father Chanse organize the wounded. A bandage wrapped her head, but she'd survived. She looked at him then, and her smile was tender and sad. He wanted to join her, to hold her, and tell her the things he'd kept hidden in his heart. But for now, his place was with his mother and twin.

Greydon held his own vigil next to the bodies of Dharien and their father. Odo sat next to him, holding Greydon as he wept, neither aware of the few bewildered looks, nor, Zander thought, would they care. Death had a way of defining what was important, what was not.

Zander felt no happiness at the end of the war. Why did he live when so many others died? Fate? Destiny? He dropped his head into his hands. Would he ever sort it out? *Could* it be explained?

Greydon was now the elder of his father's estate and a council member. Del would be charged with treason. Zander would search Del's heart. If he'd spoken true, Zander would argue for leniency. Changes were coming to Puck's Gulch, and they needed men and women willing to work for them.

The able-bodied Odwans returned to camp. When they returned with their families, Zander would use his gift, and those earnest about living in peace could stay. Moira had been right to insist he keep his favor.

When the men came to carry his father up the gulch, Zander stood and then stumbled. His wounded leg wouldn't hold him, and he slid to the ground.

In an instant, Kaiya was beside him. "Stay down. I'll get help."

He grimaced. "No, I'm the warriors' leader. I can make it."

Eyes shining, she said, "You saved the village, Zander. No one gives a damn if you need help."

Kaiya called over two warriors. Zander put an arm around each of their shoulders and limped up the gulch. And he found he wasn't the least bit embarrassed.

CHAPTER SEVENTY

Alexa

Alexa supported Mother as they followed the men carrying Father's lifeless body up the gulch and to the church. Too many bodies lined across the churchyard. Villagers and Odwans lay side by side. To what end? For Terrec to have more power? And now, he lay as dead as the others.

Leaving Mother with others grieving, Alexa walked to the cell abutting the church. She steeled herself and peered through the small window. Merindah's body lay on the cot, her patron sparrow in her arms. Alexa could almost pretend her friend was sleeping.

Coming to stand next to Alexa, Father Chanse said, "She gave too much." He broke down, sobbing. "So much death."

Finding herself in the strange position of comforting the priest, Alexa held him as he cried. War and now grief unified the village. They had to find a way to stay united in peace.

She recalled Merindah's final words. *What can happen in a brick cell?* With a start, Alexa realized her friend had already known her future.

"Without Merindah, we would have lost," she said.

Wiping his eyes, Father Chanse said, "We'll make a statue. Puck's Gulch won't forget her sacrifice."

A statue. A reminder for all generations of her role in saving the village. She patted the priest's arm. "With prayer beads in her hand and a sparrow on her shoulder."

She turned as Dharien's body was laid next to his father's, the cloth wrapping him stained crimson with blood. His love for her had killed him. She would never understand it—the panthers, his death after he'd survived the war. Moira had been silent, and Alexa didn't expect any answers. She had a lifetime ahead of her to hear Moira's wisdom. Did the why of it matter? Dharien was dead. No amount of understanding changed it.

As grief engulfed Alexa, Dorothy ambled up and stuck her nose in Alexa's hand, whiffing for a treat.

"Silly donkey," Alexa said as she leaned her head against Dorothy's neck. A vision of riding away from the village on Dorothy's back filled Alexa's head. Tshilaba had promised to train her. As soon as she could leave, Alexa would find the Raskans.

But first, she had duties to attend. With Dorothy's help, Alexa gathered cedar and built a fire next to the Quinary. She added a handful of clary sage and spelled the smoke to swirl into every home, every building. Cedar healed and guarded against nightmares; clary sage relieved anxiety. She tended the blaze until Kaiya and Gia joined her and insisted she go to bed with the promise they'd keep the fire going.

She didn't have it in her to trek to Melina Odella's cottage. Her cottage. Instead, Alexa crossed the market to the bakery. She thought she couldn't sleep, but when she lay in her old bed, Moira appeared at the foot.

"Rest, my child. You have a journey ahead of you."

Alexa fell into a deep sleep and woke melancholic, but refreshed. The scent of baking bread filled her room. So many years she'd hated the smell. Now, it was a comfort.

After she dressed, Alexa touched the scar at her neck, hesitating only a moment before adding a yellow scarf. She stumbled down the stairs. Loaves of sturdy oat bread crowded the counters. No fancy cakes, no special breads baked for the elders' families, not even a sugar biscuit in sight. "Mother? Did you sleep?"

The dark circles under Mother's eyes answered the question. "People need to eat. I baked lavender into the loaves for healing." She piled the bread onto a tray. "Will you help me carry them to the Quinary?"

Alexa filled a tray and walked side by side with Mother to join others carrying baskets of food, subdued but determined. It would take time, but they would heal. Strength wasn't often realized until needed.

Father Chanse blessed the food. The remaining elders served the peasants. Merchants filled plates for kids from the shacks. They'd come together in war, could they continue now that the threat to the village was over? Alexa glanced at the tribes. Kharok, Yapi, Chadha, Dakta, and Odwa—they'd lived in peace for two hundred years as Puck envisioned. Now, with Father Chanse and a new council, Alexa would help them live in equity. She was leaving, but she'd return. This was her home, and they needed a fortune-teller.

A ragged laugh escaped her. Father Chanse and a few red-haired kids from the shacks mingled with the others. With the added Odwans in the village, red hair would no longer be an oddity. Her laugh turned to a sob. Zeph would have loved it.

She missed him terribly.

CHAPTER SEVENTY-ONE

Zander

"You'll likely always limp," Eva pronounced as she pulled the final stitch through Zander's knife wound. "It damaged a muscle."

Zander unclenched his hand from Shadow's fur and opened his eyes. At his insistence, he was the last of the injured to be treated. He shuddered. He might be a warrior, but needles still made him woozy.

Dark circles under her eyes, Eva slumped on the bench next to him. "What will you do now?" she asked as she knotted the thread. "We won't need warriors anymore."

What would he do? He cocked his head. "I'm thinking the village is in need of a furrier."

Eva nodded, and tears glistened in her eyes. "You were a surprise when I midwifed for Lark. Alexa came out squalling. A few minutes later, you followed, quiet and with the look of an old man."

"She never stopped squalling, did she?"

Eva laughed. "Theron looked so proud when I placed her in his arms." She turned sober. "And then they were terrified to have twins. Afraid of the quest already." She rubbed her eyes. "I hated their plan to separate you. I tried to convince Lark that Moira would do what Moira would do. She was so scared for you."

"I don't blame her. I've made my share of bad decisions with the best intentions."

Eva wrapped a bandage around Zander's thigh. "Wise as an old man, too."

He didn't feel wise. "Do you think the village will ever return to normal?"

She shook her head. "With the influence of you young ones, we'll be better."

He gave Eva a long hug. "Did you sleep at all last night?"

"No, but I'm heading to bed soon." She motioned toward Cobie as he changed a bandage on one of the warriors. "He's a natural healer. That's one good thing that came out of this mess." She stood. "Come on, let's join the rest of the village."

It was a short walk to the Quinary, where they found tables laden with food. Nothing fancy like the festivals, only simple, sturdy food that satisfied. Like the villagers—dependable and steady. Still in battle clothes, the elders served the peasants. It was a good sign.

Eva headed for Lark and the group of women who'd become archers and would forever share a bond. They welcomed Eva with hugs, tears, and laughter.

Zander limped his way to Alexa, who sat alone at a corner of the Quinary.

"Hoy," he said as he sat next to his twin. The night to his day.

She turned, and he couldn't avoid seeing the secret she carried. "You're leaving?"

"Tshilaba said she'd train me. Mother doesn't need me, and you . . ." She glanced at Kaiya. "You have Kaiya." She blinked back tears. "I know I should stay and help, but I can't take the sadness. Everywhere I look, I'm reminded of loss. I'm so tired, Z."

When she hesitated, Zander knew if he asked her to stay, she would. Hells, he wanted to. He rubbed the back of his neck. "You deserve to go. The village will be fine without you, at least for a while. Promise you'll come back?"

"I will." She threw her arms around his neck. "I'd be lost without you."

When she sat back, Zander tugged at the scarf around her neck. "You don't need this, Alexa. Let people see your scars. They've made you strong."

She pursed her lips. "I'll think about it." She stood and walked to their mother. Alexa talked, and Mother nodded. Then Alexa hugged each of the women and strode toward the bakery without a backward glance.

He already missed her.

Zander stood and searched for Kaiya. He found her with Odo and Greydon. Kaiya's cheek had turned purple. She wore the tattered clothes of battle, her hair smelled of cedar, and he loved her.

Greydon turned haunted eyes toward Zander. Black stitches crossed his forehead. "I'm the head of my family now."

With his left arm in a sling, Odo put his good arm around Greydon. "You're not alone. I'm here for you."

With all the deaths in the village, Greydon wasn't the only one hurting. "No one will grieve alone. We'll heal together. It's the beginning of uniting the tribes."

"I pledge my land to your cause." Greydon glanced at Odo and took his hand. "We've been talking. The manor has plenty of room for kids. Any child orphaned from our village or the Odwans' could live there." Reticent, he said, "I'll keep the staff and cooks. It will help Mother to heal if she has little ones to care for."

And Greydon had once accused Zander of having a soft heart. "My friend, that's a generous offer. Will you talk with Father Chanse? He's worried about how to care for them. It will be a relief to have a plan."

Greydon nodded, and he and Odo wandered off. Zander took Kaiya's hand. "Come with me?"

They walked in silence to a quiet bench near the gulch. He hugged her, and a smile tugged at his mouth as he whispered into her ear, "I still think you're pretty."

When she pulled away, he expected it, and held her close. "But that's not why I love you."

She softened. "You love me?"

"You're smart, and you amaze me with your courage. You shoot as well as I do, and you're just as stubborn. You did what you thought was right, even when defying my orders. We couldn't have won without you." He made certain his shield was strong before he found her eyes. He would never take her secrets. "I love your smile and the way you cock your head when you're thinking. You never gave up on me, even when I was being an arse."

"You were an arse a lot." She laughed, and the sound was one Zander knew he'd never tire of.

"Think you could be happy with a boring old furrier?"

Her eyes widened, but she nodded. "If that furrier is you, I'm sure of it."

He took her face in his hands and kissed her. The pain of loss lifted a tiny bit. It wasn't an easy thing for him to open his heart, but the shell he'd created cracked. He'd never close it again. Not to her, not to love.

"Look!" Kaiya turned him to face the gulch.

Led by Geno, the first Odwans struggled up over the edge, looking bewildered and unsure. Father Chanse ran to greet them and guided them to the Quinary. A steady stream of men and women with tired children, almost all redheads, came up and over, carrying tattered bags.

Farther down, a gray donkey faced the steep gulch. Two small packs were tied across her rump.

Next to his side, Kaiya encircled his waist with her arms. "Where's Alexa going?"